The CONTAINER

LUCILLE LABOSSIERE

 FriesenPress

One Printers Way
Altona, MB R0G 0B0
Canada

www.friesenpress.com

ISBN
978-1-03-918584-5 (Hardcover)
978-1-03-918583-8 (Paperback)
978-1-03-918585-2 (eBook)

1. FICTION, THRILLERS, CRIME

Distributed to the trade by The Ingram Book Company

Table of Contents

Acknowledgments

I would like to thank my husband Jim for his encouragement and helpful advice throughout the entire novel.

In loving memory of Jim Kocurek, an amazing husband, loving father and grandfather, and a very special brother. You are greatly missed.

Chapter One

September 30, 11:00 a.m. –
October 2, 10:00 a.m.

THERE WAS A DEFINITE DAMPNESS in the air as September finally came to a close, and October was fast approaching in the small town of Blue Ridge. The town was unaware of the events that would soon turn their community upside down for the second time in a decade. Tom Lockman was finally going to be as free as a bird. As he sat in his prison cell, he waited patiently for a guard to drop off his get-out-of-jail-free package. Before long, a simple black duffel bag was delivered to his cell, and his door was locked one last time to keep him safe until his release. Sometimes, other prisoners would get jealous of an inmate about to be released and attack him. Or, even worse, kill him.

Tom sat on his bunk and anxiously opened the bag. Inside, he found a set of clothing, shoes, and basic underwear. Even though the clothes wouldn't have been his choice, he quickly pulled them on. He stuffed his prison attire into the bag as a reminder that he never wanted to return to this hellhole ever again. A second look into the bag revealed three small, sealed envelopes.

Opening the first one, Tom found papers with the name, phone number, and address of his parole officer, whom he would have to contact upon arrival in Blue Ridge. The second envelope contained a free taxi coupon that would take him from the prison to the local bus station. In the same envelope, several bus tickets to Blue Ridge, his final destination, were enclosed. The last envelope contained two hundred dollars to cover his travel expenses. He hadn't seen that much money in over ten years, but he knew it wouldn't last long if he squandered it.

Tom was about to stuff the cash back into the envelope when he discovered another piece of paper inside. He pulled it out; it was a note stating that the rest of his money owing would be paid in monthly instalments until he had collected what he had earned while behind bars. The bottom right-hand corner of this page had an official seal. He returned the note and his cash back into the envelope, and stuffed all three envelopes back into his duffel bag. Patiently, he waited for someone, anyone, to come and collect him. Tom soon heard footsteps approaching. He stood proud and tall, waiting for his cell bars to slide open for the final time. Taking a deep breath, he started his long walk through a series of doors that squeaked open in front of him, and then slammed shut once he had passed through. At the final door, and with tears in his eyes, he turned and watched it slam shut. Prison was now a thing of the past.

A taxi was waiting for him. Tom gave the driver his voucher for the bus station. Taking the coupon, the driver nodded for Tom to climb into the back seat. The driver glanced into his rearview mirror and watched his passenger secure the seat belt before he started the engine. Tom turned around and a single tear ran down his cheek as those towering walls disappeared into the distance. He had no idea what freedom would feel like, but he cherished the moment. He was finally on his way home to Jenny.

"It's supposed to rain today. What do you think?" the driver asked.

Tom looked out the side window. "Don't care either way."

"Where're you heading?"

"Home."

"Where's home?"

"Blue Ridge."

"Where the hell is that?"

"It's on the coast of British Columbia."

"Must be beautiful there?"

"It is."

Tom arrived at the bus depot and had a one-hour wait, so he found a coffee shop and, for the first time in ten years, bought himself a meal: an egg salad sandwich and strong black coffee. He wolfed it down and then bought a package of cigarettes. This freedom he had waited so long to experience felt good; he was at ease among normal people. No one here had a grudge against him or felt like they needed to beat the shit out of him. Tom enjoyed people-watching until he spotted his bus approach the station. It was finally time to leave, so he boarded the half-empty bus, took a seat at the back, and fell sound asleep. In total, it was a seventeen-hour bus ride with several transfers from one bus to the next before he would finally arrive home.

On the last leg of his journey, Tom was awakened when the bus driver announced, "Blue Ridge is in fifteen minutes. That's the end of the line."

Tom grabbed his bag and was about to move to the front of the bus when he discovered a phone lying on a seat and not a soul in sight. He quickly picked it up and shoved it into his bag and moved closer to the front of the bus. "Are you familiar with this area?"

"Sure am. Blue Ridge is my hometown," the bus driver answered.

"I've been away for some time, for work, and really want to surprise my wife with a getaway weekend. Is there anywhere outside of town that is nice and private? We need time to reconnect." Tom's funds were slowly depleting, but he knew he owed Jenny something.

The bus driver apologized. "Sorry, man. There used to be a motel close to town—in fact, it's just around this next corner—but it went broke years ago."

Tom looked sadly at the dilapidated sign when the bus drove by the turn-off to the motel. "Guess I'll have to surprise her some other way." Tom sat in the front seat until they arrived at Blue Ridge.

There were only a few passengers left on the bus, so once it was parked in town, Tom collected his duffel bag and waited for the other passengers to leave before him. He then started down the stairs, paused on the last step, and was about to descend when the driver said, "You getting off, man, or do I have to take you home with me?"

Without turning to the driver, Tom answered, "Sorry." He paused. "I'm getting off." He then took that final step and moved away from the bus. He heard the driver close the door behind him and drive off.

Tom was finally home in Blue Ridge and the time was seven thirty p.m. It was fall and dusk was slowly moving in, snuffing out the light of day and replacing it with the darkness of the night. Tom let out a huge sigh, as he was about to start a new chapter in his life. Ten years in prison had taken its' toll on him and he needed more than ever to reconnect with Jenny. Freedom was a rediscovered experience for him, and he absolutely had to make it work.

"I can't go back," he mumbled to himself.

Glancing around the area of the bus depot, he noticed that the old town was much the same. His first stop should have been to check in with his parole officer to let him know of his arrival, but he decided to do that first thing in the morning. Jenny was his priority. Tom had tried to contact Jenny several times while in prison, but her phone had been disconnected. Was she still here, or had she moved on?

He rushed to his house on Birch Crescent in hopes of finding her. When he arrived, he was shocked by what he saw. Their home, which had previously been kept up immaculately, was now in sad disarray. He thought that perhaps the yard was a bit like him, gone through a lot in the last ten years. The old house desperately needed a paint job and the picket fence they had built together was no longer there. In the dim light, he could see that the lawn had been freshly cut, but the flower beds needed to be cleaned up for the winter.

Tom guessed that Jenny would be in the kitchen, so he slowly walked the length of the driveway, and was about to climb the stairs when a light turned on in the window. Tom moved into the shadows and Jenny appeared in front of him, a vision of true beauty. She was running water into the sink and was starting to wash a stack of dishes set off to the side. Tom caught his breath. She was still as beautiful as ever, but was now sporting gray hair. He started to sweat and was as nervous as when he had invited her out for the first time. Without realizing what he was doing, Tom bit his lower lip and nervously fidgeted with his fingers. He shoved his hands into his pockets to try and control the trembling. How would she greet him? Would she fly into his arms? Would she reject him? More importantly, did she still love him?

Tom backed away, wondering if he should just disappear and forget about her. But that wasn't an option for him. He still loved her madly. He studied her for several minutes and was about to climb the stairs and knock on the door when a young man passed behind her. She was laughing as she conversed with this gentleman. Tom could hardly breathe. Had she moved on with a new man? At first, tears formed in the corners of his eyes, but then he got angry. Still in shock, he backed further away from the house and hid behind a tree. After a few moments of sobbing like a baby, he decided to take a walk to clear his head. Jenny was still his wife and he had to reclaim her. In the darkness that had now become complete, he found himself in a park, where he sat down on a bench, wondering what to do. He had never received any divorce papers, so that must mean she was still married to him. Was this man a fling to fill the time until he was released, or was he a permanent fixture-his replacement? She had some explaining to do.

The more Tom thought about the whole ordeal, the more he regretted taking that woman's life ten years ago. He had done his time, but his brother Charles was still dead because of Bill Smithe. Tom wasn't going to be a slave to the parole system and report to some stranger every time he wanted to do anything. He wasn't a kid who needed to report to the principal's office every day. He yelled in frustration. "I'll kill her, the unfaithful bitch. They'll never find her body." Tom never noticed a shadow in the distance that disappeared into the darkness. Had someone overheard his outburst?

He started to form a plan that didn't involve the justice system and some cheesy parole officer. He would be out of Blue Ridge by morning, and would never come back again, and he was taking Jenny with him whether she wanted to go with him or not. He was owed major wages from when he was in prison and was only going to be given a pittance each month. A plot slowly formed in his head.

Screw the system. I want more and I'm going to get it.

Unbeknownst to him, two little urchins were hiding behind a tree. The youngest whispered, "Do you think there might be food in his bag?"

The second boy whispered, "You stay here." He slowly worked his way towards the bench, determined to steal the man's bag. His tiny hand had taken hold of it, and he was about to run with the bag in tow, when Tom sensed him and grabbed him by the wrist. He glared at the small child and shouted, "How dare you steal from me? I'll kill you, or worse, I'll cut off your hands! That'll teach you a lesson. No one steals from me, especially not some snotty kid!"

The child whimpered. "Let me go. You're hurting me."

Tom was about to backhand the kid when the younger child came out of nowhere and kicked him hard in the shin. Tom released the boy and grabbed at his aching leg. The two kids were immediately off and running. Tom turned around to follow, but he could barely see them in the distance. He set off after them. "You better hope I don't get my hands on the two of you because if I do, your little game is over."

The two urchins found a tree to hide behind, hoping the man wouldn't find them. The younger of the two whispered, "What do we do?"

"Shh." He peered around the tree and could see the man slowly approaching them.

Tom was getting too close to the boys and was yelling, "If I get my hands on you, I'll take you to the old motel outside of town and kill you. No one will ever find your bodies."

Glancing down, the older boy spotted a rock that would neatly fit in his hand. Carefully picking it up, he peeked around the tree and saw the man coming dangerously close to them. "Stay here and don't make a sound." He quietly moved from behind the tree and threw the rock. It landed behind the man.

Tom panicked. If there were two of them, what was to say that there wasn't a third one stealing his duffel bag? He spun on his heel and screamed over his shoulder as he ran back to the bench. "I'll catch both of you and the police will never find your bodies."

The two urchins saw their opportunity. The older one grabbed his brother's arm and whispered, "Let's get out of here. We'll hide out at the safehouse until our uncle comes and finds us tomorrow." They both disappeared into the night.

Tom was relieved that his duffel bag still lay on the bench where he had left it. He sat down on the bench, already knowing that he would have to sleep in the park all night. But it started to rain and he didn't want to get soaked in the only set of clothes he owned, so he headed back to his house. Tom was mentally exhausted and needed to find a dry spot for the night, and since he would not be sleeping next to Jenny, his only other option was the shed in their backyard.

He scooped up his duffel bag, returned to his house, and snuck into the backyard, hugging the shadows of the trees to remain hidden from Jenny and her new boyfriend. It was no surprise that two cars were parked in front of the shed. He assumed that one belonged to the mystery man, so Jenny must own the other.

Upon approaching the car closest to him, Tom realized it was his old wheels. Further inspection revealed patches of rust along the bottom driver's side of the car. He was sure that the rust must also be eating the passenger side too. He looked sadly at his neglected car. He'd worked hard to pay for it and now it stood like a rust bucket. If he'd been around, Tom would've cleaned the rust off and repainted it, but instead he'd been stuck behind four walls of a prison a whole province away.

Tom found the car unlocked, so he quietly opened the door and slid behind the wheel. Locals never locked their cars in Blue Ridge, with the exception being the Blue Ridge Police Department and other emergency services. He reached across and opened the glove compartment and took out the insurance papers. In the darkness, he managed to read the registration papers. The car belonged to Jenny Lockman. He returned the paperwork to the glove compartment, closed it, and slid out of the car, quietly closing the door. Curiosity could have got the better of him and he could check out the papers in the other car, but he wasn't interested in the name of the man in his house, since he wasn't going to be a permanent resident.

Bypassing the second car he turned his attention to the shed and found the plastic bag where two keys were hidden behind the building just where he had left them all those years ago. One was the shed key and the second one was to the house. Even Jenny wasn't aware of the keys' location. He opened the door and slipped inside, closing it behind him. Tom knew his workshop like the back of his hand, so he didn't need to turn the light on and alert Jenny of his presence. The streetlamp provided enough light, filtering through the only window in his shop. Nothing had changed. In the dim light, he noticed that every tool appeared to be where it should have been. He felt his way along the workbench in search of his flashlight. Once it was in his hand, he turned it on. As luck would have it, the batteries were still somewhat charged.

Scanning the shed, he noticed ugly cobwebs with dried-out, dead bugs trapped within them, and a thick layer of dust covering every inch of his workspace. He always kept his work area immaculately clean, so he looked sadly at his neglected shop. Jenny never came into it, as she had considered it his man cave, and he preferred it that way. The unspoken rule was "his workshop, his domain; her kitchen, her domain."

Transferring the slowly fading flashlight to his mouth, he found his wooden toolbox sitting in the corner, holding miscellaneous tools. He emptied the contents onto the floor and started putting in items he thought might come in handy for his new plan that was slowly coming together. Its' new contents soon included a coil of rope, several packages of tie wraps, wire cutters, a padlock and key, lots of duct tape, a half-full gas can, and, finally, a pair of scissors. As he moved the toolbox closer to the door, his flashlight died, so he tossed it onto the bench. Tom found a spot in the far corner, where a dirty blanket lay in a heap, and he settled in for the night.

Even after so many years away from Jenny, he still had the same dream every night. That dream had helped him keep his sanity. As he drifted off, he was once again gently lifting Jenny from the living room couch and carrying her into their bedroom, eagerly anticipating their lovemaking. In his dream, Tom anxiously removed her clothing, tossed them onto the floor, and then scrambled to turn down the bed. With a grin on her face, Jenny watched him fumbling with the buttons on his shirt and she slowly approached him, kissing each of his trembling fingers. She helped him with the remaining buttons and then removed his shirt. Tom's clothes were now tossed onto the same pile as hers and the two quickly fell onto the sheets. Tom snuggled up to her, making sure that every possible part of his body made contact with hers. Burying his face into her hair, he was overcome by the soft scent of vanilla and a hint of lavender that mesmerized his nostrils. It always amazed him that his wife had such a crazy effect on him. Jenny was his true soulmate. Raising himself up on one shoulder, he studied her face while their eyes intensely hungered for one another's next move. Tom lowered his face to Jenny and gently kissed her lips, and the moment intensified as she answered his kiss with true passion. Tom placed soft kisses along her neck, and he felt her body trembling. He moved away from her and let his eyes wander over her nakedness as if it were a road map that he didn't need. He already knew the road to ecstasy.

Jenny grinned. "See anything you like?"

"Are you kidding? Every time I see your beautiful body, I feel like a kid in a candy store. I'll never get tired of exploring every inch of your amazing body." He slowly ran his fingers down her side and her skin was as soft as satin. He whispered into her ear. "I love you, Jenny, and I always will."

She giggled and looked passionately into his dark eyes. "I love you too. Promise me that we'll always be this happy, even when we're old and our bodies start to fall apart."

"You have my word."

The two started making passionate love, and Jenny moaned under his caresses, as Tom kissed his way down her body. She quickly took the aggressive role, flipping Tom onto his back and moving on top. He grinned, as she often liked taking the lead and he didn't mind being dominated. She ran her fingers through his hair and gently tugged at the hair on his chest. Closing his eyes, he groaned as her fingers slowly worked down his trembling body. Both were out of control with passion.

This was usually when Tom woke up, but tonight's dream was going to throw him a curveball.

A loud bang suddenly filled the room. Tom's eyes shot open, and he started to panic. Was someone in their house? He felt Jenny's body slump against him.

"Jenny, are you okay? I can't breathe, honey. You have to get off of me."

He lifted her head and looked at her face. Jenny's eyes were glazed over, and her body was limp. He knew that something was terribly wrong. Tom's eyes filled with tears as he called her name. "Jenny! Jenny, honey! What's wrong?"

He placed his hand on her back and was about to roll her off him when he realized that his hand was soaking wet. Seized with panic, he pulled it back. It was dripping with blood—Jenny's blood.

He started screaming. "No! What the hell is going on?"

He was trapped in the middle of a horror movie, but was unable to wake up. He checked his hand again; the blood was still there and was now seeping into the sheets. He managed to move Jenny off him when his eyes saw a movement in the room. A man stood in front of him, holding a gun! It was his deceased brother.

Tom watched Charles grinning as he turned and left the room in a fit of laughter. Then he jolted awake as if he had been hit with a taser, and found himself standing. He had temporarily forgotten that he was sleeping in his shed, anxiously waiting for morning, when he would approach Jenny. Sweat covered his entire body, dripping from his hair onto his face. His clothes were damp and clammy, but Tom didn't have another set to change into, so he ran his sleeve over his face so he could at least see.

Tom had to walk it off. The shed was small, but he treaded every square inch of the floor that wasn't covered in tools. He became aware of sounds outside his shed and peeked through the window. There was movement on the back porch; he saw the male stranger smoking a cigarette. Tom thought that he could easily sneak up behind the man and snap his neck, but reconsidered. That would only cause new problems.

He returned to the corner of the shed and fell asleep from exhaustion. Jenny entered his dream once more before morning. She smiled at Tom as she slipped beneath the sheets of their bed, never taking her eyes off him. Tom was about to follow her when, to his shock, he discovered another man already waiting for her in the bed.

Tom started sweating, now furious. How dare this man take his place? Jenny belonged to him, was out of bounds to other men. Tom squinted, but the man was faceless and could have been anyone.

He awoke with a start and slowly opened his eyes, which were now filled with tears. His heart felt like it had left his body and there was nothing to fill the void. He now knew what it must feel like to be heartless. Deciding he was not going back to sleep, he looked out the window. Sometime during his second dream, the male stranger must have left the premises. Jenny's car was now the only one in the driveway.

It was still dark enough outside, and Tom knew he could remain unnoticed, so he picked up his duffel bag and tossed it into the toolbox, then quietly carried it out and placed it in the back seat of Jenny's car before returning to the shed. Moving his stool in line with the window, he took a seat and waited for Jenny, not knowing the best time to confront her. He had mixed feelings. What would he say?

"Hi, honey, I'm home. Hey, baby, I'm back. Who's the asshole shacked up with you?" Nervously, he sat there and noticed the outline of a man approaching Jenny's car and peer inside the windows. Tom tensed up, but didn't dare move to confront him in case it caused a commotion. The last thing he needed was for Jenny to come out and investigate and ruin his plan. The person shone a flashlight into her car, turned it off, and then disappeared. Tom hadn't realized that he was holding his breath until the man left.

Before long, the kitchen light turned on, and Jenny opened the back door and walked out of the house, a little girl in tow, locking the door behind her. The wind was knocked out of Tom's lungs. He needed to breathe. He watched as Jenny and the small girl, who was carrying a pack-sack on her back, walked down the driveway.

So not only had she moved on with a new man, she also had a daughter.

When she was out of sight, he left the shed, unlocked the house, and relocked it behind him. He was so disappointed that he felt like smashing something. Instead, he clenched his fists and swore. "Damn you, woman."

He glanced around the kitchen and scrounged through the drawers for anything that he could use to convince Jenny to leave with him. He found his switch blade pocket knife in the cutlery drawer. He grabbed it, slammed the drawer shut, and slowly walked to his old chair. He sat down, opened the knife, and placed it on his lap. The inside of the house was also in need of some paint and minor repairs. He assumed that her new boyfriend wasn't too handy, so they had just let everything go. Maybe she had been waiting for Tom to return so she could put him to work. Now that he saw she was with someone else, there wasn't a hope in hell that he was going to start repairing anything. He was done with her.

He heard Jenny's footsteps coming up the stairs and unlocking the door before entering the house. She quickly relocked the door and moved into the kitchen area. Jenny hummed as she started tidying up the kitchen.

He watched her closely, and then spoke. "Hello, Jenny. I've returned."

Jenny spun around in fear, which gave way to shock. She could hardly believe her eyes. This shell of a man that had once been her husband was sitting across the room from her. She immediately noticed the knife on his lap. "How did you get in here?"

"My hidden spare key behind the shed. Guess you didn't know it was there."

"If I had, I would have removed it." She nervously asked, "What're you doing here?"

Tom stood up and shoved the knife into his pants pocket. "What, no hug or kiss from my wife?"

Jenny was speechless. Tom had lost a great deal of weight. At first, he seemed rather frail, but upon closer inspection, she could see the muscles flexing in his arms. She guessed that he could use a good home-cooked meal and a clean set of clothes, but she wasn't about to offer him anything. His hair was cut short and completely gray, while his face had what she guessed was at least two days of stubble on it. As she studied him more closely, she became frightened. She moved further away from him and found herself wedged up against the counter. His eyes that had once looked so lovingly into hers were now devoid of any feeling. They looked like his late brother Charles' eyes, glaring black voids that she could read like an open book. Fear set in as she waited to see what he was about to do. Charles had shot Jenny in the back and almost killed her. Would Tom do the same thing? Jenny wasn't prepared to have to defend herself a second time, but she slowly shifted into survival mode.

"I didn't know you were released."

"You would've known if you hadn't cancelled your phone."

She looked angry as she shouted at him. "Why do you think I had to change it? You killed a local woman. I was constantly getting calls about being married to a killer. When I went to work, no one would let me wait on them in the restaurant. The owner knew I couldn't survive if she laid me off, so she generously moved me to the kitchen, cooking, where no one knew I was there. It took years before I could wait tables again. I finally have my life back in order and now you appear in my house. Uninvited, I might add." She took several deep breaths to calm down and then politely asked, "When did you get into town?"

"Last night. I would've knocked on your door, but it was obvious that you had moved on without me. I spent the night in my shed." Tom suddenly rushed across the room and grabbed her shoulders, shouting, "Have your forgotten you're still my wife, and this is my house too?"

Jenny's eyes filled with tears as she stared at him. "Let go of me. You're hurting me."

"Don't talk to me about hurt! Who the hell is the man you're sleeping with?"

Shocked, Jenny shot back. "I'm not sleeping with anyone!"

"Don't lie to me. I saw that man in the window last night. The two of you were pretty friendly. He was also on the back porch last night smoking. Do you know how easily I could have come up behind him and broken his neck?" He added, "Is that you and your latest fling's daughter you were taking to school?"

She glared at him and stated, "I have no boyfriend and the girl is not my daughter." She chuckled. "Typical of you to assume before you know the facts. I don't have to explain anything to you. We're done." She then shouted, "Get out before I call the police!"

Tom laughed. "We will be calling the police, just not right now."

Jenny trembled. "What're you going to do?"

"Collect what's owed to me."

"What're you talking about? No one owes you anything. For the last time, get out!"

Tom turned her around roughly and shoved her towards their bedroom. "Pack a bag. We leave in five minutes."

Jenny turned to face him. "I'm not going anywhere with you." She shoved him aside and made a mad dash for the kitchen door; and she hoped her freedom. Tom spun around and quickly grabbed her. Jenny screamed out in pain as his hand clamped down on her arm. She felt his enormous strength, almost like her arm was trapped within a vice.

He turned her around once more and shoved her towards the bedroom. "You now have four minutes before we leave."

The look in his eyes made her realize that she had no choice. She turned and went into the bedroom, with Tom following behind her. She said, "Where're we going and how long will we be gone?"

"You leave the details to me. Just pack."

She glared at him. "I don't know what to take with me. Do I need clothes for one day or one month? When are we coming back?"

"We won't be coming back."

Jenny turned to him. "What do you mean we won't be coming back? I'm not going anywhere with you. I have a job here and friends who love me."

"You don't need your job and you have me to love you. Screw your friends."

Jenny turned and glared at Tom. "If we aren't coming back, then there's no need for me to pack anything." She glared at him before stating, "You can hold me prisoner, but you can't watch me all the time. I will escape. You can't force me to love you again. You aren't the man I married."

Tom looked hurt when she announced that she no longer loved him. He shrugged. "Suit yourself."

Jenny started to panic. What could she do to protect herself? She needed time to think. Without looking at him, she asked, "Can I at least use the bathroom before we leave?"

"Make it quick."

Jenny went into the bathroom, not knowing what to do. When she looked at her reflection in the mirror, the fear on her face stared back at her. She could scream and the neighbors might hear her, but that would only put them in danger. She remembered Tom's knife in his pocket and decided screaming could easily get her killed before she had a chance to escape. She sat on the toilet lid and mumbled to herself. "Think, Jenny. Think."

Knowing that the police would be involved she had to think how could she get a message to Don? She looked around the bathroom, trying to form a plan. The window was too small for her to fit through, so she abandoned that idea. She stood in front of the mirror once again and slowly opened the medicine cabinet. Seeing her lipstick tube on the bottom shelf, she picked it up.

Tom banged on the door and yelled, "Hurry up in there. What the hell are you doing?"

"I'm almost ready." She flushed the toilet and turned on the tap. While the water was running, she removed the cap from the lipstick tube and paused slightly. The police would figure out that Tom was out of prison once they found out she was missing, so her clue had to be something more useful. She drew a blank, but eventually glanced down at her watch. She quickly wrote "8:45" on the back of the mirror, and then put the lipstick cap back on the tube before returning it to the shelf and closing the cabinet. Hopefully the police would connect the 8:45 as the time she was kidnapped. Her clue was sketchy, but eventually the police might figure it out. She then confidently left the bathroom.

Not looking at him, she said, "I'm ready. Let's get this over with." She hadn't noticed the pillowcase he held in his hand.

On the way out of the house, Tom grabbed her purse, car keys, and cell phone. He drew the knife from his pocket and showed it to Jenny. "You so much as breathe too loud and you die." The look in his eyes showed that he meant business.

Despite everything going on, he was a perfect gentleman, even to the point of opening the passenger side of the car for her. She slid into the car, not making eye contact with him. He closed her door and opened the back door to grab the package of tie wraps from his toolbox. He slammed the door shut and then opened her door a second time. "Put your seat belt on."

Jenny did as she was told. She was horrified when she realized that he was binding her wrists together with a tie wrap, and then attaching her to the door handle with the second tie wrap. She fought furiously but was no match for him. He then threw the pillowcase over her head, closed the door and went to the driver's side.

Jenny was trembling. She knew screaming was out of the question, but maybe one of the neighbours had seen what was happening to her and called the police. "What the hell are you doing? Take this pillowcase off me. Where are you taking me?"

Tom didn't answer, but started the car and backed out of the driveway.

Jenny started to sweat. What did Tom have planned for her? Where was he taking her, and what was her next move? She mentally counted the minutes as they traveled to their destination in hopes of giving Don a clue to where he might be holding her.

At first, the road was paved, so Tom made good time. Then he made a quick left turn onto a gravel road and, judging by the condition of the road, it was abandoned, just as the bus driver had said. The location was perfect for his plan.

The car bounced along the road as the gravel turned into potholes. He was swerving left and then right, throwing Jenny around on her seat. The branches that scratched the side of her car sounded like poorly tuned trumpets.

When they arrived at wherever he was taking her, Tom turned off the engine. He slid out of the car and Jenny could hear his footsteps slowly walk away from the car. Tom already knew that Jenny would still be there when he returned.

She wondered if screaming would bring someone to her rescue, but decided that Tom was too smart for that. The bumpy road told Jenny that there was no one around to hear her screams. She mentally calculated that they had been on the road for about fifteen minutes.

How could she get this information to Don? She panicked, finally realizing that Bill might also be dragged into the case. Was Bill part of Tom's plan? Tom hated the Blue Ridge Police Department for the death of his brother, and Bill had been the sergeant at the time. Five years earlier, when Charles had held her and Claire captive, it was obvious that either Charles would die, or both she and Claire would. Charles had been the loser.

She pulled at the tie wraps but nothing gave. She even tried to shake the pillowcase off her head, but with no luck. She started to cry, feeling defenseless. The last time that she was this scared was when Charles held her and Claire captive in that dirty rundown cabin in the middle of nowhere. That was five years ago, but the memory was still vivid in her mind. In a state of panic, when Charles knew that the police force had found him, he used Jenny as a human shield and he put a bullet in her back. She still remembered the pain of the bullet passing into her body. She had to remove that memory from her mind and concentrate on the present situation.

Tom paused before approaching the motel. The once paved parking lot was now mostly full of cracks. Weeds had grown between the cracks and spread as far as the eye could see. The grass was overgrown with foliage, and the shrubs were dead from lack of watering. This was proving to be a good location for him and Jenny to hide out. Tom walked to the office, smashed the window, and reached through to unlock the door. He opened it and crossed the room to a board where keys hung in order of room numbers. He selected the key for the room that was furthest from the office and shoved it into his pocket. He then grabbed the rest of the keys and left the building. Walking slightly into the bush, he tossed the keys well away from the building. If the police did manage to find his location, they wouldn't know which room he was in. That would give him an advantage over them. He returned to the car, undid her seat belt and clipped the tie wrap that held Jenny to the door handle He roughly pulled her out of the seat, and then guided her to the room.

She felt scared and insecure. "Take your hands off of me." When she got no response, she added, "Take this stupid pillowcase off my head. I can't see where I'm going."

"You don't need to know where you're going." He stopped in front of a door and Jenny heard him slip the key into the lock and then open it. He pushed her in and led her to the bed. "Lie down."

She was tired of fighting, but didn't want him to think that she was weak, so she gave him some resistance, to no avail. She was brutally deposited on the bed, and Tom grabbed her arms. Shock set in when she realized that he was binding her to the headboard.

Jenny shouted, "You bastard! Do you think keeping me here is going to get you into my good books? What do you hope to accomplish?"

He reached out and pulled the pillowcase off her head. Smugly, he answered, "My darling, I'm going to be rich with or without you. We could be basking on a remote beach in a matter of days, sipping on fancy drinks with little umbrellas in them. That is, if you choose to come with me."

"What do you mean rich? Whatever you have planned, count me out."

"Suit yourself. I'm sure I can find a nice young lady to join me."

"Not if she has a brain in her head."

Expecting a slap across her head, she was surprised to hear him laugh instead as he left the room. Jenny was confused. What did he mean when he said they could be rich? What did Tom have planned? There was one thing Jenny knew: wealth came from honest, hard work, not from dishonesty. She wanted nothing to do with Tom, but she had to know his plans. Hopefully she could warn anyone who might be in his path of destruction, someone who could stop him and save her at the same time.

She looked around the room and realized that it had been abandoned for years. The curtains were shredded, likely from mice that lived within these four walls. Everywhere she looked, Jenny saw mouse droppings. Cobwebs and dust formed blankets over all the broken furniture. Jenny panicked when she saw how filthy the sheets were beneath her.

She had to escape this hellhole. But no matter how hard she pulled and tugged at her restraints, she couldn't break loose. Her wrists were becoming raw with each worthless tug she made, so reluctantly, she accepted defeat.

Once Tom left the room, he was ready to kill anyone who got in his way. He muttered, "How dare Jenny talk to me in that tone?"

He was starting to realize that she might be lost to him forever. Tom knew that everything that had happened over the past ten years was his fault, but he had to pass the blame on to anyone other than himself. The scapegoat at this point was Sergeant Bill Smithe. He would pay dearly.

Tom walked around the motel, getting his bearings. The side and back of the building were as rundown as the front. To his surprise, partly hidden in the bushes behind the building, there was a shipping container, its' doors slightly ajar. He walked around the container and decided it was a safe place to store his tools, maybe even hide Jenny's car. The rusty hinges squeaked when he forced the doors open. Inside, it was completely empty, dark, and gloomy. It was a good hiding spot, well away from prying eyes.

He returned to the car and drove it around the back of the building and into the container. He dropped the car keys into his pants pocket, tossed Jenny's cell phone on the front seat, and then picked up her purse. Tom removed his duffel bag from the toolbox, looked at his stash of tools and placed the scissors in his bag before slinging it over his shoulder. He filled his pocket with tie wraps and left his toolbox safely inside the container. He then locked the container with his padlock and tossed the key into his pocket before returning to the room.

He could tell from the condition of Jenny's wrists that she had tried to escape. He placed his duffel bag on the table and then tossed her purse onto the bed beside her. He sat in the chair facing her and studied his wife before speaking. "Well, Jenny, you have some explaining to do."

"I have nothing to say to you."

"Okay. I'll ask the questions, and if you don't answer, I'll know you're hiding something." He got no reaction, so he continued, "Who is your new boyfriend?"

Jenny was forced to answer, or he would assume she was guilty. She looked directly at him. "He's not my boyfriend. When you went to prison, I couldn't afford the house payments, so rather than lose the house, I took in a boarder. His name is Joseph Marks and he rents the spare room with his wife, Sally."

Tom studied her and knew she very well might be telling the truth. Taking a chance, he asked another question. "Who's the girl you walked to the bus stop this morning?"

Jenny knew better than reveal the little girl's real name, as Tom might figure out that his brother was dead because of this child. She chose her words carefully. "I babysit her every morning and after school Monday to Friday. When she's at school, I work at the restaurant." Jenny saw this as her opportunity to get a message to anyone Tom would let her speak to. She looked into Tom's eyes. "You have to let me go. She needs her medicine after school or she could die."

"Not happening."

"At least let me tell someone, anyone, who can meet her after school and make sure she gets her medicine. Please, Tom. You can do whatever you want with me, but please don't let an innocent child die because of your pride." Jenny saw Tom glance at his watch then pick up his phone. It appeared he was about to leave the room. "You're not going anywhere, buddy, until you promise me that I can talk to someone about the child's medicine. Do you want to be responsible for a child's death? You may not be the same man I married, but I'm sure you don't want to add a second murder to your already tainted record. Give me my phone. I need to call right away."

Tom conceded. "Fine, but you're not using your phone."

"Why not?"

"I have my own phone." Tom paused. "Who do you want to call?"

"Someone reliable."

"Like who?"

"I trust the police force completely. Let me call them."

"Excuse me Jenny, but I don't exactly trust you."

"You'll be in the room and can hear my conversation."

Tom laughed. "Of course you would pick the police force. We have all day before school is out, so let's not be hasty. We need to talk."

Jenny needed to talk to him too. "Okay, let's sit and talk, and then I can make my call."

"What you want to talk about?"

"I answered your questions, now you have to answer mine."

Tom swung around and scowled at her. "I don't have to answer any of your questions."

"Right. So, this is how the game is played. I had to answer your questions, but mine are out of bounds? You asshole. How can you even live with yourself?"

Tom stopped dead in his tracks. "Fine. Ask away."

Jenny let out a sigh of relief. "Thank you, Tom. Can I ask you what your overall plan is?"

"Out of bounds."

"What do you mean, out of bounds? What the hell do you think I can do to ruin your plan? I'm strapped to this dirty bed in this run-down room out in the middle of nowhere." She was frustrated, but asked a third question. "Okay, then how do you plan on getting rich?"

"Why do you care? You're not coming with me."

"Talk to me, Tom. If I'm going to die today, I have a right to know everything."

Tom took a seat across from her and grinned. "Sergeant Bill Smithe killed Charles and he's going to pay for it."

Jenny was scared, but asked, "How is he going to pay for it?"

"I'm about to call him and ask for half a million dollars in exchange for you?"

"You're not serious. How do you even know if he has that much money?"

"If he wants you alive, he'll figure it out."

"Okay, but let me speak to him."

"No way."

"Who better to make sure that the little girl gets her medicine than the sergeant? He also has to know that she is off school fifteen minutes early today."

Tom retorted, "She can stand there and wait."

"You forget that right now I should be at work. You didn't even let me call in sick, so now that makes me look irresponsible. I'm the one who's supposed to pick her up from school. Don't leave her alone and scared."

He just shrugged. "Oh, hell, if Bill doesn't come up with the money, you won't be around tomorrow to go to work or pick her up. They'll figure it out."

She looked directly at him and asked, "When are you going to call Bill?"

"Now seems like a good time."

"Please stay in the room. I need to speak to him before you hang up."

"Oh, crap, all right, but if you say the wrong thing, you die and so does the child." He then approached her and cut the tie wraps that attached her to the headboard, but left the ones around her wrists. He led her to the chair next to the table. "Call the number for the police and then hand me the phone."

Jenny did as she was told.

Chapter Two

10:00 a.m. – 11:15 a.m.

DON SAT IN HIS OFFICE, sipping a cup of coffee, and was about to enter the main area for the regular morning meeting when the phone rang at Daniel's desk. Daniel went to answer, but Don signaled to him that he would get it. The light for line one was flashing, so he picked it up and answered, "Good morning. Blue Ridge Police Department, Sergeant Don Wilson speaking."

There was a slight pause at the other end of the line before Tom responded, "I need to speak to Sergeant Bill Smithe."

"I'm sorry, but Sergeant Bill Smithe no longer works for the force."

Tom was stunned. He wondered if his plan could still work without Bill. He covered the mouthpiece and turned to Jenny. "Why didn't you tell me that he's no longer on the force?"

She shrugged nonchalantly. "You never asked."

He threw her a dangerous glare and then removed his hand from the phone. "Where is he?"

"Who is this?"

"I'm just an old friend who'd like to catch up with him."

"I'm sorry, but he's not available."

"I really need to speak to him. How can I reach him?"

Don became suspicious as the voice on the other end of the line turned urgent. "I'm sorry. We aren't allowed to give out information on our officers."

Tom started to sweat. Would his plan still work if he dealt with a different sergeant? His revenge was personal, so it had to be Bill or no one. He wasn't about to walk away without a half million dollars in his pocket, so he inquired, "Is he deceased?"

Don became nervous. Why was this man on the other end of the phone inquiring about Bill? "I'm sorry, but if you have a problem, you either have to deal with me, or I can pass you on to another officer on duty." He then waited for a reply.

Tom was now out of control as he yelled into the phone. "I'll only speak with Bill Smithe!" He then took a few deep breaths to calm down. "I assume he's still in town. Call him and get him into the office. You have one hour before I call again. If he's not there, he'll be responsible for a death." He then ended the call and slammed down the cell phone.

Don immediately jumped up from his desk and ran into the common area. "Heads up, guys. Morning meeting's been cancelled. I just received a strange - no, I should say, a rather eerie phone call that involves Bill. Put out your feelers and see if we can learn anything that could identify who this person is."

His day shift workers flew into action. In no time at all, the room turned from a group of officers sipping on coffees and preparing for their morning meeting to a beehive swarming with activity. Some desks were occupied by officers picking up phones, while others were looking through files of active or unsolved cases.

Don returned to his office to call Bill.

Bill Smithe had been retired for several years, and they had been peaceful years with his wife Beatrice. He and Beatrice were sitting in the kitchen enjoying a leisurely cup of coffee when Beatrice asked Bill. "What do you want to do today?"

He got up from his chair, walked around the table, and placed a kiss on her cheek. "Anything, as long as it involves you."

She suggested, "If it warms up later, maybe we could have a picnic on the beach."

"Sounds like fun. Count me in."

When the phone rang, Bill crossed the room to answer it. Seeing that it was from the police station, he became nervous. He looked at Beatrice. "It's the station. Hopefully all is well." Not knowing which officer was calling, he picked up the phone and answered, "Hello?"

Don was apologetic. "Sorry to bother you, Bill, but we have a situation here that involves you. You need to get in here pronto."

Shocked, Bill paused before responding, "I'm on my way." He hung up the phone and slowly turned to Beatrice. "I'm sorry, darling. Not sure what's going on in the office, but they need me. You may have to put our picnic on hold."

Beatrice stood up, crossed the room, and hugged him nervously. She moved out of his arms and studied his facial expression, but got no indication as to what was happening. "Any idea what it's about?"

"No, but it sounded urgent."

She looked at him and spoke in a trembling voice, tears already running down her cheeks. "Don't you go and get yourself shot again."

Bill wiped away her tears and smiled. "Not a chance. I've already done that once. I'll call you when I know what's going on." She was slow to release his arms, but he reassured her. "I'll be fine."

Both Bob Billings and Jack Spencer sat at their desks, each man scrolling through their list of contacts. Bob found the phone number for Mike Johnson, the local parole officer for Blue Ridge, and called the number.

Mike picked up the phone. "Hello?"

"Mike, this is Officer Bob Billings."

"Hi, Bob. I was about to call your office."

"Interesting, we have a situation here and it sounds like you might be able to shed some light on it."

"Maybe I can. I don't know if this is related to your issue, but three days ago, I was notified that a Tom Lockman was granted early release from the Edmonton prison. He was put on a bus and should have arrived here last night. He was supposed to report to me upon arrival, but since his bus didn't get here until evening, I thought he would check in this morning. So far, I haven't heard a word from him." He paused. "He was very lucky to get out of prison early, so I hope he didn't screw up the one and only chance he had for freedom."

"He may have done just that." Bob noticed that he was gripping the phone far too tight, but he always did that when his job became overwhelming. He relaxed his grip on the receiver and added, "Sounds to me like a breach of parole, so once we find him, he's back behind bars. He really screwed up. Thanks, Mike."

Mike said, "Keep me updated. I have to notify Edmonton that he was a no-show. It won't go well for him."

"Talk later." Bob hung up the phone, crossed the room and entered Don's office. "I have an update and it isn't good."

Don stopped what he was doing. "What've you got?"

"I just talked to Mike Johnson, our local parole officer, and it appears that Tom Lockman was released from prison three days ago and is now in town. As of this morning, he hadn't checked in with him."

Don shot out of his chair. "Oh, shit! Get over to Jenny's place and check on her! If she isn't home, go to her workplace and make sure she's aware that Tom's here!" he shouted as Bob left his office. "Just make sure you take backup!"

"I'm on my way."

Bob left the office, Jim Banks in tow, and the two officers drove the short distance to Jenny's house. Before leaving the cruiser, both men assessed the front yard and the side of the house they could see. Bob turned to his partner. "It looks clear so far."

Cautiously, the two officers left their cruiser. Jim glanced up and down the street. "Pretty quiet on the street too. I'll take the front of the house and you take the back. Let's meet up at the back porch."

Both walked in opposite directions, checking first the house and then the yard, looking for possible footprints that shouldn't be there. Behind the house, Bob noticed that not only was Jenny's car gone, but also her tenant's, so hopefully she was at work. Bob watched Jim come around the back of the house. "You got anything?"

"Nothing out of the ordinary on this side of the house."

The two men each pulled on a set of evidence gloves in case they had to enter the building. They cautiously climbed the stairs and Jim tapped on the door. When there was no answer, he quietly opened the door, calling, "Jenny? Are you here?" Both men slowly drew their weapons and entered the kitchen, moving from one room to the next, carefully looking for any signs of disturbance. Once they had swept the entire house, Jim commented, "There's no one here. Let's head over to her workplace."

"Right behind you, partner." Once outside the house, both men removed their gloves and shoved them into their jacket pockets.

The two officers left and drove over to the diner. They walked in and glanced around, looking for Jenny, but she was nowhere to be seen. The owner was behind the counter, so Bob approached her. "I was looking for Jenny. Have you seen her this morning?"

The owner answered, "She never came into work today. I called her house, but no one answered, so I assumed that she was on her way in." She added, "There must be a problem if you officers are here. I sure hope she's okay."

"I'm sure she is. Please don't hesitate to call the precinct if she shows up."

"Of course." The owner suddenly looked scared. "Oh my God, has something happened to her?"

"I'm sorry, but I can't give you any information at this time."

"That poor woman has been through hell."

Bob responded, "Yes, she has. Please call if she shows up."

"For sure, officer."

Both men returned to the office, and Jim reported to Don. "She's not at her house and never showed up for work this morning. Her car's missing."

Don thought before speaking. "Jim, put out an APB on Jenny's car."

"Right on it, boss!"

Don could feel the stress set in. He looked at Bob. "Shit. We have a real problem. If Tom took Jenny forcefully, and I'm guessing he did, then we have to find her. We don't know what Tom's capable of doing. Being behind bars can change a person, and often not for the better. If she resists him, he could hurt her or possibly even kill her." He then added, "I called Bill and he's on his way in. I'm not sure why Tom has to bring Bill into the picture, but he's likely out for revenge. Poor Bill should be enjoying his retirement, but instead this asshole shows up and throws a wrench into his life. I hate to say it, but we need that damn whiteboard again."

Bob looked nervous and then asked, "Do you think Jenny will be able to send us any messages or clues about where he's keeping her, like when Charles held her hostage?"

Don answered, "I hope so. If we're lucky, he won't be any smarter than his brother was."

Bob sighed. "I'll get the damn whiteboard out and set it up." As he passed Jack Spencer's desk, he said, "Well, we know who the asshole is."

Jack looked up from his desk, waiting for a name.

"Do you remember Charles Lockman?"

"Who could forget? He was the nutcase who kidnapped Claire, shot Jenny, and almost killed Bill. Please don't tell me he's back from the dead."

"Not exactly, but his brother Tom Lockman was just released from prison and is now in Blue Ridge. Jenny is also missing."

Jack responded, "I'll call the Edmonton prison and get the details of his release." He looked puzzled. "Why weren't we notified of his release?"

"I'm not sure, but we certainly should have been."

Jack Spencer looked up the prison's phone number and called it. At the other end of the line, a receptionist answered the phone. "Good morning, Edmonton Maximum Security Prison. How may I help you?"

"This is Constable Jack Spencer of the Blue Ridge Police Department. I need to speak to someone about the release of a prisoner."

"I'll patch you through to the head of the prison, Mr. Al Grant. Hold the line, please."

"Thank you."

Jack waited for several minutes before a voice answered, "Good morning, Constable Spencer. How may I help you?"

"I understand that three days ago, a prisoner, Tom Lockman, was released from your complex. I need to ask you a few questions about his release, if I may."

"Of course."

"Why was the Blue Ridge Police Department not notified of his release?"

"It isn't standard procedure to notify police stations if an inmate is released. We notify the local parole officer and it's up to them to notify your department if there are any problems." He then asked, "Is there a problem?"

"At our end, there's a major problem. He never checked in with his parole officer and since he arrived, it appears he's kidnapped his wife, and we're not sure what he's capable of doing." He then asked, "He was given early parole. Can you tell me how it was granted?"

"Just give me a minute. I'll put you on hold while I grab his file."

Jack waited patiently while soft music played in the background.

Al returned and apologized. "Sorry, I had to get my secretary to locate the file. I'm not much good at the paperwork side of the prison." He continued, "Mr. Lockman applied for day parole six months ago and it was granted. He worked in the local town as a mechanic and was well respected. Inside these walls, Tom was a model prisoner, did his job, and minded his own business. That doesn't mean it was easy for him. When I look at his file, he was sent to the infirmary regularly and suffered brutal beatings. He worked hard and it looks like he had very few friends. Actually, only one. The one prisoner he knew the best, Big John, was murdered a few months before Tom was released. When he applied for full parole, the board studied his file extensively and made the decision based on his health, frail condition, and good behavior. The board knew that if he was not released, he would likely also be murdered. Tom stood in front of the board and didn't plead for his life, but spoke directly to Mr. Wilks about how sorry he was for destroying his life. The board saw a sensitive side of him and, after hours of deliberation, decided he was not a threat to society. He was to report to his parole officer in Blue Ridge once he arrived there. I'm sorry to hear that he never checked in."

Jack was frustrated. "We only just found out this morning that he never met with or notified his parole officer of his arrival."

"A big mistake on his part."

"That's for sure. Thanks for the information, Al."

"Keep us updated."

"Will do." Jack hung up his phone and then went into Don's office to update him.

Don asked, "What you got?"

"I just spoke to the Edmonton prison, and it sounds like Tom got out on good behavior."

Don was upset. "Horseshit. Kidnapping Jenny is not good behavior. We have to find her."

Bob appeared, carrying the whiteboard, and set it up outside Don's office. Don emerged and looked at it. Picking up the marker, he wrote "Tom Lockman" at the top. Beneath his name, he wrote "phone call 10:00 a.m." and beside the time he wrote "Jenny hostage." Underneath he finally added "Called Bill Smithe." Next he wrote "Check out Jenny's house and work place Bob and Jim".

He turned around and saw Bill walking into the room. The shock on his face was obvious when he saw the whiteboard with Tom Lockman's name at the top. Don pointed to his office and Bill followed him in, then the two sat down. "I'm sorry to drag you into this, Bill, but we have a serious problem and, unfortunately, it involves you."

"Of course it does." Bill ran his fingers through his hair. He had to think. "Any chance I can get a cup of coffee?"

Bob was already ten steps ahead of him, and in a flash, the mug was set down in front of him. "Thanks Bob."

Bill looked at Don. "Beatrice is going to be pissed when she finds out about this."

"I'll bet." Don got up from his desk and went to the window. "We just found out that Tom Lockman was released from prison three days ago and arrived in town last night. He was supposed to check in with his parole officer first thing, but I guess, instead he went to visit Jenny. I have to assume that his homecoming wasn't what he expected. I got a phone call at ten this morning asking for you, and when I informed the person at the other end of the phone that you no longer worked here, he blew up. My team has since confirmed that the call was from Tom Lockman. I had one hour to get you here before his next call or someone would die. That someone has to be Jenny."

Bill looked down at his watch. "We have fifteen minutes before he calls again. Is everything set up for recording?"

"It is. I'm really sorry about this, Bill."

"I know you are. Let's hope this is the last asshole coming after me."

"Are you going to call Beatrice?"

Bill paused. "Not right now. I need to clear my head and get ready for my call."

Bill left the office and walked aimlessly around the common area, trying to kill time, saying hi to every officer in the building. As eleven o'clock approached, he took a seat across from Daniel Straume, who would not only be recording the call, but also attempting to track the phone.

"You ready for this, Bill?"

"I sure as hell hope so, but I might be a bit rusty." When the phone rang, Bill jumped and then reached for the receiver. Once he saw that the phone-tracking device was set and the "record" button had been pushed, he answered, "Hello?"

"Is this the famous Sergeant Bill Smithe?"

"You should already know it's me." Bill paused. "You must be Tom Lockman. I haven't had the pleasure of officially meeting you, except at your trial and at the prison when I informed you of your brother's death. The prison was pretty pissed off that you broke one of their phones." Bill paused again. "On the other hand, I had some dealings with your departed brother Charles. He was a good adversary, but not good enough to beat the Blue Ridge Police Department." When Bill got no response, he continued, "What can I do for you?"

"Funny you should ask." Tom was feeling very confident. "You probably already know that I have Jenny with me."

Bill ignored him. "This isn't Jenny's phone, so where'd you get the phone, Tom? Prisons don't hand them out."

"Found it on the bus. Someone's loss is now my gain."

"So now you've added theft to your already tainted record."

"Hey, it was lost. Finders, keepers."

"If you say so. Let me guess, when you arrived in town and she didn't exactly greet you with open arms, you must have been pissed." Bill paused. "Ten years with you out of her life made her very independent."

Tom became angry. "She's still my wife and I had every right to take her."

"Maybe if she was willing to go with you, but kidnapping her is a different story. She doesn't want you anymore, so what do you hope to gain by forcing her to leave with you?"

Tom laughed. "Since she no longer wants me, she's now my means to an end."

"What the hell does that mean?"

"Come on, Bill. I'm sure you know how this will end."

"I do. You will either be back in jail for failure to report to your parole officer, or in a body bag." Bill added, "If you turn yourself in now, I could talk to your parole officer and tell him you were delayed. That gesture would give you a second chance on the outside."

Laughter on the other end of the phone sent chills down Bill's spine. "You must be on drugs if you think I'm going to turn myself in to you. You're the man who murdered my brother. Tell me, Bill, why didn't you get sent to prison for murder?"

"I work for the law, not against it. Your brother kidnapped a child and then Jenny. He was a terrorist and unstable. We tried to bring him in peacefully, but when he shot Jenny, that sealed his fate." Bill looked at Daniel and mimed, "Are you getting this?" Dan nodded. Bill turned his attention back to Tom. "Okay. You have me here, so what do you want?"

"Funny you should ask."

Bill was outraged. "You think this is funny? Do you have any idea what you're doing? You were given a second chance at life and you seriously screwed up. You kidnapped Jenny!"

Tom shouted into the phone. "She deserved to be kidnapped! I was going to take her away and start over."

"I guess she didn't want anything to do with you."

"I told her we could start a new life somewhere else. She could either come with me, or I was going to take her. I had a bright new future planned for the two of us and she turned me down."

"That had to hurt, but that's no excuse to hurt her back. You have no idea what she went through while you were in prison."

"What about what I went through?" Tom shouted. "It wasn't a piece of cake inside those four walls. I was beaten regularly because of my size. My best friend was murdered just because he was my friend and protector."

"I'm sure it wasn't easy for you, but why should Jenny be penalized for your mistake? You forget that you killed Joan Wilks, an innocent woman out buying milk for her family."

Tom was becoming agitated. "Let's cut the bullshit and get down to business."

Bill was adamant. "Not until I talk to Jenny."

Tom insisted. "Business first, then you can talk to her."

"Cut to the chase, Tom. I don't even know if she's still alive."

"She is."

"Then let me talk to her."

"You better not try anything stupid, or she dies." He then passed Jenny the phone.

Jenny's voice was nervous as she spoke. "Hello, Bill."

"Are you okay?"

"I'm fine, just scared." Her voice broke.

"Has he hurt you?"

"Not yet." Jenny spoke slowly, as if that would help Bill better understand her words. "Bill, it looks like I won't be home to pick Nancy up after school. Please make sure she gets home safely."

Puzzled, Bill glanced at Daniel, who also looked confused. "I'll make sure she's picked up."

"Thank you. She also needs her medicine right after school. It's inside the medicine cabinet in the bathroom."

Bill listened carefully, as he knew there were likely hidden messages in their conversation. "I'll take care of it personally."

Tom was standing beside Jenny, ready to grab the phone from her. She spoke quickly. "One more thing. School ends fifteen minutes early. I don't want her to think that no one was coming for her."

"Don't worry. I'll make sure someone is there to pick her up."

"Thank you." She then added, "Tell her I love her."

"She already knows that. Stay strong and we'll find you, I promise."

Tom came back on the line. "Okay, now that you know she's still alive, let's get down to business. While I was in prison, my wages were a pittance. You need to compensate me for that. I want five hundred thousand dollars in exchange for Jenny."

Bill was incredulous. "Where do you think I can come up with that much money?"

"Not my problem. You might want to take up a collection in the office, since all of your officers were responsible for my brother's death. It would also be a good idea to hit up Doctor Jackson, after all, he did testify at my trial. I'm sure he has a healthy salary and would probably make a donation in exchange for Jenny."

"You're as crazy as your brother," Bill said, "You can still turn yourself in and save face with the justice system."

"Nice try, but I want what's owed me."

Bill now knew what he had to do. "Okay, Tom, your brother gave me eight hours to find him and my team located him just before the time expired. How much time are you going to give me?"

Tom grinned. He knew that Bill had no choice but to pay up or sacrifice Jenny. He still hated using her as a pawn, but she had rejected him, so her loss would become his gain. "If you start right now, you should have the funds in place by nine a.m. tomorrow."

Bill was stunned. "So, you really want to play this game. Tom, you know you can't win against my team. You're just another Lockman asshole." He paused. "Okay, let's up the ante. I'm guessing my team will find you well before tomorrow morning and then you'll be back behind bars." Bill knew he had to keep in contact with Jenny, so he asked, "When can I talk to Jenny again?"

"Not going to happen."

"Then you won't get your money. I have to talk to her at least every two hours to know that she's still alive. If I don't hear her voice, then the deal's off. So when can I expect your next call?"

Tom felt a headache coming on and rubbed his forehead. "Fine, I'll call at one o'clock." Tom ended the call on his cell phone and dropped it onto the table.

Daniel turned off the tracking device and looked at Bill. "My tracker says the call came from Florida. It must be a burner phone. These devices come with scrambled locations built into them. His next call will show a different location."

"It's not your fault. What were the odds that the phone he found on the bus would be a burner phone?"

"Guess he lucked out when he found it."

Bill paused before asking, "I thought the police force could track burner phones."

"They can if they have the right equipment. Blue Ridge is just a small town in the middle of nowhere. By the time we get the proper equipment here, it could be too late for Jenny."

"Listen to the replay and let me know if you hear anything in the background that will tell us where he's hiding out," Bill said.

Daniel stopped Bill as he was leaving the desk. "Sorry I couldn't locate where he is."

"I thought we might have gotten lucky, but scrap that idea. We'll have to locate him the good old-fashioned way." Bill went to the whiteboard and picked up the felt pen. He added. "Tom called 11:00" under that he wrote "Claire's new name Nancy." Below that, he wrote "Medicine behind bathroom mirror", next clue was "School out fifteen minutes earlier 2:45", and finally, "Tom using burner phone."

Don came to stand beside Bill, and the two looked at the four clues that faced them. Don asked, "Why do you suppose Jenny changed Claire's name to Nancy?"

Bill answered, "Jenny's probably not sure if Tom knew that Charles had used Claire as the ticket to getting him released, and she's protecting Claire again. Jenny is one strong lady."

"We have to find her, Bill."

"I agree. As far as the second clue is concerned, Claire's medicine is for her diabetes, so it's kept in the fridge, not in a medicine cabinet. I'm not sure about school getting out fifteen minutes earlier. He managed to get a burner phone so we couldn't track his location. I'm going to head over to Jenny's and check out the medicine cabinet in the bathroom."

Don called Greg over and said, "Please accompany Bill to Jenny's house." Don added on the whiteboard. "Bill and Greg check Jenny's house".

Greg nodded and the two men left the building, Greg behind the wheel. They arrived at Jenny's place and before going inside, put on disposable gloves. Once inside, a quick glance around the home, told both men that they were the only people there. Bill went straight to the bathroom. Greg watched as Bill slowly opened the medicine cabinet door, revealing 8:45 written on the back side of the mirror.

"What do you think it means?" Greg asked.

Bill studied the time for several moments before speaking. "Right now, all I see is a time. What was she thinking when she wrote it down? Was she alone when it was written or did Tom force her to write it down, in order to throw us off his trail?" Bill glanced around the bathroom, but the message behind the mirror was the only thing he spotted. Frustrated he turned to Greg. "Jenny is on borrowed time and here we both are wasting time on a silly clue."

Greg responded, "No clue that Jenny might have left is silly. We just need to figure out what it means."

"All I know is Jenny's on borrowed time and we really need to find her fast. Why couldn't she have been more specific?" Frustrated, Bill shut the mirror and looked at his reflection. He was an old man trying to do the job of two younger ones. "I'm too old for this shit."

"Hang in there, Bill. The team has your back."

"For how long?"

"As long as it takes."

"Maybe Beatrice and I should move away."

"Not a good idea."

"Why not?"

"If someone else appears down the road, looking for you, you'll be too far away to come back." Greg added, "Besides we'll all miss the two of you. Eventually, we'll have caught everyone connected to you and you can be as carefree as a bird."

"Maybe when I'm in my eighties."

"You could live to be well into your nineties. According to my math, you'll have ten plus years of peace and quiet."

"That's encouraging." The two men left the bathroom and did a quick scan around the rest of the house, looking for more clues. "There are lots of dirty footprints on the floor, so we need to get a forensic team here and sweep the house. Maybe Jenny left more clues," Bill said.

Greg responded, "I also saw lots of footprints outside. I'm almost positive that Don has already thought of that, but I'll check with him when we get back to the office. Let's get back to the precinct." Both men left Jenny's house and drove back to the station.

Don approached Debbie Mozer's desk and nodded for Eric Simpson to join them. "Debbie, I need you and Eric to go over to the school and pick up Kimberley and Claire, and then go over to Richard's office and pick him up too. Fill them in on the situation. Take them to their house. Eric, you stay there until this is all over. Debbie, I need you back at the office. I'll call the school and Richard's office to let them know you're on your way."

Debbie nodded. "Will do." The two officers left the office. Debbie slid into the driver's seat while Eric took the passenger side of the cruiser. The two officers left for the school.

Don picked up the phone and called the school number and spoke directly to the principal. "Hello, this is Sergeant Don Wilson."

"How can I help you, Sergeant?"

"I've sent two officers to your school to pick up Kimberley and Claire Jackson."

"Okay. Is there a problem?"

"I'm not at liberty to say right now. Can you please make sure they're ready when the officers arrive?"

"Of course, Sergeant. I'll look into it immediately."

Don had a gut feeling about one of Jenny's clues, so he asked, "One more thing, is school over fifteen minutes earlier today?"

There was a slight pause at the other end of the line, and then the principal responded, "No. Classes go until three p.m., as usual. Why do you ask?"

"I was under the impression that classes ended earlier today. Sorry, my mistake. Thank you." Don hung up the phone and approached the whiteboard and placed a question mark next to "school out 15 minutes earlier." He already knew that the fifteen-minute difference must have been a clue from Jenny, but at this point, he couldn't make any connection, or any sense of it, for that matter. Jenny was a clever woman, so it must be something important.

Bill and Greg had just arrived back at the office, and after going to the whiteboard, Bill added the time of "8:45" next to the medicine cabinet. He also noticed that school wasn't out fifteen minutes early.

Don approached him. "Was that written on the back of the mirror?"

Bill responded, "It was, and my only guess is that might be the time that Tom kidnapped her."

"That's a good assumption." He then added, "If that's true then Tom had her for ninety minutes before he called the station at ten o'clock this morning. At least it gives us a possible time line from when she was taken, and where he might be holding her."

Bill glanced at the board. "What's going on with school being out fifteen minutes early today?"

"I'm not really sure. The principal told me that school was out at the regular time, so we have a fifteen-minute discrepancy. Why do you suppose Jenny told us the wrong time for Claire getting out of school?"

Bill studied the board in front of him. "There is a difference of fifteen minutes, so that must be our clue."

"Why don't Jenny's clues make any sense?"

"If they did then Tom would know she was sending them. It's up to us to figure them out." Bill stood silently before he spoke. "Let's work on the clues that make sense for now."

Don said, "That hour and a half window scares me. He could cover a lot of territory in that time."

Bill's face turned white and he started to sweat. He turned around and looked at the officers busy at their desks. Trying not to act defeated, he said, "Shit. That takes in the flats again. How could Tom know that we took down Charles in that area?"

Don shrugged his shoulders. "There's no way he could have. Do you think we should send out a team to check out the cabin?"

"Might be a dead end, but still worth checking into it. At least it will eliminate that area."

Don called Eli Watson and Bob Billings into his office. "The two of you head out to the old cabin where Charles was killed and make sure Tom isn't hiding out there with Jenny. If there's any sign of them, call for backup at once. Don't be heroes."

Eli answered, "On our way, boss." The two left the building, jumped into their cruiser, and sped off.

Don was still baffled over the fifteen-minute difference, and once again posed the problem to Bill. "Why is Jenny telling us that school is out fifteen minutes early if it isn't?"

Bill answered, "Guess that's the ten-million-dollar question. One thing I know for sure, we need to take clue classes from Jenny. She's probably wicked at word guessing games."

"I'll bet she is."

Kimberley heard her name called over the PA system. "Mrs. Jackson, could you please report to the office immediately?"

Kimberley looked across the room at a parent who was helping out for the day and then spoke to the students. "Class, please turn to page twenty and work through the questions until I return. Meanwhile, Sara's mother is in charge of the class." She then left for the office.

Kimberley was surprised to find Claire waiting on a chair just inside the door. "What're you doing here, honey? Are you okay?"

"I'm fine, but I don't know why I'm here, Mommy."

Kimberley turned to the principal, who motioned her into the office and closed the door behind them. "We just got a call from the police station saying that two officers will be coming to pick the two of you up."

"What's this all about?"

"Not sure at this point."

Debbie and Eric entered the school and went into the reception area, where they saw Claire sitting patiently. Debbie smiled. "Hi, Claire, is your mom here?"

"She's in with the principal." Tears started to form in the corners of her eyes. "I think I did something wrong, but I don't know what."

Debbie comforted her. "You didn't do anything wrong, sweetheart. I'm just here to take you and your mom home."

Debbie tapped on the principal's door.

"Come in."

Debbie opened the door and saw the puzzled look on Kimberley's face.

Kimberley asked, "What's going on here?"

Without any explanation, Debbie said, "You and Claire need to come with us right away. We'll be picking up Richard and taking the three of you home. I'll explain everything once we're at your place."

Kimberley looked at the principal. "What about my class?"

"I'll cover for you."

"Thanks."

The two officers left with Kimberley and Claire. Kimberley was confused, but she knew better than to ask questions in front of her daughter.

They stopped at the hospital to pick up Richard. He was just as confused as Kimberley, but like her, didn't ask questions, likely knowing it had to be something important if he was being pulled away from his office with no notice.

Debbie drove them all back to the Jacksons' house. Once they were safely inside, Debbie turned to Claire. "I bet you would love to go and play in your room while I talk to your mom and dad."

Claire was gone in a flash.

Eric whispered to Debbie, "I'll check the perimeter of the house while you fill them in on the situation."

Kimberley and Richard watched Eric leave, and then took a seat in the living room with Debbie.

Debbie looked between the two of them before speaking. "I guess you're wondering what's going on here."

"Yes, we are," Richard answered, "Are we in danger?"

"At this point, we don't think so, but there's a situation that somewhat involves the three of you." Debbie looked at Kimberley and Richard gravely before continuing, "Tom Lockman was granted early release from prison and is now in town. He's kidnapped Jenny and is holding her hostage."

"You must be frigging kidding," Richard said angrily.

"Not in the least. He's forced Bill out of retirement." Debbie paused, letting her words sink in before continuing, "Richard. Lockman mentioned your name, and until this is over, you and your family need protection."

Richard saw that Kimberley was upset. He took her hand. "It'll be okay, darling. I'm sure we won't need protection for long. The force will find Jenny, and this will be all over in no time."

Kimberley looked at Richard. "How can you be so sure?"

"Because I know the police force will work their butts off until the case is solved."

"I hope you're right."

Eric returned and nodded to Debbie. "The perimeter's secured." He then turned to Richard and Kimberley. "I'll be with you until this is all over. Sorry about all this."

"Thanks, I think," Richard said, "It looks like the nightmare is starting all over again."

"Why is this happening?" Kimberley inquired, "Haven't we all been through enough with Charles and now Tom shows up to threaten us again." She suddenly looked worried. "Is Bill okay?"

Debbie nodded. "He is for now."

Richard cut in. "Tell him I'm available for the takedown, just in case Jenny is injured."

"I'll let him know, but right now, I have to get back to the office."

"Thanks, Debbie," Richard said as she left the room. Then he turned to Eric. "I need to call my office and cancel all my appointments for today."

"Not a problem, but once your call is made I'm the only one who will answer any incoming calls until this is all behind us."

Eric was about to secure the inside of the house when Claire ran out of her bedroom and asked her mom. "Can I go outside and play?"

"Not now, honey."

"But Mom, why can't I?"

Richard smiled at his daughter. "Because you, Mommy, and I are going to play a game."

Claire looked at Eric. "Is Eric going to play too?"

Eric answered, "Not today, Claire. I'm working."

She looked puzzled. "But you don't work here; you work at the police station."

"You're right, but today I'm playing policeman at your house."

Claire was surprised but impressed. "Cool."

Eric worked his way around the house, closing all the curtains and checking that the front and back doors were locked.

Upon arriving back at the station, Debbie went to her desk and started studying the papers spread across it. Don approached her and inquired, "Everything set up at the Jacksons'?"

"Eric walked the circumference of the house while I filled them in on the situation. I left once he was inside watching the family."

"Perfect. What're you working on?"

"I'm studying the map of Blue Ridge and the surrounding area, trying to find empty buildings. Wish I could blindfold myself, shove a pin into the map, and magically find his hideout."

"That would be a trick for the books. Once the team narrows the search area down, your research could very well help us pinpoint exactly where he's holding her. Keep me updated."

Don returned to his office and looked out the window. Ideas were muddling around in his head. *What do I do first? How can we find Jenny?* He closed his eyes and said a silent prayer. "We'll find you Jenny, just be strong."

Don spun around and returned to the common area, signaling for Muhammad and Sam to join him in his office. He glanced between the two officers. "Go over to Jenny's and search her house, the outbuilding, and the bushes for any clues. Talk to the neighbors. See if they saw anything."

Sam responded, "You got it."

Don wrote on the whiteboard. "Searched Jenny's house Sam and Muhammad Collect evidence".

Bill slowly approached Don. "Can you handle the situation here without me for a short time? I won't be long, but I'd like to head home to fill Beatrice in on the situation. I'll be back well before one p.m. and my next call with Tom. This asshole is messing with the wrong person. Beatrice and I were supposed to go for a picnic lunch today and he's interfered with our plans. She's going to be pissed."

"Go." He added, "What do we do about the ransom?"

"Absolutely nothing. We have to find Jenny because there's not a hope in hell that he's getting a dime out of me."

Bill left the station and went home to Beatrice. She was waiting inside the front door, trying to read the expression on his face, when he entered the room.

He looked sadly at her. "Looks like I could be working for the next day or two."

Beatrice started to tremble. "What's going on, Bill?"

He gently took her into his arms. "Do you remember Charles Lockman?"

She pulled away from him. "What about him? Isn't he dead?"

"Yes but his brother Tom just got out of prison, and he's alive and well."

"What does that have to do with you?"

"I guess he's out for revenge. He's kidnapped Jenny and is holding her for ransom."

"You're not serious?"

"I'm sorry, darling, but the team needs me. He won't deal with anyone but me."

"You can't do this. The team has to learn how to work without you."

"Honey, Jenny protected Claire and put her life on the line to keep her safe. I owe her—no, *we* owe her this."

Tears ran down Beatrice's cheeks, as she collapsed into his arms. Bill could feel her trembling and held her even closer. He spoke softly. "I'm going to make arrangements for your protection."

She looked up at him. "Do you think that's really necessary?"

"I'm not taking any chances with you. Charles was delusional and I can't afford to underestimate Tom and put you in danger." Bill crossed the room, picked up the phone, and called the number of his old friend, Glen Forner.

"Hey, Bill. Good to hear from you. What's up?"

"I need you again, buddy."

"It sounds serious. Where are you?"

"At home with Beatrice and come armed."

"I'm on my way."

Glen arrived to find Bill standing on the front porch. "What's up, Bill? It must be serious if I had to take my weapon out of storage."

"Do your remember Charles Lockman?"

"How could I forget? He shot you. But your team killed him, so what's the problem?"

"His brother Tom was just released from prison. He's kidnapped his wife Jenny and is holding her for ransom."

"The bastard. What does he hope to gain?"

"He wants half a million dollars from me, and I think putting a bullet in my head would be the icing on the cake."

"That's not going to happen. What do you need me to do?"

Bill took a deep breath before speaking. "I need you to protect Beatrice. Take her anywhere, but I don't want to know where she is. It will be safer if I don't know. I'll call your cell number to keep you updated. I really hate to ask you to do this, but you're the best, besides the local team, and they're all busy trying to figure out where Tom is hiding." Bill went on. "Jenny has already sent us a few clues. She's very good at sending us messages while not alerting Tom to what she's doing."

"What about Kimberley, Richard, and Claire?" Glen inquired.

"Don has already set up security at the Jacksons' house. Eric is there keeping them safe. I just really want you to make sure the asshole doesn't get close to Beatrice."

"You can count on me. Let's go inside so I can assure Beatrice that it will all work out."

They went inside to find Beatrice sitting on the couch, Kleenex in hand. She rose when she saw Glen. "It's nice to see you again. This time you only have one damsel in distress to protect."

Glen winked. "It's nice to see you again, too, Beatrice. It looks like we'll be spending some time together again."

Tears ran down Beatrice's cheeks, and Bill put his arms around her, not really wanting to let her go, afraid it might be the last time he'd ever hold her. But he had to. He felt like he had been kicked in the stomach a second time. These Lockman brothers were taking a toll on him. "I love you, Beatrice. Glen will keep you safe. I'll call whenever I have a chance."

Beatrice pulled away from him, tears still streaming down her cheeks. Trying hard to compose herself, she smiled. "I'll expect you home for dinner tonight."

"I can't make any promises."

"I love you, Bill."

"I love you, too." He glanced over at Glen, nodded, and then he left for the office.

Glen turned to Beatrice and spoke softly. "Pack an overnight bag, Beatrice. We can't stay here."

"Where're we going?"

"Somewhere safe, where Tom wouldn't expect you to be."

She turned and slowly climbed the stairs to pack a few personal items.

While she was out of the room, Glen picked up his cell phone and called a number. "Hi. It's Glen here. Bill has entrusted Beatrice into my protection. She's not safe here. I'm bringing her over."

Beatrice came back downstairs holding a small bag. "I'm ready."

Glen opened the front door and the two left in his vehicle.

Chapter Three

11:15 a.m. – 12:30 p.m.

MUHAMMAD AND SAM LEFT THE station and drove to Jenny's house. Her street was like an oil painting, the fall colors on full display, but both men were focused only on their task. Sam turned into her driveway, and before they left the cruiser, they glanced up and down the street, looking for anything unusual. There was nothing out of the ordinary. They left the vehicle, one from the driver's side, the other from the passenger's side, their evidence kits in hand. Muhammad signaled to Sam that he was taking the left side of the house, where the driveway was located. That meant that Sam would go around the front and then down the right side of the home.

Muhammad walked the length of the driveway and examined all the windows along that side of the house, looking for evidence that someone might have tried to enter the home. Glancing at the residence next door, he noticed a curtain fall back into place, as if someone had been watching him.

Returning his focus to Jenny's driveway, he saw tire tracks indicating that two vehicles had been parked behind the building; both vehicles were now gone. He knew one of the vehicles belonged to Jenny, which meant the second one most likely belonged to the couple who were renting the spare room. The rain from the previous night had left distinct impressions of tire tracks and footprints in the damp soil. Glancing behind him, Muhammad noticed these footprints were also visible coming from the road and down the driveway. These dirty footprints were also on the steps leading up to the back door. As he waited for Sam, he walked along the back of the house. Glancing up, Muhammad noticed that most of the leaves had already fallen off the trees, covering the ground with rich colors of red and yellow. There was also a chill in the air, as fall was fast approaching. A slight breeze would soon strip the few remaining leaves off the trees, leaving them bare until the next spring.

Meanwhile, Sam had worked his way around the front of the house, but had not found anything unusual. All the windows and the front door seemed intact. No one in Blue Ridge ever locked their doors, but Sam thought Jenny might have locked hers, given the threats she'd received after Tom killed Joan Wilks. Time had certainly worked to her advantage, as most people had eventually forgotten about the incident and returned to their everyday routines.

Nevertheless, Jenny was still cautious; she would likely have wanted to make sure she and her renters were safe behind locked doors at night. He climbed the steps and turned the front door handle. Sure enough, it was locked. If Tom had knocked on that door and Jenny had opened it, not knowing who was on the other side, maybe the outcome would have been different. Maybe she could have slammed the door in his face and called the police.

Sam guessed that Tom had entered the house from the back door. Regardless of how Tom had entered the home, Sam would fingerprint both doors.

Tom definitely had a criminal record, so his prints would be in the system, along with his mug shot. His prints would give the police an iron-clad case once Tom was apprehended.

He went back down the stairs and continued his walk around the right side of the house, checking the flowerbeds for footprints indicating someone might have been peering inside, but the soil was undisturbed. As he glanced at the neighbor's house, he noticed all the curtains were still closed.

He met up with Muhammad at the back porch. "There's nothing out of the ordinary on this side of the house," Sam said.

"I can't say the same for my side. Apparently we have a nosey neighbour. I'll question them later," Muhammad added, "There are lots of footprints on the driveway that lead to the shed, one of the vehicles, and then onto the back porch." He set down his evidence kit on the bottom step and opened it, taking out his camera and tape measure. He placed the tape measure next to several sets of footprints and snapped some photos. "I expect at least one of these footprints belongs to Tom Lockman."

"That's a pretty good guess."

They walked up the back stairs, put on gloves, and opened the door, already knowing it was unlocked because Bill and Greg had entered the house earlier.

Sam announced their presence. "Blue Ridge Police Department. Is there anyone here?"

When there was no answer, the two men entered the house. Sam set down his evidence kit. "I'll dust both doors for prints, even though we already have a good idea who some of them belong to."

"The only question is which door did he enter?"

Sam gestured to the back door. "I expect this one, because the front door was locked when I tried it."

Sam dusted the back door with powder and found lots of prints, which wasn't surprising as Jenny's would be there, plus the renters' and Claire's. Taking a strip of tape and placing it over the handle, he lifted the prints and sealed them inside a plastic bag. He then labeled the bag, dated it, and noted the time.

Next, he went to the front door and did the same. Several prints showed up, and he repeated the tape and bagging process, carefully labeling and identifying the samples. They likely belonged to Jenny and the other two people who lived in the house, but some could also belong to Tom.

With both doors finished Sam announced. "I'll take the bathroom."

"I'll process the kitchen."

Sam entered the bathroom and glanced around. Setting his bag on the floor next to him, he opened the medicine cabinet and saw "8:45" written on the back of the door in lipstick; the tube still lying on the bottom shelf. He opened his bag and drew out his camera, snapped a photo of the message, then returned the camera into the bag. He picked up the lipstick tube and dusted it for prints, then placed it in an evidence bag and labeled it. If the prints were Jenny's, then the message behind the mirror was in her handwriting. If it was Tom's writing, the team could be in trouble. He could have written the wrong time down, so the police wouldn't be able to figure out how far Tom drove before his phone call. Forensic analysis would solve that in short time.

He closed the cabinet and started dusting the surface of the mirror. There were several sets of prints, so he lifted all of them and carefully sealed the bags and identified each one individually. Cases were won or lost based on the quality of evidence collection. Both Sam and Muhammad knew the importance of being thorough and accurate.

When he returned to the kitchen, Muhammad looked at him and asked, "Any luck in the bathroom?"

"Lots of prints, but at this point I'm not sure if Tom entered the bathroom. Took a photo of the message left behind the mirror. Any luck here?"

"There are fingerprints everywhere. I've just bagged and tagged them all. At this point, they could belong to anyone."

Sam looked around the kitchen, noticing all the patches of powder on the areas Muhammad had dusted. "Looks like you had a field day."

"You know the old saying. 'The kitchen is the heart of the home.'"

Sam chuckled and allowed his eyes to follow the faint, dirty footprints from the back door to the kitchen and then to an old chair in the living room. Apart from them, everything was neat and tidy. "I wonder if this was Tom's chair. It makes sense that he would sit where he was most comfortable while waiting for Jenny to come home after dropping Claire off at the bus stop." Sam set down his evidence kit and drew out the camera and tape measure. He placed the tape measure next to the dirty prints and took a photo of them. "We can compare these prints with the ones outside and hopefully see if they belong to Tom."

"Maybe yes, maybe no," Muhammad said from the kitchen.

"What does that mean?"

Muhammad responded, "They could also belong to one of the renters."

"Are you serious? Look around you. The place is immaculately clean. Jenny would have insisted that anyone entering her house remove their shoes."

"You have a point, so most likely they do belong to Tom."

Sam dusted the arm rests, lifting several sets of prints and bagged them. Upon further inspection he commented, "These prints are similar to the ones that were on the back door. He added, "They're probably Tom's." He shook his head. "I don't know about you, but I find this whole scene creepy. Poor Jenny has been through so much, and now this." He continued, "It's disturbing, but not the craziest case we've ever worked on. I wish Jenny knew that he was watching the house. She could have called the force and it would have ended last night."

"I agree," Muhammad said, "It looks like Tom walked from the driveway to the shed in the backyard, hugging the fence, maybe trying to avoid the downpour we had last night, and he spent the night in that shed. Judging by the location of the window on the shed, he was probably watching the house all night."

"He's definitely a disturbed man." Sam then moved towards Jenny's bedroom and started dusting for prints. None of the prints he found in her room looked the same as those on the chair in the living room, or the back door, so he guessed they belonged to Jenny. He bagged the prints and once again meticulously labeled each bag. He then returned to the kitchen. "Are you finished in here?"

"Sure am. Let's check out that shed?"

They picked up their evidence kits, left the house, and walked to the shed.

Before opening the door, Muhammad set down his bag, opened it, and dusted the handle for prints. He then opened the door and switched on the light, commenting, "I would have thought the door would be locked, but apparently I'm wrong."

Sam responded, "No one has come in here for years. It was probably locked when he was living here, and also the entire time he was in prison. Look at the state of this shed, it's a disaster. Tom must have had a key hidden outside and let himself in. He has a lot of very expensive tools here, so it would have been stupid of him to leave the shed unlocked. Anyone could have come in and stolen all his tools. The only thing that puzzles me is why he didn't lock the door again when he left."

"That's a very good question. Maybe at that point he didn't care about his tools. He only wanted Jenny." Muhammad stopped dead in his tracks when he noticed the stool facing the window that overlooked the back of the house. "This guy is crazy. He was watching the house from this spot. We need to catch Tom before he gets to Bill, or worse, kills Jenny."

"We'll get him, buddy."

Muhammad dusted the light switch for prints and found nothing. "Guess he never turned on the light."

"If he did, it could have alerted Jenny and she would have called the police."

"I really wish he had turned it on. Then none of this might have happened."

"True, but now that it's happened, we have to deal with it."

Off to his right, Sam spotted a dirty blanket lying in the corner. "Looks like the creep spent the night huddled in this corner waiting for morning and at some point sat on that stool."

Muhammad lifted a clean set of prints from around the rim of the stool, bagged it, and again carefully identified them.

Sam moved towards the bench and noticed the dust and cobwebs hanging from the ceiling, and spotted the tools strewn all over the floor. Turning his attention back to the bench, Sam noticed a flashlight that appeared to have been touched and then discarded. He almost didn't have to process it, as the prints were engrained in the fine layer of dust on it. Still, he lifted the prints and not only bagged them, but also sealed the flashlight in a larger evidence bag and labeled it "garden shed."

Muhammad scanned the entire area around him and shrugged with disgust. "This shed is a disaster. What do we hope to find here?"

Sam answered, "I know this area is overwhelming, but let's look at the scene differently. I know that we're looking for anything that would help us to find Tom. But what if we looked at the scene, thinking about what's not here?"

"What do you mean?"

"There are cobwebs and dust everywhere. Why is there a somewhat cleaner spot in that corner?" He pointed to the spot in question, drawing Muhammad's eye to that part of the floor.

Muhammad studied the clean area. "It looks like there could have been something rectangular there, possibly a toolbox?"

"I agree. The tools that are strewn next to it tell me he didn't need what was in the box." Sam looked around the room. "So we're looking for what's not here rather than what is." He drew out his notepad as they studied the surface of the work bench and then the floor.

Muhammad spoke first. "There's a lawnmower here, but I don't see any gas."

"Sam commented, "I see that. The yard is in dire need of a fall cleanup, but the grass has been recently cut. Who do you suppose is cutting it?"

"Good question. Maybe a friend or neighbor. We can ask the neighbors when we question them."

Sam added, "I guess that's possible; or maybe Tom took the spare fuel for Jenny's car? He would want to get as far away from here as possible before he stopped at a station."

"I suppose."

Regardless, Sam jotted down "gas can missing."

Muhammad glanced around the shop again. "I don't know about you, but to me, it seems that every workshop should have rope in it."

"I agree." Sam added "rope" to his list.

They spent a few more minutes looking around the shed, but neither could think of anything else that was obviously missing.

Muhammad shook his head. "I'm almost positive that he took more than those two items with him, but for the life of me, I'm not sure what they are."

"Let's not spend any more time in here, then."

Muhammad picked up the camera. "I'm going to take photos inside the shed just in case we need to review the location."

"Excellent idea." Sam stepped outside to allow Muhammad the space to snap the pictures.

When he was done, Muhammad turned off the light and they regrouped at their cruiser. They placed the evidence kits in the back seat of the cruiser and locked the doors, securing their evidence.

Muhammad indicated the house next door. "I'll go talk to this neighbor and see if anyone there saw anything."

"I'll talk to the people on the other side of Jenny's house."

They went in opposite directions. Muhammad approached the neighbor's house and knocked on the door. The door slowly opened, and an older lady peered outside. "What do you want?"

"I'm Officer Muhammad Salomar. I'd like to ask you a few questions, if that's okay."

"If it's about the house next door, there're things always going on over there."

"What kind of things?"

"People moving around at all hours of the night. I've been watching the place."

"Did you notice anyone prowling around last night?"

"Sure did. Someone was walking around the back yard."

"And you didn't think to call the police and report it?"

"I thought it was the fellow who rents the room from her, besides it's none of my business. He wasn't on my property."

"Did you see anything this morning?"

"I only watch the place at night," the woman said rudely. "That's when I feel vulnerable. Nothing ever happens in the daytime." She then added, "The lady's at work during the day."

Muhammad was angry, but he managed to keep his opinion to himself. "Thank you. You've been a big help." He left the house, shaking his head, and returned to the vehicle.

Meanwhile, Sam had approached the house on the other side of Jenny's and noticed the sign on the front door: "Night shift worker, please don't ring doorbell." He quietly knocked, not knowing if anyone would open the door. A slight woman peeked through the window. When she saw him, she slowly opened the door.

"How can I help you, officer?" she whispered.

"I'm Officer Sam Lawson. Do you mind if I ask you a few questions?"

"Not at all. What's going on?"

"Did you notice anything suspicious in the area last night or early this morning?"

"Nothing." Looking scared, she asked, "Is Jenny okay?"

"You know Jenny well?"

"Sure do. After that incident with her husband, I felt like she needed a friend, so I kept in close contact with her. At first, I said hi over the fence, and once she was comfortable being around me, I walked over and delivered some baking. Jenny was so appreciative." The woman rubbed her face as if she was trying to clear a headache. "Is she okay? What's going on? What's happened to her? She's supposed to be at work right now. Is she okay?"

Sam couldn't keep up with all her questions, so he pushed them aside and asked once again. "Did you notice anything late last night or early this morning?"

"No. My husband was working night shift and now he's sleeping, so the curtains on that side of the house are almost always closed." Tears trailed down her cheeks and Sam could see stress overtaking her body. "I always call her a couple of times a week to check in on her. I should have called last night, but got too busy. It's my fault, I should have called her."

Sam felt bad for the woman. "Thanks for caring about Jenny. She's lucky to have a friend like you."

"Has something horrible happened to her?"

"I'm not at liberty to say right now, but so far, everything is fine." Sam hated lying to her, but he could see the woman was in distress.

"Where is she?"

"We're actively looking for her."

"So she's missing?"

"Rest assured that we'll find her." Sam paused. "By any chance, have you noticed anyone cutting her grass?"

"Sure, my husband cuts it for her. Jenny struggles to keep up the yard work so my husband helps her with the grass. Apparently the shed in the back yard is locked and her mower is inside. She didn't want to break the lock and get into trouble with her husband when he came back to town."

"That's very kind of your husband. Thank you for speaking to me." He then returned to the vehicle and talked to Muhammad. "Poor woman was in distress. I felt bad leaving her up in the air, but couldn't tell her anything about Jenny. Apparently she was a close friend. I did solve the mystery about the grass. Her husband was cutting it for her, as Jenny couldn't get into the shed for her mower. Apparently she was worried that Tom would be upset if she broke the lock."

Muhammad asked, "Do you think that Jenny was afraid of Tom?"

Sam responded, "At first, probably not, but once he murdered Joan Wilks, she was most likely unsure what he was capable of doing." He nodded in the direction of the neighbor's house. "How did you make out over there?"

"Woman was full of criticism. Saw someone around last night, but didn't report it."

"Damn, this wouldn't have happened if she'd just picked up the phone and called us."

"She thought it was the man renting the spare room." Muhammad nodded at the homes across the street. "Let's talk to them."

"They have a clear view of Jenny's house, so hopefully they either heard something or, even better, saw something."

Muhammad knocked on the door directly across from Jenny's. There was no answer. Knocking a second time, he heard someone slowly shuffling towards the door. The door opened and an elderly gentleman stood in front of him, a dog sitting obediently by his side. The man leaned on a cane, and Muhammad realized that the man was blind. He wore a pair of sunglasses to cover his eyes.

"Good morning, sir, I'm Muhammad Salomar of the Blue Ridge Police Department. I'm so sorry to bother you." Muhammad felt awkward and wasn't sure what to say next. He'd never interrogated a blind person before and wasn't sure how to proceed.

"Good morning, officer. I'm John Simpson. How may I help you?"

"Actually, I'm not quite sure if you can."

The man chuckled. "I may be blind, but I see more than people give me credit for. My other four senses kick into play and compensate for me. I can tell you that last night, it rained, as I could hear, smell, and taste the moisture in the air. I was sitting out on my porch, my trusty companion next to me, and I could feel the arms of my chair were damp. Would you like to come in?"

Muhammad was impressed. "I'd like that."

The man may have been blind, but he walked straight to his chair, his faithful companion next to him, and sat down. "Can I get you anything? A cup of coffee, maybe a donut?" He chuckled. "I'm just messing with you."

Muhammad laughed despite the overused joke and took a seat across from the man. "I'm fine, thanks. My first question to you is did you hear anything last night?"

"I enjoy sitting outside in the early evening, especially if it's raining. The rain relaxes me." He paused to pet his dog. "I can sit in the dark and no one even knows I'm there. It's kind of a game that blind people like to play." He laughed before continuing, "At first, I was rather confused. Even though it was raining hard, I could hear footsteps coming up the street and pausing in front of the house across from me. As the person started walking again, I thought he was continuing up the street."

"Why didn't your dog start barking?"

"He's trained to only bark if I'm in danger. Like me, he just listened."

"Did you hear anything else?"

"Sure did. It was weird. Sounded like a scraping sound, but I wasn't sure what it was. I assumed it was the fellow who rents a room from her, so I went inside."

"Did you hear anything this morning?"

"The lady across the street has the same routine during the week. This morning, I heard her walking a child out of her driveway. Nothing makes me feel happier than a small child's laughter first thing in the morning. It brightens my day. I have to assume she was taking the child to the school bus, and I waited until I heard her coming back before I went inside. It's kind of my daily routine."

"Did you hear anything else?"

"Strange that you should ask. I thought I heard the doors close on a vehicle three times and then drive away, but I wasn't outside to confirm it."

"Are you sure the car doors shut three times?"

"Definitely. I may be blind, but my hearing is impeccable."

Muhammad smiled. "Did you hear anything else?"

"Like I said officer, I was inside and starting my daily routine."

"You've been an incredible help. I'd love to spend the day with you but unfortunately, I need to get back to work." Muhammad got up from his chair.

"Is everything okay, officer?"

"Yes. If I have any more questions, I'll be sure to come back."

"You're always welcome, officer."

Muhammad crossed the street, returning to the cruiser to wait for Sam.

Sam knocked on the door, and it was opened by a man who was still in his pyjamas. "Good morning, sir. I'm Officer Sam Lawson." He paused before continuing, "Do you mind if I ask you a few questions?"

"Ask away, officer." He then glanced across the street and saw the cruiser in Jenny's driveway. "Is Jenny okay?"

"When did you see her last?"

"I saw her walking Claire to the bus stop this morning." He looked directly at Sam. "What's going on?"

"Did you see her come back after dropping Claire off at the bus stop?"

"No. The wife called me to breakfast, so I went to eat. The kitchen is at the back of the house."

"Did you notice anything out of the ordinary last night?" Sam asked.

"Nothing." He then added, "That poor woman has been through hell. Please tell me she's okay."

"You know her well?"

"Not really, but the wife and I keep an eye on her. She doesn't have too many friends. We wave to each other if we're outside or going for a walk. Wasn't her fault what happened years ago."

"You're right about that. Thank you for answering my questions."

"Do I dare ask what's happening?"

"We're just asking questions for now. Thank you for your time." He crossed the street and met up with Muhammad in Jenny's driveway. "Any luck?" he asked.

Muhammad said, "Believe it or not, a blind gentleman answered the door and invited me in."

"How did that go?"

"He may have been blind, but he was very helpful. He was on his front porch last night, enjoying the rain, when he heard someone walking down the street. That person stopped in front of Jenny's. He thought that whoever it was had continued down the street. He also heard a scraping sound that could have been the shed door opening, but he thought it was the renter outside. He also heard Jenny and Claire leave for school this morning, and shortly after, Jenny returned. Apparently it's his daily routine to listen for them." He paused before adding, "But he said that this morning, he heard a car door shut three times."

Sam looked puzzled. "Was he sure?"

"I was given a lesson on how his hearing is impeccable, so I believe him."

"Okay, but why three times?"

"Beats me." Muhammad spoke up. "Do you remember the missing tool box from the shed? Do you suppose Tom was putting it in Jenny's car?"

"That's a fair assumption."

Muhammad then inquired, "How did you make out?"

Sam pointed to the house across the street. "Fellow saw her leave this morning, but didn't see her return. Sounds like he and his wife watched out for Jenny too."

"Nice to have concerned neighbors, but there's always one grouchy one on the block." He nodded towards the house with the grumpy lady in it. "We should get back to the station and report our findings."

The two climbed into their vehicle and drove back to work, where they handed over the evidence they had collected to the lab for analysis.

Don approached them. "How did it go at Jenny's?"

Sam answered, "Collected lots of evidence, plus photographed the message on the back of the mirror, and Muhammad took several photos of footprints outside. We turned all of our evidence over to the lab team. We also interviewed four of the neighbors. They were all very helpful, although one of them was rather negative."

"Excellent work, men."

Muhammad added, "That's not all, boss. Once we left the house, we followed a set of footprints that led to the shed. Both of us were surprised to find the door unlocked. We believe that it must have been previously locked, as there were lots of expensive tools inside that someone would have stolen, given the opportunity. The inside was covered in a thick layer of dust. There's a good chance that Tom had a key hidden outside and let himself in. I managed to get a clean fingerprint from the door handle, but there were no fingerprints on the light switch, so he never turned the light on."

Sam added, "I found a flashlight on the bench that had been recently handled. I fingerprinted it, plus bagged the flashlight as evidence. We suspect that he spent the night in the shed, sleeping in the corner on a dirty blanket, waiting for the right time to confront Jenny. She wasn't aware of his presence on the property."

Muhammad cut in. "At some point, we know that he was watching the house, as a stool was placed by the window giving him a clear view of the house. I lifted prints from the stool and they most likely belong to Tom. When we looked around the shed, we noticed a clean spot on the floor surrounded by a pile of tools. We suspect that a toolbox must have previously been there, its' contents emptied on the floor, and the box refilled with items that he thought would help his cause. We both studied the workshop trying to figure out what was missing."

Sam interceded. "Neither one of us found any rope, but more disturbing, there was a lawnmower, but no gas container. There very well could have been more items missing, but not knowing what was there to begin with put us at a disadvantage."

Don was in shock. "What kind of a game is he playing, and why the hell would he need rope and gas?"

"Possibly rope to tie Jenny up, but he very well could have taken the fuel to top up Jenny's car instead of stopping at a station for fuel."

Muhammad added, "Oh, one last thing, boss. Before we left the shed, I took as many photographs as possible inside. We may very well need them later."

Don rubbed both hands over his face, trying to think. "I'm not sure how Bill handled Charles five years ago, but I'm sure glad he's here now. Nice work, guys. Right now, we all need to get back to work and catch this bastard."

As Sam and Muhammad returned to their desks, Don walked over to the whiteboard and reviewed the clues that were still in front of him. He was still unsure what the fifteen minute gap meant, but knew his team would figure it out.

He only hoped it was sooner rather than later.

Chapter Four

11:15 a.m. - 1:00 p.m.

ELI AND BOB HOPPED INTO their cruiser and headed up the highway, towards the intersection that led to the cabin. That infamous turn-off was close to thirty-five minutes away, which felt like a lifetime for the two officers.

Eli was behind the steering wheel. As he drove, he glanced at his partner. "Well, who would've thought we'd be back in this neck of the woods?"

"Not me. What're the chances we'll find anything here?"

"Not sure, but at the very least, we'll be able to eliminate the area."

Bob was deep in thought as he asked his partner. "Do you think Tom would've figured out that his brother was killed at this cabin?"

"I really doubt he would've seen the report on Charles' takedown. Those files are closed to the public, and especially to a murderer."

"So, this road trip could very well be a waste of our time."

Eli shrugged. "It's never a waste of time. Finding a criminal is a matter of elimination. As a team, we investigate all potential areas, and eventually we'll close in on the bad guy, in this case, Tom. If we find him here, that's a bonus. We contact the team and take him down. If he isn't here, then it's most likely the entire flats are clear. When we were last in this area, this was the only cabin that was habitable." He then added, "It's just too bad that the drive takes so long to get here. But if it's a dead end, maybe by the time we get back to the office, we'll be closer to finding out where he's holding Jenny. Let's just hope she's okay."

"She's stronger than she looks. How can a man be so in love with his wife at one stage of their relationship and then turn so vindictive?"

"My guess is prison took its' toll on him."

Bob shook his head in disbelief. "But Tom had a second chance with Jenny. Why didn't he take it?"

"I expect prison changes everyone. He must have gotten out expecting Jenny to greet him with open arms. Instead, he saw that she was surviving beautifully without him. That had to hurt. He probably lived a life of hell behind bars, and she carried on like he never existed."

Eli turned off the highway, and the vehicle bounced over the bumpy road. The ground was muddy from the previous evening's rain, and it splashed onto the hood and sides of the cruiser. Both men were silent as they drew closer to the infamous cabin, each collecting their thoughts.

Just short of their destination, Eli pulled the cruiser off the road into a sheltered area. They got out and started the short walk to the cabin. "Damn, should've worn my boots," Eli said.

"You'd think we might've remembered, from our last experience in the area, that fall is the rainy season."

Eli sighed. "Who knew that we'd be coming out here today? Just another good pair of footwear destined for the garbage."

As they approached the last bend in the road before the cabin, both men drew their weapons. Eli signaled that he would take the left side of the building, so Bob knew that the right side was his approach. The cabin walls were starting to rot, leaving gaps between the boards that allowed cool air to penetrate the interior. A thick layer of moss clung to the roof and drooped over the edges. The door was slightly ajar, alerting the officers that it was likely abandoned. Eli glanced into the one window of the cabin, but not seeing anything, he continued around the back.

They met up behind the cabin and recognized the path that led into the forest where Bill had taken a bullet to the chest. Brushing that terrible scene from their minds, they carefully moved to the front of the building. Suddenly, they heard a sound that immediately put them on high alert, adrenaline pumping.

Eli slowly moved towards the front door. He whispered to his partner. "On the count of three."

He raised his fingers one at a time. On three, he pulled open the door, weapon pointing at anything or anyone who might make a move towards him. He stopped dead in his tracks when he was greeted by two grey wolves glaring back at him. Two young pups were huddled in one corner. The smell of urine alerted Eli that these wolves had marked their territory, and they were intruders. The attack on them was inevitable.

The wolf closest to the door was ready to defend their den. It snarled and crouched backwards, lips curled to expose deadly fangs. Its' green eyes bore into Eli's. The fur on its' back stood erect, and its' tail was parallel to its' body, signaling an imminent attack. Eli already knew that a pack could consist of eight wolves or more, so the rest of the group was likely not far away, probably hunting to feed the young pups inside the cabin. The growls grew more intense, telling Eli this wolf was not happy with their intrusion.

He pulled the door closed and both officers started to run towards their vehicle, gasping for air, wondering why they had left the cruiser so far away from the cabin. He heard a howl from inside the cabin behind them before the door exploded open.

"We're screwed," Bob panted. "That damn wolf is calling for backup."

Eli struggled to speak. "Wish we could call for backup too. Just keep moving and maybe we can outrun them."

"I doubt that. We have two legs and they have four, plus we're grossly outnumbered."

"Just keep moving and cover your back."

Both men were gasping for oxygen and terrified as they approached their vehicle. The sound of the wolves galloping behind them meant they'd have to stand their ground. Only a short distance from their vehicle, they turned to face their fate. Half a dozen wolves stopped dead in their tracks, hackles raised, fangs dripping with saliva, and slowly began to surround them. Eli and Bob stood back to back, trying to protect each other from the angry wolves.

Eli hissed over his shoulder. "Tell me you have a plan?"

"I was about to ask you the same thing."

Eli pulled the car keys from his pocket and pushed the panic button. The horn started to honk loudly, startling the wolves enough that they backed away a bit. Now that the officers had a slight advantage, they carefully moved towards their vehicle. When they were close enough, Eli unlocked the doors with his fob and he jumped behind the wheel.

Bob was not so lucky. Before he could enter the vehicle, a wolf crunched down onto his arm. He hollered out in pain as the fangs sank into his skin. Pulling away wasn't an option, as the fangs were deeply embedded.

Eli drew his pistol. "Lean back! I can't get a clear shot!"

Bob could barely hear his partner, but saw that his pistol was drawn. Time was of the essence, as the rest of the pack was regrouping. He flung himself out of the way, even though it sent the wolf's fangs deeper into his flesh.

Eli pulled the trigger. The wolf's body went limp, releasing Bob's arm. "Get in and shut the door!" Eli yelled.

Even though the pain was excruciating, Bob managed to pull himself into the vehicle and slam the door shut with his good arm. The wolves were swarming the cruiser, some jumping onto the hood, saliva dripping onto the windshield. Eli started the engine and shifted into reverse, hoping to either scatter the pack or run over them. Once the cruiser was on the road and accelerating towards the main highway, the wolves were forced to jump off the hood before they were thrown off.

With the hood finally free of wolves, Eli was able to clean the windshield with his wipers and washer fluid. In the rearview mirror, he watched the pack chasing the vehicle, but eventually they lost interest and turned back. He drove what he thought was a safe distance from them and pulled over. "How're you doing, partner?"

"What do you think?" Bob snapped. "Damn wolf tried to eat me. Hurts like hell."

"Let's have a look."

Bob gingerly exposed his arm to Eli. The wound was turning his sleeve red with blood. Eli slipped his belt off and looped it around Bob's arm. Looking at his partner with sadness, he announced, "Sorry, buddy, but this is going to hurt."

Bob turned away. "Just do it!"

Eli quickly cinched the belt tight around Bob's arm and secured it.

Bob screamed. "Shit man that hurts!"

Eli looked sympathetically at his partner. "Sorry. That was the only way to slow down the bleeding. I'm going to call it in and then I'm taking you to the hospital." Eli picked up the radio and reported to the police station.

Daniel responded, "I was starting to get worried about the two of you. How did you make out at the cabin?"

"We've just checked it out, and it's clear, except we were attacked by wolves," Eli paused. "Bob is injured. Call the hospital and let them know we're on our way." Eli was about to hang up when he added, "Fish and Wildlife should be notified. I had to shoot one of the wolves. And also tell them there are two pups involved."

"Copy that. I'll call the hospital first, then Fish and Wildlife. Keep us updated on Bob."

"Will do, we're on our way."

Eli pulled back onto the road and managed to miss as many potholes as possible. The drive was slow until he hit the highway. Once back on the pavement, he pushed the pedal to the metal. He watched as his partner cradled his injured arm close to his chest. "How're you doing?"

"As well as can be expected. It doesn't hurt as much if I don't move it."

"In that case, I suggest you try not to move it."

Bob looked at his partner. "Do me a favor. If I pass out before reaching the hospital, make sure they give me a tetanus shot." He paused. "Maybe a rabies shot too."

"Consider it done. You rest and I'll get you there as quick as possible."

Back at the station, Don saw the concern on Daniel's face and approached him. "What's going on?"

"Eli and Bob just checked in. The cabin's clear, but Bob was attacked by wolves."

"Shit, how is he?"

"Not sure, but Eli is taking him directly to the emergency room. We'll get an update after that. I'm just going to notify the emergency room of their impending arrival."

Don looked troubled. "Let me know when you hear from Eli."

"You'll be the first to know."

Daniel watched Don approach the whiteboard and put a line through "Searched cabin Charles died at."

When Eli pulled into the hospital parking lot, he helped Bob out of the cruiser and the two entered the emergency door entrance. Bob was conscious, but in extreme pain. Two attendants helped him onto a gurney, and wheeled him behind a curtain. Eli took a seat in the waiting room. He called the precinct on his company radio with an update.

Daniel answered, "You must be at the hospital. How's he doing?"

"They just took him in to see the doctor. If I'm not needed at the office, I'm going to stay here until I get an update on him."

"You stay until he's released and then drop him off at his house."

"He's not going to like that."

"Not his choice. The boss wants him at home resting."

"Okay, then. I'll be there as soon as possible."

Eli waited in the emergency room for about half an hour before Bob walked out, his arm bandaged and in a sling.

"Okay, partner, let's get back to the office. We have work to do," he said.

"You're not going anywhere except home."

"Like hell I am. They've patched me up and filled me full of painkillers, so I'm more than ready to go back to work." He added, "They also gave me that tetanus and rabies shot, so I'm good to go."

"Don doesn't want you back at the office."

"That's just too bad. I may have been attacked by a wolf, but my head is clear and I need to get back to work." He chuckled. "That wolf wasn't so lucky. I bet his buddies aren't very happy about him taking that bullet to the head. Nice shot, I might add. Thanks."

"You're welcome."

The two left the hospital and returned to the station. Don approached them and asked, "How're you feeling, Bob?"

"I'll live. I can't say the same for that wolf, but I do feel bad that Eli had to shoot it. Did anyone notify Fish and Wildlife yet?"

Don answered, "Daniel already notified them. I expect they will have to go out there and retrieve the body. You need to go home and get some rest."

"Bullshit, I do. They pumped me full of painkillers, so I may not be able to drive, but I'm perfectly able to shuffle paperwork. I need to be in the loop." He added, "How about I stay for now, and if I find it's too much, I'll go home?"

Don nodded. "Fine, but the moment you show me any signs of pain and discomfort, you're out of here."

Don returned to his office while Eli and Bob went to their respective desks and filled out their report on the cabin search.

Chapter Five

11:15 a.m. - 1:00 p.m.

AFTER THE CALL TO BILL, and having slammed the burner phone onto the table, Tom glared at Jenny, his dark eyes boring into hers. He didn't enjoy seeing the fear in her eyes, because he still loved her for what she once was - but not for what she was now. She had written him off.

Anger overtook him, and he asked her a second time, yelling now. "Why the hell didn't you tell me Bill was retired?" Before she could answer, he glared at her. "How dare you say that I never asked?"

He lunged at Jenny and pulled her off the chair. His fingernails bit into her flesh, and she cried out in pain. "Stop it, Tom, you're hurting me! Let me go! Let me go, or so help me, I'll kill you myself!"

Tom was livid. "You really think you're a match for me? You forget that you're soft, while I spent ten years in jail. I learned how to deceive people, avoid people, hurt people, and, most of all, survive, so don't you talk to me about hurt and what you're going to do to me," he spat. "Do you have any idea what it was like living—or should I say dying—within those four walls of my cell day after day?"

Trembling, Jenny whispered, "It wasn't easy for me, either."

He released her and shoved her back into the chair. "Yeah, right. I was fighting daily to survive, and you were sitting in our house collecting money from your renter, slopping tables in that greasy café, and babysitting someone's brat. Sure sounds like a tough job." He smugly added, "Heaven knows how you survived in such deplorable conditions."

Jenny shot back. "I know you think I didn't have a worry in the world, but you're wrong. I had so many phone calls from people threatening that if I didn't leave town, they would burn my house down, preferably with me inside. The middle of the night was worse. The phone would ring at all hours, and all I would hear was someone breathing at the other end. I reported every incident to the police department, and they finally placed me and my house under protection. I eventually changed my phone number just to get some reprieve from the harassment." She saw that he was about to speak, but then he closed his mouth. In a gentle voice, she said, "I'm really sorry, Tom. Would it help if you talked about it?"

Tom glared at her before responding. "I don't want to talk about it. You don't give a damn about me anyway. You're so wrapped up in"—Tom paused before continuing—"'oh, poor me!'"

"We have nothing but time on our hands, and you know that I've always been a good listener. Talk to me Tom."

Tom paced around the room for several minutes, mumbling under his breath, before he took a seat in the chair across from her. He was about to relive his nightmare. He started to sweat, and his eyes became heavy, and then a single tear ran down his cheek. Part of Tom hoped Jenny never saw his weakness, but secretly, he wanted her to know how much he hurt. Prison had changed him, and it was important that she understood why he was so bitter.

Jenny had been rubbing her sore wrists, but now she shuffled her chair closer to him, intent on understanding what her husband had endured over the past ten years. Tom's face, which had once showed so much passion for the wonderful future they should have had together, now showed only defeat and despair. His hair was short, the tell-tale brush cut that prisoners wore while behind bars. His face was deeply creased now, and he hadn't shaved in several days. He'd aged rapidly while inside those four walls.

She coaxed him to speak. "Talk to me, Tom. Help me understand how being behind bars has changed you. I look at you and all I see is a shell of the man I once knew; defeated, trusting no one, not even me." She chose her words carefully. "How could you think that I would be unfaithful? I didn't sleep with any man after you." She waited patiently as she watched Tom gather his thoughts. "I know it couldn't have been easy for you, and I'm truly sorry for what you went through."

Tom made eye contact and appeared to be entering a horrible past that he was about to share with her. Speaking softly, almost as if he didn't want anyone but Jenny to hear his story, he lapsed into his nightmare. "My last day of freedom was when I got off the bus outside that horrible prison. I was herded towards a large gate that was already open to receive the line-up of new prisoners. My hands were handcuffed in front of me and my legs were in shackles as I joined a group of about ten men in single file, like children tied to a rope to keep them in control. There was no welcoming committee, just guards yelling and directing us inside.

"The building was a brick structure with guards stationed on towers at the two front corners. I'm sure that the two back corners had the same setup. The walls might have been five feet thick and twenty feet high, and the top was strung with barbed wire. The area around the prison was bare of buildings and growth. It was in the middle of nowhere. The prairies were so flat. I was used to the mountains of British Columbia, and here, I felt totally exposed.

"The guards brutally herded us all through the front gate. All I heard was 'Move it, scumbags. We don't have all day.' I kept my eyes down as we shuffled into the prison, helplessly pushed forward by the man behind me and pulled by the man in front of me.

"Once we were all inside, the dampness sent chills down my body. The rest of the prisoners must have experienced that same coldness. I jumped when the gate slammed shut behind us. I still recall the harsh scraping of metal upon metal, and then the locks falling into place. It sent shivers down my spine."

Jenny reached for his face but stopped short of touching him. His eyes were now filled with tears, and they ran freely down his cheeks, dripping onto his pants. She needed to comfort him, but couldn't bring herself to hug him. She said three simple words: "I'm so sorry."

Tom made no effort to wipe away his tears. "I remember thinking that maybe I was just stuck in a bad dream, but I also knew this was my new reality. We were pushed forward like cattle into rail cars, being led to the slaughterhouse. I remember there were three or maybe four sets of doors before we all entered the final room." Tom sighed before continuing, "A single guard unlocked our cuffs and shackles, while several other guards held their weapons ready in case a brawl erupted. I'd never been that terrified before. What if I did something wrong? Would they kill me? And if they did, would you ever know what actually happened to me?"

He stole a look in her direction. "You know that behind those walls, I was just a number. No one inside cared if I lived or if I died; it would just be one less mouth to feed." Tom looked away, and appeared to be deep in thought. "Next, all our heads were shaved. Head lice are a real problem that prisons try to avoid." A crooked grin appeared on his face. "You used to love my hair. I remember lying in bed next to you with your face buried in my locks. You would giggle as you inhaled the fresh scent of shampoo and conditioner."

His facial expression returned to despair as he continued, "At least with short hair, I no longer needed a comb. They never provided the prisoners with one. Guess they thought we could make a weapon out of anything, maybe even something as innocent as a comb. And they were right. I remember noticing that the entire floor was covered in human hair as we were pushed by yet another guard who was yelling, 'Okay, losers. Strip down to the buff.' While we removed our clothing the guard shouted again: 'Hurry up. Don't be shy.'"

Visibly uncomfortable, Tom looked away from Jenny. "We were then sent into the showers." Tom started to tremble, and he whispered, "After the shower, we were all strip searched, one man at a time, while the rest of the line watched. I felt humiliated and abused as a guard manhandled every inch of my body. Flashlights looked up my nose, into both ears, under my arms . . . but the worst was when I had to bend over and let him check my private areas. At first, I objected, but a quick punch to the stomach stopped me dead in my tracks."

Jenny reached for his hand, but Tom moved away from her, not wanting to feel her closeness to him. "It's okay, Tom," she said. "Hopefully talking about it will help me understand what you went through."

Tom composed himself before continuing, "Another guard yelled, 'Move to the first table for your new uniform, underwear, socks, and shoes.' I found my size and swept the pile into my arms before looking for somewhere safe to get dressed. While pulling on my orange jumper, I realized that some of the other prisoners were eyeing me up." Tom took a deep breath. "No one had ever seen me completely naked before, except my parents, my brother, and, of course, you. I kept my eyes down and couldn't get dressed fast enough.

"Last stop was down a long hall and through another set of doors leading to the cell block. This room was vast, three stories high, and cold and damp, with bars running the full length of the room on both sides, on all three floors. The air was stale and there was a whiff of vomit that was hard to ignore. One by one, men in front of me were pushed into a cell that would be their home until they had done their time. The guard mumbled something to each prisoner, but I wasn't able to hear him until it was my turn. Do you know what he said to me?"

Jenny looked sadly at him. "No, I don't."

"'Welcome to your new home. Enjoy your stay.' I was brutally shoved into my space and cautiously looked around. It was a dark, tiny cell. The ceiling, walls, and floor were solid concrete, and I could feel the cold passing through my shoes and socks, sending shivers through my entire body. A small window that looked out to a brick wall made my cell feel less dark and dingy. Within my four walls was a chipped sink with patches of rust around the downspout, while off in a back corner stood my toilet. Besides there being no toilet seat or lid, and no privacy, the water inside the bowl was a dirty rust color.

"Feeling overwhelmed, I sat down on my single bed. It was so hard that I felt underneath myself, checking whether there was even a mattress there. I was scared shitless and felt like a total failure. The men around me were huge, burly men, and I wondered if I would survive even one night, let alone ten to twenty-five years. I just covered my face and cried like a baby. I felt totally vulnerable and abandoned. I had seriously screwed up and no one could help me. Charles had always fought all my battles for me, so I'd become totally dependent on him, and now, in here, I was a loner, stuck with murderers, rapists, and other criminals. You should know that I never planned on any of this happening. I'm really sorry I let you down." Tom composed himself. "A guard passed by my cell and saw me whimpering. Do you know what he said to me?"

For the first time in Jenny's life, she was almost speechless. "No, Tom, I can't even imagine."

"He said, 'Not exactly the Hilton, is it, but what did you expect? Prisoners don't get a five-star hotel. And no matter what your crime is, whether it was murder, rape, or anything else, you get treated as equals.' He laughed as he left, and then he added, 'You'll get used to it.' I quickly realized that the guards constantly overstepped their limits. Every day, some unfortunate prisoners would be gut punched for not following the rules. These beatings at first bothered me, but before long, it became the norm." Tom's mood changed dramatically. He appeared to slip deeper into depression, and his body started trembling.

He composed himself before continuing, "My first winter was a reality check. It didn't take me long to realize there was almost no heat in the cell block. Colds became my new norm and with only one well-worn blanket on my bed, I often fell asleep shivering.

"I was fortunate enough to be strong and healthy, which kept me from getting too sick. I also worked in the laundry department, so I managed to warm up during the daytime. Thank God I wasn't on any life-saving drugs, as apparently, medical records never followed the prisoners. Several inmates died before they received the medications they needed."

Jenny looked at him with sympathy. "I'm really sorry you had to deal with all of this. It makes my problems seen minor."

Tom's voice softened. "Being separated from you never seemed minor. To me, it was a major problem, which, I might add, was entirely my fault." His voice cracked as he continued, "I don't know how to make things right."

Jenny looked at his defeated face, not knowing what to say.

Tom went on: "Once I managed to survive my first winter inside, the spring and summer should have been a piece of cake. Not so. Although there was air conditioning on site, it was only available in the offices and infirmary. I spent each night sweating profusely. Luckily, working in the laundry department saved me again. Daily, I snuck my sweat-soaked sheets down to the laundry room and exchanged them for a dry set. I got pretty good at sneaking back and forth between my cell and the laundry. No one ever caught me remaking my bed." Tom paused, lost in thought. "I think the hardest thing for me to get used to, was the constant distractions. At night, some inmates felt they had to disrupt the entire cell block. I often used my pillow to try and block out the continuous yelling, and in some cases, the screams from an inmate being abused either by a guard or another prisoner."

Jenny cautiously asked, "Were you ever abused by a guard or inmate?"

Tom looked at her before answering, "Not sexually by a guard, but I came close once with a group of inmates. While I was taking a shower one morning, several prisoners attacked me from behind. Do you know what one of them said?"

Jenny just shook her head.

Tom shuffled in his chair, obviously uncomfortable about sharing the humiliations he suffered inside the prison. "One of them said, 'Look what we have here. Fresh meat.' The other two prisoners started laughing. One of them approached me. 'Should we show him how it works when you're the new guy?' I started trembling. I was scared shitless.

"Another one grabbed me and shoved my face against the shower wall. 'You go first while I hold him down.' Even though my body was slippery from the soapy water, I couldn't get away from my attackers. I fought, kicked, and scratched to no avail.

"But then another prisoner, Big John, entered the shower and saw the scene in front of him and came to my rescue. He was a rather husky man, but obviously somewhat simple. I learned later that he was arrested for beating up a man who was attacking an innocent woman on the street. Unfortunately, the man died and Big John was now paying the price for trying to help. Seeing me at a disadvantage, he knew he had to stop them from raping me.

"I still recall his voice saying, 'Hey, guys. What's going on?' All three men turned and saw Big John. 'Best you turn a blind eye and get lost. We only need ten minutes with this one and then you can come back.' I was so scared, but didn't want anyone to see what these men were going to do to me, so I yelled, 'Get the hell out of here!'

Tom trembled before continuing: "Big John was on top of the man closest to him and threw him against the opposite wall. The other two men quickly picked up their friend and rushed out of the room. My naked body slammed against the shower floor. One shouted over his shoulder, 'We're not finished with either of you. Watch your backs.' That was the day Big John became not only my friend, but also my bodyguard."

Tom got up from his chair and walked towards the window to look outside. His voice trembled as he continued, "I was a small man in a prison full of large men that enjoyed beating me when no one was looking. At one point, they broke several ribs, and I spent a lot of time in the infirmary. But at least the beds were nicer there and I had warm blankets. That's the only time I felt truly safe. There was a doctor and nurse there twenty-four hours a day, seven days a week."

Tom turned and faced her. "I'm so sorry, honey. I wish I could turn back the clock and once again be working as a mechanic and coming home to a hearty meal that you lovingly prepared for us every night. I still ask myself every day, why did my parents' death hit me so hard? They had abandoned Charles and me years before, so there didn't seem to be any reason why I would use drugs, let alone buy a gun. I should have talked to you about my feelings rather than shut you out." Tom sounded defeated as he continued, "In a matter of a few days, I went from being a free, married man to a killer."

Tom saw the tears in Jenny's eyes. He approached her and raised her up from the chair and passionately kissed her.

Jenny struggled, beating against his chest to get away from him. He released her in utter disbelief. He'd thought that she wanted him as much as he wanted her.

"You stay away from me!" she screamed, wiping her mouth with the back of her hands, which were still tightly bound together. "You had no right to kiss me!"

Tom was mortified. "I thought you wanted me to."

"I already told you it's over between us. I was willing to listen to you with the hope that it might help you heal, but that's all I was doing."

He brutally turned her around, forced her towards the bed, shoved her down, and then secured her wrists to the headboard. She fought him, but once again lost the battle. "Stop it, Tom. You're really hurting me." For a moment, Jenny was worried that he was going to rape her, but instead, his face was full of disappointment.

Tom had to get some fresh air. Confident that she was unable to escape, he left the room, slamming the door shut behind him.

Outside, he jabbed his fist into a post on the front of the building. He screamed in agony, not just from the pain in his knuckles, but also from knowing that Jenny no longer loved him. They had pledged their love to each other all those years ago, and it was his fault that she didn't want anything to do with him now.

Was he capable of killing the love of his life? If he did, then he was no better than his brother, who had tried to kill her. What had Charles been thinking? Was he delusional, or did he just feel invincible? Was Tom no better than his brother? How could he expect to win when he was not only going up against Bill, but also the entire police department? Tom's strategy for winning had to be different than Charles's. And he had to win because going back to prison wasn't an option.

He sat on the chair next to the door and lit a cigarette. With each drag, he tried to think of ways to win Jenny back. Maybe if she fell in love with him again, she could get Bill to talk to his parole officer and straighten everything out.

Could Bill really turn the tables around for him? Should he turn himself in?

Tom quickly brushed that idea aside; it was too late for Bill to help him. Plus, Bill owed him, and he really needed the money so he could truly start over. It was sad that Jenny wouldn't be part of his new beginning. He butted out his cigarette and decided to stroll along the front of the complex to clear his head.

Entering the main office, at the opposite end of the building, Tom took a look around. Judging by the dust covering every surface, the place must have been derelict for some years. He stepped behind the counter and noticed a series of drawers, some partially open, while the others were completely closed. Glancing into each drawer, he came upon a flashlight. Amazingly, it still worked, so he put it in his pocket. Then he spotted a stack of dusty books lying on a table below the window. He crossed the room and picked one up. Tom blew the dust off the cover. Coughing, he looked closer and discovered the books were Bibles waiting to be delivered to the now-vacant rooms. He smiled. If he gave one to Jenny, she might see the correct path to follow: walking away with him into the sunset.

He opened the good book and searched out a particular reading. Once he found it, he tore out another page and used it as a marker. With a wide grin on his face, he tucked it under his arm and returned to the room, tossing it on the table.

She inquired, "What's that?"

"Just some spiritual reading that will help you find your way back to me. I need to clear my head but when I return, I'll share a section that applies to you and we can discuss it."

Tom grinned and left the room again. He walked around the back of the building and found a trail leading into the woods. He needed to burn off his frustration, so he decided to explore where it went. He walked for several minutes and came upon a clearing near a running creek. He bent down and splashed the cool water over his face. For a moment, he felt revived, but then became confused, unsure what his next move should be. He was physically exhausted and his mind was rambling.

He sat on a rock, trying to unscramble all the emotions that were going through his head. Reflecting on his past made him feel even worse. His parents had been failures; Charles had been no better. But what was his excuse? He didn't have one.

Standing up, he skipped from one rock to the next to get to the other side of the creek. He continued to explore until the trail came to a dead end. Glancing around, he spotted another clearing to his left. As he peeked between the trees, something shiny caught his eye. At first, he thought it was his imagination, but once he climbed over a few fallen trees, he came upon a makeshift fire pit with some half burned logs, surrounded by rough stumps that someone might sit on. Empty beer cans were strewn around the site. At some point, people might have used it as a hangout.

As he glanced to his left, Tom found the shiny object that had caught his eye. It was a perfectly good axe embedded in a tree. The tree was covered in notches, as if the axe had been thrown at it multiple times. Tom approached the tree and pulled out the axe. He wasn't quite sure what purpose it would serve as he already knew that he couldn't kill Jenny with it. Touching his pants pocket he felt his pocket knife. Both weapons could only be used to protect him if he was close to his enemy. Neither could be used if his enemy was too far away, but at least he was no longer unarmed. He took the knife out of his pocket and found a section of the tree that wasn't covered in axe marks and started to carve a heart deep into the bark. He then added his initials within the heart shape and was about to add Jenny's initials when the tip of the knife blade broke off. Tom wasn't sure if this was a sign or not but in frustration he threw the damaged knife and its' sheathing into the brush.

He walked back to the motel with the axe in hand, and again quietly sat outside on the chair with a cigarette. Tom ran his finger gingerly over the tempered edge of the axe blade. Although it wasn't sharp, Tom wasn't sure if he could even use it. He knew that eliminating Jenny wasn't going to be easy. He thought about just climbing into her car and driving off into the sunset, leaving her to starve in the room. He already knew that the police force would actively be looking out for Jenny's vehicle, so if he left, it would have to be on foot.

Tom was starting to feel exhausted. He dropped his cigarette butt and stepped on it to extinguish it. Somehow, he had to convince Jenny they still had a chance. Then he could have not only her, but also the half million dollars that Bill owed him. Tom would just have to turn on his charm and win her over once again.

He took the axe into the room and set it on the table. He noticed Jenny glaring at him. "What're you looking at?"

She shook her head sadly. "A very delusional man who's trying to take on the world. What do you hope to accomplish by holding me hostage? You're expecting the impossible of Bill. How in hell do you think he can come up with that much money?"

Tom remained calm. "He will if it keeps you alive"

"And what if he can't come up with it in time? Are you just going to kill me and run away?" She let him think for a few moments before adding, "They will hunt you down and either kill you, or put you back behind bars. Is that what you want?"

Tom became angry. "I want what's owed to me. Bill will pay, or I will not only kill you, but also hunt him down and eliminate him too."

"Do you honestly think the police force is going to let you get close to Bill? They're a close-knit family. Bill and his team helped me to survive after you went to prison. I already told you about the threats from people in the community and how the police set up twenty-four-hour protection until everything settled down. You kill me, and they'll hunt you down like the animal you are." She glanced at the table and spotted the axe. "Where did you get that?"

"I found it in the woods." He laughed. "I now have a weapon. It's not sharp but it could still cause a lot of damage to a person."

Jenny whimpered. "What happened to the man I married?"

"Come away with me and you'll find him again. I still love you, Jenny, and I know that deep down, you love me too."

"Sorry. I'm not interested."

"I can change."

"It's too late for that."

"So be it." He studied her. "Now that I think of it, I'm better off without you. You had me eating out of the palm of your hand. Being around you made me weak, a pushover. Charles always said you were controlling and now I believe him." He sneered at her. "He never did like you. He actually discouraged me from marrying you, but I refused to listen. Lesson learned."

Jenny turned her face away from him. "I guess I thought I knew you, too, but was obviously wrong." She turned and looked at him. "What's going on in that head of yours?"

Tom grinned. "Do you really want to know?"

"Of course. Why else would I ask?"

"I'm thinking about how, if I have to eliminate you, what would be the best way to do it and hide your body?"

Jenny started to tremble. "You won't find me an easy person to kill. Even if I die, I'll fight you to the end."

Tom laughed. "You're no match for me. I could snap your neck in a second."

"I guess you saw a lot of death in prison. Just answer me one question. Did you ever kill anyone inside?"

Tom ignored her question. Instead, he responded, "I saw a lot of death inside, but the worst was when Big John was killed right in front of me. He was killed for not only being my friend, but also for protecting me. No one ever got close to me when he was around."

"I'm so sorry about your friend." She paused before speaking again. "I thought of you a lot over the years, wondering how you were doing. With you being gone for so long, I had to learn to take care of myself. It wasn't easy. I had to make house payments, so that's why I took in the two boarders, continued working at the restaurant, and babysat during the week."

Tom turned to her. "This Nancy that you babysit ... who are her parents?"

Jenny thought quickly. She didn't want him to connect "Nancy" to Kimberley or Richard, so she conjured up another lie. "Her mother is Kimberley Parker," she said without volunteering any more information.

"What does this Kimberley Parker do for a living?"

Jenny looked directly at him, hoping she sounded convincing. "She's a school teacher."

Tom became suspicious. "If she's a schoolteacher, then why do you have to pick up her daughter after school? Can't she go home with her mother?"

"Ms. Parker has after-school classes twice a week, and on the other days, she stays to tutor children who are struggling. I pick her daughter up after school every day and her mother drops by my house around four o'clock to fetch her before heading home. She also drops her off before school."

"What about her father?"

Jenny answered, "The bastard abandoned her when she told him of her pregnancy."

He shrugged. "Guess she should have been more careful."

Jenny hated lying to Tom, but she needed to survive long enough for Bill to rescue her. She was terrified for her life but didn't want Tom to know it. She looked at him with defiant eyes and said, "Please untie my wrists. They're aching." Seeing him hesitate, she added, "Let me sit in the chair and you can fasten me to the arm rest again. I promise I'll behave."

"I guess you can't go anywhere as long as you're tied down." He clipped the tie wraps and watched as she rubbed her red, swollen wrists. She got up and walked to the chair, allowing him to fasten her there.

Jenny started shivering, so Tom picked up the blanket and draped it over her legs. "Thank you." Looking at him, she said, "It's going to get dark in a few hours. Have you seen any candles or matches we can use until morning?"

Tom laughed. "How about when it gets too dark, we just call it a day." He pulled the flashlight out of his pocket. "Found this in the main office, but the batteries are weak. You may want to save it in case of an emergency." He placed the flashlight next to her on the table.

"What about heat?"

"Do you want me to light a fire in the middle of the room?" Tom growled.

"No, of course not, but could we light a campfire outside to keep warm?"

"Not a chance. I'm not sending any signals that will give away our location."

"Where the hell are we, anyway?"

"Somewhere close to town, but not too close."

"What kind of answer is that?"

Tom studied her. "If I tell you, then what's to prevent you from telling Bill at our next call?"

"You honestly think I'm so stupid that I would tell him where we are? If I did, you would kill me and then you'll never get your money." She added, "I'll help you get your money, but then I want you to get the hell out of my life."

Tom needed to think without Jenny staring at him, so he picked up the axe and left the room. He took a seat in his chair just outside the door and was running possible ideas through his mind. Would she actually help him get the money? If she did, but refused to leave with him, he would still have to eliminate her. How would he get rid of her? He started to sweat. Tom refused to believe that his plan wasn't perfect, but it was too late to modify it. He was now forced to wing it, and hope for the best.

Tom was thinking hours ahead. How would Bill deliver the money? What would be the best way to exchange her for the money and still escape? Bill wouldn't come alone, so how would he get away from the motel once the swap was done? Maybe he could do it from a distance, undetected. He could hide at that fire pit deep within the woods and call Bill from there. But then who was to say Bill wouldn't take Jenny and also keep the cash?

Tom rubbed his forehead, realizing there was no way out for him. He had backed himself into a corner. That stupid axe was useless. He wouldn't even get a chance to throw it before there would be a bullet between his eyes. He wondered how it would feel to die from a bullet wound. Hopefully it would be quick. He paced in front of the motel room. It was clear that he would die trying to collect his money, so he might as well leave and take Jenny with him right now. Yes, she would resist him. Did he have the energy to watch her twenty-four hours a day, seven days a week? Could she learn to love him once again? Was it a dying cause? He was slowly losing perspective on the situation.

Back in the dingy motel room, it was cold, and Jenny was thankful for the blanket across her legs, even though it was filthy. With the movement of the early afternoon sun, shadows started to appear around her turning the room into a place of horror. Jenny tried to turn and look out the window, but all she saw were trees. She was unable to figure out where she was. Jenny knew that Tom was just on the other side of the window, as she could feel his presence there. A cloud of smoke appeared occasionally, indicating that Tom was smoking. He'd never smoked before he went into prison, so that must have been a bad habit he picked up while behind bars.

Terror descended onto her as the shredded curtains, once innocent-looking, now seemed like ghosts passing in front of the window. Scurrying sounds in the corner of the room told her that the mice had returned and were seeking shelter from the elements. Jenny's body slowly succumbed to the chill that closed in on her, and in horror, she watched the mice now running on the bed that she had earlier been bound to.

Tom had told Bill their next call would be at one p.m. It was important that she get another message to Bill, but would Tom allow her to speak to him again? Tom didn't trust her, so she would have to be careful to not trigger Tom's suspicions, or it was over for her.

As she sat in her chair, Jenny's brain started to work overtime. She didn't know if Bill had been able to decipher all the clues from her first call, but somehow, she had to give Bill another clue as to where they were hiding. Jenny already knew that Kimberley, Claire, and Richard would be placed into protective custody, but Tom wouldn't know that. The only clue that came to her mind was the dreadful road leading to their location. Jenny wasn't even sure where she was, as Tom had blindfolded her when they left the house and only removed it once she was inside the building. Judging from her surroundings, it appeared to be a rundown motel. If Tom was telling her the truth, it was somewhere close to town, but not visible from the highway. But what if he was lying to her?

Jenny started to cry, knowing that the man she had once loved was now capable of killing her. It would be a fight to the end. If Tom was going to kill her himself, she would force him to look into her eyes as she died.

Her mind went back to that horrible bumpy road that led to this location. Her mind tossed around ideas, but nothing seemed believable. She was stressed to the limit. She closed her eyes and forced herself to think of ways to tell Bill about that treacherous road. She had to think fast, as one o'clock couldn't be far off.

Outside, Tom sat on the chair and lit another cigarette. He was becoming bored with this waiting game. He had to put pressure on Bill, as he didn't want to wait until morning to collect his money. Surely Bill would know by now whether he could raise the funds. If not, the game would end, simple as that.

Before he was sent to prison, Tom had had no idea that ten years later, he would be planning his wife's death. The more he thought about it, the easier it became. She would only die if he never got his money and Bill was too late to save her.

Stamping out his cigarette, he picked up the axe and went behind the building. He needed to unwind, so he picked a tree for target practice. Looking at the dull blade, he threw the weapon, hoping to sink it deep into the bark. He missed the tree completely, so crossed the clearing and picked it up. He continued throwing it again and again, but it was no use; it always bounced sideways and fell to the ground.

"Damn useless thing. How can I possibly protect myself with this piece of shit?"

However, Tom persisted, and after numerous throws, he finally sank it deep into the tree. He shouted, "Yes! Finally!" He practiced until, each time he threw it, it was a direct hit. Proud of himself, he went back inside the motel room and placed the axe on the table.

Tom was about to call Bill when Jenny stopped him. She suddenly knew what her next clue to Bill was going to be. "Before you call, it's important that I speak to Bill again."

Tom scowled at her. "What now? You forgot to put the milk in the fridge?"

"No. Bill told you he'd need to talk to me frequently to make sure I'm still alive, remember? I'm just trying to give you a heads up on how he works. When Charles kidnapped me, Bill did the same thing--insisted that he speak to me every hour, just to make sure I was still alive. One time when he called and Charles refused to let him speak to me, he hung up.

Charles was livid, but then he understood Bill's rules. If I don't speak to Bill each time you call, he will assume that I'm dead."

"At this rate, you will be."

"I hope that if I'm able to help you get your money, you'll let me live. Take my car now and hide it well away from here. Once you have the money, you can hike to it and escape. You know the back roads like the back of your hand, so you could be out of the area before anyone finds you."

Tom seemed to be thinking. "What do you need to tell Bill this time?"

Jenny swallowed nervously. "He needs to know that two of the three roads leading to the school are under construction."

"He lives in town, so wouldn't he already know about the construction?"

"He's retired, Tom, so no, he may not already know."

"He'll figure that out once he gets there."

"You don't understand. He'll have to detour twice and that would add fifteen minutes to picking Nancy up from school." Jenny went a step further in her explanation. "Nancy has had anxiety issues ever since her father abandoned her and her mother. She would be traumatized if no one was there to pick her up."

Tom was skeptical, but conceded, "Fine, but no tricky business."

"I promise."

Jenny told Tom the number of the station. She watched him enter it, and then waited patiently for Bill to answer.

Chapter Six

12:50 p.m. - 1:45 p.m.

THE STRESS IN THE STATION mounted as each hour moved faster than the officers wanted it to. It was already the afternoon, and some of Jenny's clues still remained unsolved. Bill crossed the room for the third time and topped up his coffee mug. Even though he knew the caffeine was hard on his system, Beatrice wasn't there to stop him. At his age, he was having a hard time keeping up with the fast pace in the station. Bill was too old to be still doing the job—that was why he chose retirement—but life doesn't always play fair. Jenny had protected Claire when she was held hostage and now it was Bill's turn to repay that favor.

He turned to Daniel. "I'm stepping outside to have my coffee and clear my head. I'll be back before my call. If not, come find me. Hopefully you won't find me dead on the sidewalk."

"I hope so too. We really need you."

Bill left the station and sat on the front steps, hugging his mug. He wasn't ready for another roller coaster ride that would throw him into a tailspin. He breathed deeply, trying to slow his heart rate and clear his head. His thoughts went back to Beatrice; she had married him for love, not his job. Bill had found it increasingly difficult to separate his work life from married life, so he'd taken early retirement. Bill thought he was finished working for the force and now had suddenly been dragged back to work.

This was not the time to abandon Jenny. He only hoped that this was the last time history would come back to haunt him. The outside air was cool, and it helped clear his head, plus the mug warmed his hands. Every case he'd handled in his career had been unique, but they'd also had similarities to each other. Some cases were connected, and in this case, the common thread was the Lockman brothers. Charles had been delusional, and Tom was not that different from his brother. He was disconnected from reality and also displayed signs of schizophrenia. The only difference here was that Tom had been corrupted while behind prison bars, whereas Charles had been tainted after having to defend himself and his brother their entire lives. When their parents committed suicide and the boys were removed from their home, they scrounged for food and their everyday needs, while living in the elements beneath overpasses. Tom was bullied constantly and as a bigger brother Charles fought not only his own battles, but also his brother's. This unstable background had affected both boys at a very young age, and carried on into adulthood. If the child protection system had stepped in when they were young, this could have been corrected.

Charles had lost his mental health battle when he challenged the Blue Ridge Police Department. It was starting to look like Tom might also fall victim to the same disease.

Bill took the last sip of his coffee then returned inside and sat next to Daniel.

Daniel smiled. "I see you survived the outdoors. You ready for your one o'clock call?"

"Not really, but I have no choice."

"You're good at this stuff, Bill. Don't underestimate what you're capable of."

Bill sat down and nervously waited for the phone to ring. When it did, Bill glanced over at Daniel to confirm that he was ready to record before picking up the receiver. "Hello, Tom. How's it going?"

"I should be the one to ask you that. Do you have my money yet?"

"I'm working on it."

"Are you really?" He paused a moment. "Just as long as you have it by tomorrow morning."

"If you'd asked for a couple thousand dollars, I could have had it in less than an hour, but since you wanted much more, it'll take time. All you need to know is I'm working on it. Half a million dollars doesn't just appear out of mid-air. It takes time."

"Well, the clock's a-ticking, so don't screw up. It will cost Jenny her life."

"Speaking of Jenny let me talk to her."

"Sure, but no tricks." Tom covered the phone and spoke to Jenny. "You slip up and I'll kill you right here and now." His face turned ugly. "Imagine how Bill would feel hearing you take your last breath." He cut one of the tie wraps and passed the phone to her.

Jenny nervously took the phone. "Hello, Bill."

"How're you holding up, Jenny?"

"I've had better days."

"Are you hurt?"

"Not so far, but Tom's really starting to scare me. He's out of control."

Tom grabbed the phone from her. "Tell him what he needs to know, or this conversation is over."

Jenny took the phone back and watched Tom as she spoke. "Bill, two of the roads leading to Nancy's school are full of potholes, so you'll have to make two detours. The city is in the middle of repairing them before winter. You'll have to allow another fifteen minutes at least to get there in time. Please make sure that Nancy isn't left waiting outside alone."

Bill knew that those repairs were not happening, so she was sending another clue, but what? This was the second time that the clue about fifteen minutes had entered their conversation. "I'll deal with it myself. You hang in there," Bill said, "Put Tom back on the line."

Jenny passed the phone back to Tom. "He wants to speak to you."

Tom grabbed the receiver from her and took control of the call. "Let's get back to business."

Bill cut in. "New rule, asshole. You harm Jenny or use scare tactics on her I'll personally hunt you down and put you back in prison, or six feet below the earth. Either way works for me. We'd prefer to bring you in alive, as an officer can drown in paperwork when a criminal dies. But I would be more than happy to stay an extra day or two to complete those papers. She's been through hell since you were arrested, and the entire force will back me up." Bill ran his finger through his hair. "Answer me one thing, Tom. How in the hell did you manage to get early release?"

"Funny you should ask."

"I don't find it the least bit funny."

"I'd written a speech on how I realized my mistake and prison had changed me. I was a reformed man and fit to be returned to my hometown. I was pleading for my life, so I turned to this guy and spoke to him directly."

"I'm assuming you mean Mr. Wilks."

"Is that the name of the guy whose old lady I killed?"

"If you showed any remorse, you would already know his name."

Tom shrugged. "I'm lousy with names."

"Thought you might remember the woman you killed, and her husband, but I guess not."

Tom was irritated. "You want to hear my story or not?"

"Sorry, you can keep rambling on and I'll take notes. They'll come in handy when you are back behind bars."

"Write to your heart's content, but I'm not going back to prison."

"We'll see about that."

"Shut up and let me tell my story," Tom snapped. "I chose to wear my prison attire, as I would only wear civilian clothes if I was released. I thought that would get me on the good side of the parole board."

Bill had to agree that not wearing civilian clothes would help his plea, but he wasn't about to admit it out loud.

"When the guard came to fetch me, I was scared. Could I convince the board that I was ready to return to a normal life? I was sweating profusely in that confined room. I didn't know that whatever was said inside those four walls would be recorded and reviewed extensively by the committee in front of me. It was at that point that I had to change my strategy." He started laughing. "I was brilliant. Actually, I should have gotten an award for my presentation."

Tom glanced at Jenny and saw that she was disgusted with him. She looked sick to her stomach.

He got up, went to the window, and looked outside before continuing, "The board asked this Wilks guy to speak. I didn't need to hear anything from him, so I just ignored what he had to say."

"Why the hell did you ignore him? After all, you ruined his life, and his children's."

"Stop interrupting. I'm getting to my award-winning performance. Rather than address the committee, I spoke directly to this Wilks guy. By speaking directly to him, it made me sound compassionate. I knew that would work to my advantage. I even managed to turn on the tears. I had Wilks and the committee eating out of my hand. I told him that I have no children, but someday I hoped to have some. That my wife Jenny and I had a perfect marriage, and I threw it all away in a matter of days. I was smart and added that I had no memory of killing his wife, but there wasn't a day that went by that I didn't regret doing it. That two-hour session was exhausting. I only had to hope that my performance was enough to sway the committee. I'm living proof that it worked."

"It sounds to me that your award was undeserved."

"Quit interrupting! Do you know what the board asked me?"

"I can't wait for you to tell me."

"They had the balls to ask me if I had known of my brother's plan to get me out of prison."

"What did you tell them?"

"I knew something was in the works, but wasn't sure of the details. The bastards brought up my parents' death. They had no right to snoop into my past."

"They're the parole board. They had the right to check into your past." Bill then asked, "What made you snap? And don't tell me you didn't snap."

Tom chuckled. "I was in complete control, but imagine how I felt when I was told that I had to be in constant communication with a parole officer in Blue Ridge. I didn't need a babysitter. I just needed to get back home and reconnect with Jenny."

Bill interjected. "Well, we know that didn't go so well."

"When I got into town and found Jenny in the kitchen with a man standing behind her I was devastated."

"Did you ask her about him?"

"Sure did, and do you know what she told me?"

"Let me guess. She told you he was renting the spare room in the house." Tom was irritated. "Can you believe that she would lie to my face?"

"Have you ever considered that she may have been telling the truth?"

"I know my wife. She's a very passionate woman. There's no way she would've stayed faithful."

Bill said, "My guess is you left her so devastated that she was turned off men permanently. You might find this hard to believe, but your life now is based on lies and deceit. You wouldn't know the truth from a lie, even if it was thrown into your face."

Tom shouted into the phone. "The guards were the first to make me realize she probably wasn't waiting for me."

"How did they come to that conclusion? They didn't even know Jenny."

Tom turned back to face Jenny. "They know everything about all the prisoners. There were no secrets on the inside. If you could think of something, anything, they knew about it. You only had to make one mistake and you were marked for the rest of your time inside. No one got any sleep. The guards walked along the corridors some nights, dragging their pistols across the bars and laughing, and creating a disturbance."

Tom collected his thoughts. "I must have been talking in my sleep one night, because a guard shouted at me, 'Keep it down in there, other prisoners are still asleep!' I jolted awake and shouted back at him to leave me alone. The guard shone his flashlight into my cell and realized he must have woken me up. With a chuckle in his voice, he said, 'Don't make me come in there to shut you up!' I quietly sat up on my bunk, not wanting to irritate him. He studied me like I was an open book. He finally asked me, 'What's going on in there, anyway?' When I didn't respond, he almost sounded concerned when he asked, 'Are you okay?' I knew he didn't really care how I felt, but I whispered that I was fine. The guard turned off his flashlight and leaned against the metal bars. Do you know what he said next?"

"What's that?"

"The bastard said, 'You having another dream about your missus?' I was in no mood to respond, let alone discuss my wife with a total stranger. I saw the smirk on his face as he looked directly into my eyes. 'She's probably already moved on without you. Could already have a new boyfriend and a few kids in tow.' He struck the bars once more and laughed as he walked away. That was the day that I knew Jenny might be lost to me forever. I had hoped the guard was wrong." His next few words were a mere whisper. "I guess he was right all along."

Tom looked at Jenny and then at the Bible that lay on the desk. He picked it up and flipped through the pages until he found the New Testament,

Gospel of St. John, Chapter 8, verses 1–11. Tom composed himself and changed the subject. "How well do you know your Bible, Sergeant?"

"Pretty good, but I wouldn't expect you to be a Bible-thumper. I hope you're not like Charles and misread the true meaning of the stories within the book."

Tom grinned at Jenny, extremely proud of himself. "In the Bible, if a woman was caught in adultery, she was stoned to death."

Jenny froze in disbelief. How could Tom compare her to women who committed adultery? She might have been lonely while he was behind bars, but she wasn't a whore.

Bill became nervous. "Why do you bring this up now?"

Tom laughed. "I thought we could share a section of the Bible, and possibly discuss it further. Let me refresh your memory." He started reading. "It states that a woman who had committed adultery was brought before Jesus. Do you recall that section of the Bible?"

"I do."

"It states, and I quote: 'Teacher, this woman has been caught in the act of adultery. In the Law of Moses, the woman should be stoned to death.'"

Bill took a chance and asked, "What about the bastard who slept with her? If he showed his face, he would have been stoned too. Guess he was a coward."

"I'm not talking about the man. I'm referring to the woman."

"Maybe the man should come into play. I think he should be stoned too."

Tom was becoming agitated. "Don't try and change the subject. The woman was guilty. If Jenny lived back then, she would already be dead."

"And you would be the first one to cast a stone, right? If you recall that reading, you missed what Jesus said to the Scribes and Pharisees: 'Let him who is without sin among you, be the first to throw a stone at her.'"

"That's bullshit. They should have stoned her."

Bill continued, "'Jesus looked up and said to the woman, "Where are they? Has no one condemned you?" She said, "No one, Lord." Jesus then said, "Neither do I condemn you; go, and from now on sin no more."'"

Bill waited to see if these words would have any effect on Tom, but there was complete silence at the other end of the phone. "This is the part where forgiveness comes into play. You do know what forgiveness is?" Frustrated,

Bill added, "Do you only take sections of the Bible you like and dismiss the ones you don't? That's not why the Bible was written. The idea is to read the entire section, not eliminate parts of it. If everyone read the Bible that way, it wouldn't make any sense."

Tom was silent for a moment. "You make a lousy preacher, but as an officer, you're pathetic."

Bill didn't skip a beat. "I'm not an officer, I'm a sergeant, and I'm very good at my job."

"That's a matter of opinion. You haven't found Jenny and me yet."

"You have no idea how close we are even as we speak."

Tom became very agitated. "She got to sit in our home, under the watchful eye of your famous police friends, while I almost died several times. No one cared about me." Tom was shaking as he asked Bill. "Do you have any idea what I had to go through just to survive?"

"I could probably guess and almost hit the nail on the head," Bill said. "Why don't you talk about it and I'll listen?"

"Why would I? You don't give a flying shit about me."

"You might be pleasantly surprised. I've heard lots of crazy stories, plus I'm a very good listener."

"That's what Jenny said before she listened to me talk and then told me to stay away from her. She's always hurting me."

Bill knew Jenny was in danger, but when Tom said she rejected him, he went on high alert. Somehow, he had to try and calm Tom down. Bill spoke in a soft voice, hoping Tom would respond. "Talk to me and help me understand what you've gone through. Share with me one incident that happened when you were inside the prison."

Agitated, Tom said, "Tell me, big-shot sergeant, have you ever taken a ride in a heavy-duty laundromat dryer?"

Bill was taken aback, but remained calm. "I can't say that I have. It must have been awful."

"It was scary. My first job in prison was in the laundry. The work was hard. You have no idea how much laundry my team and I had to sort through, clean, and then get back to the inmates. One morning, I wanted to get an early start, so I went in alone. Big mistake. I soon heard a group of men come up behind me. Do you know what they said?"

"I'm listening."

Tom spoke slowly so Bill could absorb the full impact of what had happened to him. "They said, 'Are you alone again? You are such a sucker for punishment.' I was just there doing my job. I already knew a beating was about to happen, so I thought I might as well earn it. 'Don't you assholes have somewhere to be?' That was the wrong thing to say.

"One of the guys grabbed me and shouted, 'Cocky prick, aren't you?' Before I knew what was happening, they scooped me up and tossed me into the commercial dryer, which was filled with damp sheets, and slammed the door shut. I watched in horror as they turned the dryer on, and I started smashing against the dryer walls. The assholes had the balls to shout above the sound of the machine, 'Enjoy your ride.' They thought the whole ordeal was funny, especially when they saw the horror on my face.

"I was slowly sucked into the middle of the damp laundry. The heat and tumbling made me feel dizzy, and I almost passed out. I was slowly suffocating, but no matter how hard I pushed and kicked at the door, it wouldn't budge.

"Within a matter of moments the men scattered. I knew my friend Big John must have arrived, and not a moment too soon. He yanked open the dryer door and carefully pulled me out of the machine.

"Big John was pissed. 'The sons of bitches. Are you okay?' I wasn't; I was dizzy and nauseous. I asked my friend, 'Why do they all hate me?' Big John said, 'Don't worry about it. They're all losers.'"

Tom added, "I ended up getting a few bruises out of it, and now I hate being closed in. That's why I'll never go back to prison. You'll have to kill me first."

Bill was sensitive. "I'm really sorry that you had to go through that. The system could've offered you counseling if you had asked."

"I don't need counseling, I need half a million dollars to start over. This conversation is finished."

Bill jumped in before Tom could hang up. "I need to talk to Jenny at two o'clock."

Tom balked. "You told me every two hours."

"I've changed my mind."

"Who's writing the rules here?" Tom snapped.

"Looks like both of us. Trustworthiness isn't exactly your best suit. I'm only thinking of Jenny's safety."

Before Tom ended the call, he said, "Fine. Sixteen ninety-two. Look it up." The line went dead. He then proceeded to tie wrap Jenny's free arm back to the chair.

Bill put down the phone and turned to Daniel. "Let me know, when you replay the tape, if you hear anything that could help us find her."

Daniel was already on it.

Don watched Bill walk over to the whiteboard and approached him. "How did it go?"

Bill was trying to compose himself. "He's going to drive me into an early grave. We talked about the Bible, and how women were stoned for committing adultery. This fellow is like a walking time bomb. We have to find Jenny before he snaps completely." He picked up the marker and wrote "2 roads to school under construction 15 minute delay."

"There's that damn fifteen minutes again," Don commented. "We need to figure this out."

Bill then added "1692 ?" to the whiteboard.

Don was confused. "What the heck does that mean?"

"I'm not totally sure, but Tom told me to look it up."

Don pulled his cell phone out of his back pocket and opened the internet. "Let's see what it means." He searched for 1692 and then his face turned white as a ghost.

Bill looked at Don. "What does it mean?"

Don spoke slowly, as if he didn't want to reveal what it meant. "The Salem witch trials started in the spring of that year."

Bill felt like he had been kicked in the stomach. "Oh, shit. Is that to be Jenny's demise?" Next to the year, he added, with a shaky hand, "Salem witch trials?" He was so overwhelmed that he threw the marker at the board and left the building.

Don picked up the marker and placed it back on the ledge before following Bill outside. "You okay?"

Bill said nothing for several moments as he tried to get ahold of himself. "Charles was a big enough challenge for me, and now his brother Tom has me questioning my capabilities." He turned to Don, looking totally defeated. "What do I do? How can I beat someone who is so delusional? He's not working with a full deck."

"I think we already figured that out." Don paused. "He may think that he's holding all the aces for the moment, but don't forget, jokers are wild. We can beat him. We just need to work the case and follow the evidence." Don shook his head. "I'm calling the whole team together to see if any of us can make sense out of the whiteboard, especially that fifteen-minute clue that Jenny has sent twice."

Bill agreed. "Sounds like a good plan. Just give me a few minutes to compose myself and I'll be right in."

"Take your time. Are you going to call Beatrice?"

"I can't think straight right now. I'll call after our brainstorming with the team."

Don walked into the main area and Daniel handed him an envelope. "What's this?" he asked.

"Forensic just dropped it off. It's the results of all the evidence that Sam and Muhammad collected from Jenny's house."

Don opened the envelope and scanned the report, just as Bill returned. Bill looked over Don's shoulder. "What've you got there?"

"The forensic report from Jenny's place. The fingerprints from the back door, the arms of the chair in the living room, the stool inside the shed, and the flashlight all belong to Tom Lockman."

Bill answered, "That's no surprise."

Don continued, "At this time the footprints outside the house can't be identified as Tom's. We don't know what size he wears or the style of sole on the shoes the Prison issues. We need to contact Edmonton to confirm they are his. But we do know that he was at the house, so it doesn't really matter which ones are his."

Daniel returned to his desk when a woman in her mid thirties entered the building. "Can I help you?"

"I'm looking for an officer. I don't know his last name, but his first name is Sam. Is he here?"

"He is. Who may I say is here to see him?"

"Name's Sarah Brooks."

"I'll let him know that you're here."

Daniel walked over to Sam's desk.

Sam stopped what he was doing and turned to Daniel. "What you got?"

"There's a lady, Sarah Brooks here to see you."

Sam looked over to the entrance and spotted the lady. He got up from his chair and followed Daniel over to her. "I'm Constable Sam Lawson. How may I help you?"

"I understand that you came to my home this morning inquiring about Jenny Lockman."

Sam was intrigued and gestured her towards his cubicle. Once the two were seated Sam looked at the woman. "I did speak to your husband this morning. He said he never heard anything unusual."

"I had just served his breakfast so called him in to eat. When he sat down I left the room for only a few minutes to collect the newspaper from the front porch."

"Are you telling me that you heard something?"

"Yes I did. I heard Jenny's car leaving her driveway and head down the street."

"Did you see if she was alone in the car?"

"She was in the passenger side of the vehicle, but I couldn't see who the driver was." She then added, "I figured whoever was driving, was taking her to work."

"Do you recall the time?"

"It was just before 9:00."

"I wish my husband had called me when you were at the door and I could have talked to you sooner."

Don turned to the board and started his brain storming session. "I received a call at ten this morning from someone who wanted to talk to Bill. When he found out Bill was not here, he insisted I get him in the office before his next call at eleven a.m., or someone would die. I immediately called Bill and told him he needed to get here pronto."

Bob cut in. "I called our local parole officer, Mike Johnson. He informed me that Tom Lockman was released from prison three days ago, but had not yet checked in with him. I then told Don that the call was most likely from Tom Lockman and that his wife Jenny could very well be missing."

Jack Spencer spoke next. "When Bob told me that Tom hadn't checked in yet, I called the Edmonton prison and spoke to Mr. Al Grant, the Warden. He confirmed Tom's release and when I asked why the Blue Ridge police weren't informed of his release, I was told that if he never checked in, then the local parole officer would contact us."

Don added, "I immediately sent Bob and Jim to check out Jenny's place."

"Jenny wasn't at home, so we went to her workplace," Bob said.

Jim nodded. "She wasn't at work either, so that confirmed our worst nightmare. Tom had taken her most likely, against her will."

Bill leaned against the wall listening to the team trying to unscramble the whiteboard clues. "You can't imagine how seeing that whiteboard affected me. I felt like my past was coming back to haunt me once again."

Don looked at Bill sadly. "I really hated to call you in, but I had no choice." Don continued with his recap. "I immediately sent Debbie and Eric to pick up Kimberley, Claire, and Richard and put them under protection. Tom knows that Richard testified against him at his trial. I wasn't going to take a chance with their family. Eric stayed at their home, while Debbie returned here." He then asked the group. "Do any of you have any questions or queries?"

Debbie turned her attention to Sam and Muhammad. "Were there any signs of forced entry at her home?"

Muhammad responded, "None. We all know that Jenny always kept her doors locked so if he got in, there had to be a hidden key outside. When we went inside, everything was in its' place. There were no signs of a confrontation between the two of them. The only thing that indicated that he came inside the building, were the dirty footprints on the floor."

Don glanced at the board and turned to Bill. "We're now up to your eleven a.m. phone call. Do you want to add anything here?"

Bill moved to the front of the group. "Tom called and allowed me to speak to Jenny. I could tell from her voice that she was scared, but secretly, she managed to send us three clues. First, she changed Claire's name to

Nancy. She must have done that to protect Claire. Second, she told me that Nancy needed her medicine right after school and it was behind the mirror in the bathroom. I knew that was wrong because Claire has diabetes, so her medicine would have been in the fridge. Her third clue was that school was out fifteen minutes earlier today."

Don interrupted. "Do you mind if I add something at this point, Bill?"

"Not a problem."

"When I called the school, I spoke directly to the principal about arranging to pick up Kimberley and Claire. I inquired about school being let out fifteen minutes earlier today and was informed that classes still go until three p.m. That fifteen-minute window had to be a clue from Jenny, but as of now, we aren't sure what it means." Don then turned to Bill. "Do you want to continue?"

Bill nodded. "I then had a most unpleasant talk with Tom, who sounds just as crazy as his brother Charles. It seems that Jenny didn't greet him with open arms." He added, "No surprise. He blames not only me, but also the entire force for Charles's death. He wants five hundred thousand dollars before tomorrow morning, or she dies." Bill collected his thoughts before continuing, "I just got off my one p.m. call and the bastard started quoting the Bible to me, but I set him straight." Bill looked defeated as he slowly walked back to his spot against the wall.

Don continued, "I sent Sam and Muhammad over to gather evidence at Jenny's place. Muhammad do you want to share what the two of you found?"

Muhammad glanced over at Sam who was still busy with a woman, and spoke on his behalf. "We were both able to confirm that Tom entered the building by the back door as the front one was still locked. Footprints led from the street to the shed, vehicle, and eventually into the house. I took impressions of several sets of footprints, but the evidence was inconclusive. The back door was unlocked so that confirms that Tom had keys hidden somewhere in the back yard. The kitchen sink was full of soapy water, but the water itself was cold indicating that Jenny had been gone for some time. I dusted the kitchen for prints and there were lots of them, but I couldn't tell if any belonged to Tom."

Seeing Sam still busy with the woman, Muhammad continued, "Sam went into the bathroom and behind the mirror was the time eight forty-five written in lipstick, so he took a photo of it, for evidence and also sealed the lipstick tube into a bag. He also dusted the room and found numerous sets of prints, but was almost positive that Tom never went inside the bathroom. Next, he returned to the living room and followed the footprints from the back door to a chair. When Sam dusted the chair, he got several partials. Tom must have sat in that chair waiting for Jenny to return home that morning after taking Claire to school."

Muhammad again glanced over at Sam who still wasn't available for comment. He then continued, "We both left the house and went to the shed. The door was unlocked, so we went inside and turned on the light. The shed hadn't been opened for years, maybe not since Tom was put behind bars. The entire room was a mass of dust, dirt, and cobwebs. He had very expensive tools that would've been stolen if the shed was left unlocked. There had to be a key hidden outside that Jenny wasn't aware of. But more disturbing was what I found in the far corner. A dirty blanket lay in a heap. It appeared that Tom might have slept in that corner waiting for morning."

Muhammad added, "At some point during the night, he sat on a stool facing Jenny's house. He had to have been watching the residence all night. Sam and I also found something else disturbing. A clean patch on the floor told us that at sometime, a toolbox may have sat there. Around that clean area, tools were strewn all over the floor. The only conclusion that Sam and I came up with was that he didn't need any of those tools. Tom had emptied them onto the floor and picked up other items he thought would come in handy. Sam and I tried to imagine what Tom might have put into the empty toolbox. We only came up with rope and a gas can."

Muhammad added, "Sam and I then interviewed four of the neighbors. The first one I interviewed was a real piece of work, very negative. She saw Tom arrive and go into the shed, but never reported it. Guess it didn't involve her, so she ignored it. She told me that Jenny should have moved away." He paused before continuing, "One of them was very close to Jenny and concerned for her safety. Her husband was even cutting Jenny's grass to help her out." He continued, "The gentleman across the street that I questioned was the most interesting. He was blind, but he heard everything. Even though it was raining, he heard a man walking down the street, but thought the man must have continued along the road. He also heard metal scraping on metal and then nothing. He assumed that noise was the man renting the room from Jenny going into the shed. The next morning, he heard Jenny leave to take Claire to the bus and then return home. The interesting fact is he heard a car door slam shut three times before it left Jenny's house."

Bill jumped in. "Why was the car door shut three times? Tom and Jenny were the only two people in the house."

Muhammad answered, "The only thing Sam and I could figure out was sometime during the night, Tom must have put his toolbox behind the seat. The next morning, the third time the door shut was when he opened the back door and took something out of his toolbox."

Muhammad continued, "Sam took the last neighbor, but we learned nothing from him."

Across the room, Sam smiled at the woman. "Thank you for coming in. You've been a big help."

Sam now entered the group of officers and said, "I have an update. I just had a visit from one of Jenny's neighbors. Her husband didn't see anything, but was unaware that his wife had. When he was eating, she went outside to collect their morning paper. She saw Jenny as a passenger leaving in her car. She thought that Jenny was wearing a white shawl around her head, but wasn't quite sure why. Unfortunately she couldn't see the driver. She confirmed that the vehicle left the residence just before nine o'clock this morning"

Don cut in. "So that confirms that the eight forty-five was about the time that Jenny was kidnapped."

Sam nodded. "I would say so."

Muhammad continued, "I just mentioned to the team that the shed had no rope in it, plus there was a lawnmower with no gasoline. He must have taken those two items with him. Neither one of us could see anything else that might have been missing."

Bill started to hyperventilate. "Hold it team! In my last call Tom quoted 1692. That was the year of the Salem witch trials."

Muhammad responded, "They hung witches back then." He directed his next question to Bill. "Do you think he took the rope so he could hang Jenny?"

Bill felt like the wind was knocked out of him. "Oh hell, I sure hope not." Bill was then somewhat puzzled. "So where does the fuel come into play?"

Sam responded, "Maybe he took the gas can so he could get as far away from here as possible before he would have to refuel."

Don directed his next question to Sam and Muhammad. "Do either of you have anything more you want to add?"

Muhammad concluded, "I took photos of the inside of the shed, just in case we need to revisit the scene."

Don responded, "Thank you, gentlemen." He then looked at the board. "It was a long shot, but I sent Eli and Bob to check out the cabin on the flats where we took Charles down."

Eli took the floor. "We found no sign of Tom there but, unfortunately, as you all may well know, we were chased by a pack of wolves. We almost made it inside the vehicle when one got hold of Bob's arm. I was forced to kill the animal. It was an unfortunate accident."

Bob interjected, "I'm fine. The hospital filled me full of painkillers, so I will continue to work unless the pain returns."

Don responded, "Glad you're okay, Bob." He then turned back to the board. "This now takes us to Bill's latest call. Do you want to speak on that, Bill?"

Bill took the floor. "I once again got to talk to Jenny, and her most recent clue was confusing, so hopefully, between all of us, we can figure it out. She said that two roads to the school are under construction, so it would take an additional fifteen minutes to get there. We all know there's no construction happening there, so once again, we are faced with the time of fifteen minutes. Can anyone shed some light on this?"

Bob took the floor. "Do you think she mentioned fifteen minutes twice, forgetting she had already told us?" He then added, "Maybe she meant for us to combine the two and thinking thirty minutes instead of two fifteen minutes?"

Debbie Mozer appeared to be running scenarios in her mind. She was deep in thought. "I don't think so Bob. If we are looking at a thirty minute radius that would almost take us back to the cabin where Charles was taken down; and we have already searched that site." She glanced around the room.

Bob continued, "Okay, so maybe the second fifteen minutes has nothing to do with the time, but our clue is the road construction."

She responded, "That's a possibility, except there isn't any construction going on in town."

Don cut in. "Do you have another theory Debbie?"

She looked up. "I know we're only tossing ideas around right now, so I might be onto something, or else way off base. Either way, here goes." She looked at the whiteboard before continuing, "We already know that Jenny was kidnapped at eight forty-five, but Don didn't get a call until ten o'clock. That leaves a window of one hour and fifteen minutes. We're assuming that Tom drove that entire time, which puts him the other side of Sidville." She paused. "But what if he didn't travel that far? Wherever he went, he probably wouldn't have phoned right away. He would have had to restrain Jenny, scout his surroundings to make sure no one was around, hide the car, and get his bearings."

Don interjected. "What're you saying?"

"Jenny has given us two clues of fifteen minutes. What if she was telling us that wherever he took her, it's only fifteen minutes from her home? Her second clue of fifteen minutes could be confirming how important that time is."

Don stared at the whiteboard. "That's an excellent observation."

"You have a good point, Debbie," Bill said.

Debbie nodded. "I've been talking to the city and making a list of locations around town that are vacant. There are several buildings we could check out. There's the old cannery in the industrial area that has been derelict for years, and also a house at 22 Oak Crescent that recently had a small fire. The house is boarded up until the insurance comes through for the homeowners to start repairs. But the last location might surprise all of you. There's an old bunker a few miles from town on the road that leads to the Panorama Room."

Don sounded excited. "Good work, Debbie. How do we find this bunker?"

"Once we make the turn off the highway heading to the Panorama Room, there's a road called Mountain View Road. Apparently, it is quite overgrown, so you have to know it's there or you'll miss it."

Don added the locations to the whiteboard. "Greg and Jack, you take the old cannery. Jim and Muhammad you go to the house on Oak Crescent. Debbie and Eli, you take the bunker. Be careful out there. If you need backup, you call immediately." He wrote the names of all six officers next to the locations they were going to.

Don and Bill went into the office and took a seat. Don looked at Bill, who appeared to be distracted. "You okay, Bill?" Not receiving an answer, he repeated his question.

Bill glanced up and ran a hand over his face. "Truth or lie?"

"Well, I prefer the truth, but I know you're a lousy liar, so I could probably see through your lie anyway."

Bill laughed. "I was thinking that I should have been a plumber rather than a police officer. Less stress."

"Sounds like a shitty job to me. You probably wouldn't have lasted."

Bill had to chuckle. "How do you know that?"

"Plumbers deal with shit every day, while a police officer only has to deal with it occasionally. Don't second guess yourself. You're in the right job."

Bill hesitated, then got up from his chair and walked to the window. Don watched him with concern. Bill's shoulders were slumped as if he was carrying a heavy load. His voice trembled as he asked, "What if I can't save her?"

Don got up from his chair and approached Bill, placing a hand on his shoulder. "The big question here is what if you can? When we find out where he's holding Jenny, the force will be there to back you up. We got Charles, and we'll get Tom too."

"I suppose." Bill turned to Don and smiled. "Thanks, I needed to hear that. Do you mind if I use your office for a few minutes? I need to call Beatrice. She's probably worried sick."

"No problem."

Don left his office and closed the door behind him. Bill picked up Don's phone and called Glen's cell number.

Glen answered, "Hi, Bill. Was wondering when we'd hear from you. I know this is a stupid question, but is everything okay?"

"As well as can be expected. How is Beatrice?"

"Worried, like both of us, but she's a trooper. I'll put her on the line."

Beatrice answered, "Hello, Bill."

He could tell from the tremble in her voice that she was worried sick.

"What's going on? Are you okay? When can I see you?"

Her questions fell like a row of dominoes that Bill couldn't stop from falling. "Darling, slow down. I'm fine."

"Have you found Jenny yet?"

"Not yet, but the team is working hard," he reassured her. "Jenny is one clever lady and has already sent us lots of clues. We just need to decipher them."

Her voice broke as she asked, "When can I see you?"

Choked up, Bill answered, "As soon as the case is solved."

"You're not coming home tonight?"

"Darling, kidnappers don't work regular business hours. I can't come home until Jenny is found. The team will be here until the case is closed. I'll be standing next to them throughout the entire night if it takes that long."

Beatrice was devastated. "I miss you."

"I miss you too. I'll call when I get another chance, and hopefully with good news. I hope Glen is taking good care of you and not driving you crazy."

"He's quite a talker, but I'm enjoying his company, considering the circumstances. He's very professional, always checking out the rooms, and making sure that the windows, and doors are secure and curtains drawn. If I get a chance, I'm going to ask him about juicy stories of you from before we were married."

Bill laughed. "Don't believe a word he says. It's all lies." He sobered quickly. "I have to go now. Bye, honey."

"Bye, Bill."

Bill hung up, then immediately called the Jackson residence.

Eric picked up the phone. "Hello?"

"Hello, Eric, this is Bill. How's it going over there?"

"All quiet here, except Claire wants to play outside and her parents have to keep finding other ways to keep her busy. That's a real challenge. We all have to watch her like a hawk. You know from experience that when you're protecting a family, the first rule is to keep all curtains closed and doors locked. So Richard and Kimberley have their work cut out for them."

Bill went to the window and noticed the sun was covered in a stray cloud that made the day appear further along than it actually was.

The slight pause raised concern so Eric inquired, "Are you okay Bill?"

"I'm not totally sure. I just realized that I'm not afraid of dying, but I am concerned for my family that would be left behind to mourn me."

"Richard's standing next to me and you should be glad that he can only hear my side of the conversation. You hang in there."

"I will. Can I speak with them?"

"By them, you must mean the entire gang. May I make a suggestion?"

Bill responded, "I'm listening."

"Kimberley and Claire are in the bedroom playing dolls so it would be a shame to disturb them. Instead I'll just put Richard on the line." He passed the phone across the room.

"Hi Bill."

Bill's voice broke as he inquired, "How's the family holding up?"

"We're fine. How about you?"

"I'm holding up." Bill paused. "Richard I may need you professionally once we locate Jenny. She very well could be traumatized before this is over. It was awful enough when Charles kidnapped her, but now it's her husband that may be out to kill her."

"You know where to find me; all you need to do is catch the bastard, and bring Jenny safely home."

"That's my plan. Say hi to everyone for me."

"Will do. Be safe."

"Thanks. We'll talk soon"

Both men hung up their phones.

Chapter Seven

1:20 p.m. – 2:15 p.m.

GREG AND JACK DROVE TO the old cannery in the industrial part of town. Five years ago, when Charles had taken Jenny and Claire, this site had been thoroughly investigated, but with no luck.

Maybe today their luck would change.

The building was occupied by the homeless, so they expected to find at least someone inside—hopefully someone who could tell them if they'd seen Jenny and Tom here. With some luck, they might be one step closer to finding Jenny.

They parked the vehicle a few blocks away and approached the building from the back, hugging the water's edge. The massive cannery was in disarray. One entire section of the roof had fallen in, leaving more than half the building in a heap of rotten lumber and tangled sheet metal. Large sections of the walls had fallen into the channel and were now floating around the pilings. The tide was on its' way in, so there was a distinct line of seaweed and branches slowly moving towards the pebbled beach. Seagulls perched on the floating debris, resting, waiting to scrounge for their next meal. The smell of seaweed filled the air. What remained of the structure's roof was covered with a thick blanket of moss, making it look as if it had just received a fresh coat of bright green paint.

Greg looked at the crumbling building and noticed a set of stairs that would take the two of them to the second floor. He turned to his partner. "What do you think? Should we try to go inside here?"

"It's far too dangerous. Let's keep to the back of the building for now. I'd feel much better if we checked out the perimeter before going in. I don't want any surprises."

Greg nodded. "That's probably a good decision. It makes our job somewhat easier."

"What do you mean?"

"Well, look around you. Half the building's missing."

Jack chuckled. "I can see that."

The two officers climbed over piles of lumber, avoiding protruding nails and stepping over broken glass. Once they'd cleared the debris, they walked to the far end of the cannery and carefully looked around the corner before proceeding. The coast was clear, so they headed towards the front of the building.

"I think now is a good time to check inside," Greg said.

Jack nodded. "What do you think we'll find?"

"Maybe some homeless who can shed some light on the case."

"That certainly would make my day."

They moved to the first door and were about to draw their firearms when Greg paused. "I don't think we'll need our weapons here. If there are indeed homeless people here, there's no need to frighten them."

"Yeah. We'll never get them to open up to us if we appear to be a threat to them." Greg pushed on the old door, cringing when the rusty metal hinges squealed. It sent shivers down both officers' spines.

Greg slipped inside, followed by Jack. Glancing down the long building, they could see a gaping hole where part of the building had once been. The afternoon daylight lit that end of the cannery, showing how exposed the building was to the wind and rain. The building was silent. Most likely abandoned.

Greg turned to Jack. "I think it's safe to assume we're alone here, but let's check it out."

"Right behind you."

They turned on their flashlights and scanned the back section of the cannery that was in shadows. Most of the windows in the building were either broken or missing, allowing the cool fall air to flow into the room. It cut through the officers' uniforms and left them both shivering. The floor was strewn with soggy blankets, balled-up newspapers, and empty bottles, some broken and others intact. The ceiling had partially collapsed. Signs of rat droppings were everywhere, and there wasn't a single spot that wasn't covered in dust or cobwebs. The air smelled putrid, causing both officers to heave. They quickly worked their way towards the second room, which had better air circulation. Once inside this part of the cannery, they were able to turn off their flashlights. There was enough natural light coming from the gaping hole in the building.

Greg glanced around. "Well, my guess was correct. We're all alone."

In the center of the room stood a massive fireplace that looked like it hadn't been lit in a long time. Rain had clearly been pouring down the chimney for some time, and the air smelled of wet soot. "There's no way that anyone could have lit a fire here," he observed. "Even if they could, the fire wouldn't have provided much heat from the outside elements."

Jack asked, "Where do you suppose the homeless went?"

"Not sure."

Off in the far corner was a small blue tarp covering something. Jack crossed the room and lifted the tarp. Beneath it was a neatly stacked pile of dry firewood. "The cannery may be empty right now, but this tells me someone comes to collect firewood. I don't think they would just leave it behind."

Greg looked confused. "I agree, so what're you thinking?"

"The wood stays dry here."

"So, they must be close by."

Jack responded, "Grab an armload of wood."

"Why would we do that?"

"We're going exploring. The homeless must be close by, and if we arrive with an armload of wood, it would be a display of goodwill."

Both officers loaded up their arms and worked their way back to the entrance. At the door, Greg inquired, "How are we going to find them?"

"I'm not sure right now, but let's have a good look around the building."

They walked around the back of the cannery. Jack stopped when he spotted what looked like a path leading into the woods. "Bingo. That trail looks reasonably well traveled. Let's see where it goes."

Jack took the lead while Greg followed behind. Not too far along the path, they heard voices.

Greg whispered, "I think we found them." As they approached, he identified himself: "Blue Ridge Police Department. We come in peace, bearing gifts."

Jack laughed. "You sound like the Magi bringing gifts to Mary and Joseph."

"I guess I do."

Several scruffy men clad in dirty, tattered clothing glanced in their direction. "What do you want?"

Greg answered, "We've just been in the cannery and noticed that it's no longer habitable. We found your pile of wood and knew that you would be close by, so decided to find you and deliver some firewood. Sorry that half of the building is destroyed. I expect that within a year, the entire building will be a pile of rubble."

He looked around the camp. The tents were huddled in a close circle and positioned below a tight clump of trees that offered some protection from the rain and wind. A fire was blazing in the center of the circle. Greg and Jack went to the small pile of firewood and unloaded their arms, brushing the dust from their uniforms.

"Do you mind if we warm up by your fire?" Jack asked.

The scruffy man spoke. "We're not breaking any rules here, so what do you want?"

Jack answered, "We'd like to ask you a few questions, if you don't mind."

"What do you want to know?"

"Have you heard of anything suspicious happening in town this morning or even last night?"

"Always something suspicious happening in Blue Ridge. You're going to have to be more specific."

Jack continued, "Maybe someone arriving in town last night and disappearing this morning."

The homeless man grinned. "Might have heard something."

"Care to share what you heard?"

"It'll cost you."

Jack was caught off guard. "What do you mean, cost me?"

"Information as important as this doesn't come cheap."

"What do you want?"

"How about a truck load of firewood? The winter is fast approaching, and we can't find enough to survive without a bit of help."

Jack looked at his partner, then back at the homeless man. "Consider it done. It may take me a few days, but I'll make it happen."

"Then we have a deal." The two men shook hands.

The homeless man took a seat on an empty stump, and Jack and Greg sat across from him. "The old cannery was large enough to hold our kind—you know what I mean, homeless—but one evening, when we were all asleep, there was a loud crash, and we discovered half the building was gone. We knew that the next day we would be looking for new accommodations. Our group split in half. We stayed here, close to the building. You'd think we'd be used to living in the elements, but it took time for us to adjust to our new location."

Jack asked, "So, where is the rest of your original group?"

"You probably aren't aware of the other homeless camp just outside of town."

"No. Where is it located?"

"It's a short distance past Suicide Hill."

Jack froze and instantly was thrown into the past when Bill's fiancé Evelyn Parker had died at that location years earlier. The road was twisty and her vehicle hit a patch of black ice and she lost control of her vehicle. Her death devastated Bill.

The homeless man continued, "At the far side of the hill, we forged a trail through the woods. It's much easier to get through from there, and the camp is sheltered from the weather. Once we all chipped in to set up the second camp, some of us returned to the cannery."

Greg cocked his head. "So what does this second camp have to do with anything?"

"I know someone there who knows something."

"And where can we find that someone?"

"I just told you. At the bottom of Suicide Hill."

Greg became skeptical. "How accurate is this person's information?"

"Guess you'll have to talk to him yourself and find out."

"Do you know what this person saw?" Jack inquired.

"Officers, we scrounge around town in the evenings looking for scraps of food and things we can use to keep warm. This particular person saw something. That's all I can say for now. He'll have to tell you himself."

Jack nodded. "Thanks for your help. Guess we're headed to the bottom of Suicide Hill."

The two officers left the camp and walked back to the cannery. As they neared their vehicle, Jack stopped dead in his tracks and Greg almost plowed into him.

"What the hell!" Greg snapped.

Speechless, Jack pointed at the water.

Greg froze when he saw what Jack had seen: a sneaker in the water, and it had a foot inside it. "How could we have missed that earlier?"

"I'm not sure, but my guess is the current shifted and brought the body ashore."

Greg sighed. "Well, this complicates matters. I'll call it in, and then let's see if we can drag the body onto the rocks." He picked up his radio and called the station.

Daniel answered, "Hey, guys. How did you make out at the cannery?"

"Not good. The cannery is clear, and we did manage to talk to a few homeless folks, but we've had to put our investigation on pause."

"What's going on?"

"We just found a body in the water. Can you send out the coroner?"

"Definitely. Are you heading back to the precinct?"

"Negative, we have another location we need to look into. We'll stay here until the coroner arrives and the body is removed from the scene."

"I'll call the coroner right away."

At the precinct, Daniel put down his radio and turned to his phone to make the call.

Stuart Mann answered, "Coroner's office. What can I do for you?"

"Daniel here, Greg and Jack just found a body at the old cannery. They need you to head over there and collect it."

"Any details?"

"All I know is there's a body floating in the water."

"Okay. I'll grab my assistant and head right over."

Don waited for Daniel to end his call before approaching his desk. "What've you got?" he asked.

Daniel looked up at Don. "Not good news. Greg and Jack found a body at the cannery. The coroner is on his way to pick up the deceased."

Don asked, "Do they know who it is?"

"At this point I'm guessing no. They're waiting there until the coroner arrives and the body is safely on its' way to the morgue."

"So, they'll head back to the precinct once the body is removed from the location?"

Daniel shook his head. "Apparently they have another lead to follow up on first."

"Any idea what it might be?"

"Not a clue at this time."

"Keep me updated." Don walked up to the white board and drew a line through Old cannery."

Once Greg had placed his radio back in his jacket pocket, he turned to Jack. "Okay. Daniel's notifying the coroner. I'm not sure how long before he arrives, but we can't leave the scene until he's here and the body is removed from the site."

Jack sighed in frustration. "Damn, we're losing valuable time."

"I agree but for now, let's see if we can get this body out of the water."

They put on rubber gloves, and Greg knelt on the jagged rock and reached into the water. Jack held onto the belt of Greg's pants to keep him from falling in. Greg managed to get a grip onto the sneaker, and with great difficulty, he dragged the body ashore, just as the coroner and his assistant arrived.

"What you got guys?" Stuart asked.

Jack answered, "Well, I wish it was Tom Lockman, but unfortunately, it appears to be a homeless man. I'm only guessing, but I suspect that when the cannery collapsed in on itself, the poor soul couldn't escape. He must've been in the water for some time. Wonder why the homeless group never mentioned that one of them was missing?"

"Don't know, maybe they are used to some of the group being away for long periods."

Jack and Greg took a seat on a fallen down tree a short distance away, giving the coroner and his assistant room to work. They watched as the remains were placed in a black bag and zipped up. The body was then placed on a straight board, and Stuart and his assistant carried it back to their vehicle. Jack and Greg followed them, and once the body was loaded into the van, they parted company.

Greg called the station again and Daniel answered, "Any update, guys?"

Greg responded, "The coroner and his assistant have just bagged the body and are heading back to the morgue. I wish I could tell you it was Tom, but it's likely some poor homeless person who got caught when the building collapsed."

"Copy that," Daniel said. "See you back at the station."

"Negative, we have to make that side trip."

"Oh, right, I forgot. It's crazy in here. Where're you heading next?"

Greg answered, "We got a tip from one of the homeless people that there's a second camp in this area."

"Where is it?"

"At the bottom of Suicide Hill."

Daniel was taken aback. "How the hell can you get down there, let alone up again?"

"Apparently there's an easier way to get there. There's someone in that camp who may be able to shed some light on our case."

Daniel responded, "Copy that. Keep us updated."

"Will do," Greg said. "Oh, I almost forgot. I made a promise to the homeless people that, for their help, we would deliver a load of firewood. I'm prepared to make that offer to the second camp. If we want their help in the future, they need to know that any information they give us is worthy of a reward. If Don has a problem with it, I'll pay for it myself. To me, it's money well spent."

"The boss won't have a problem with that. Keep us updated on your progress."

"Talk soon."

Jack and Greg climbed into their vehicle and headed for Suicide Hill. The afternoon was quickly slipping away, and both officers were wondering what might be waiting for them at the second camp.

Greg turned to his partner. "I noticed that the mention of Suicide Hill hit a sensitive spot. What happened there?"

Jack responded, "I was young rookie then. You weren't on the force yet. Bill's fiancé Evelyn Parker died on that corner; has to be about thirty-two years ago. Bill was devastated that day, and in the days that followed. He slipped into depression and drank far too much, but eventually managed to get his head on straight. He had to be strong for Beatrice and Kimberley. The three of them mourned together and came to depend on each other. No one in the force saw it coming when Bill announced that he and Beatrice were engaged. Their marriage was a way for the three of them to move forward and continue to heal."

Before Greg could reply, Jack chuckled and changed the subject. "Do you remember that case where a woman reported that some of her laundry was stolen off her clothesline in the middle of the night?"

"Actually, I do. Heaven forbid, what made you think of that case right now?"

"Guess I was trying to get my mind off Evelyn's death. That accident was so long ago. I'm glad Bill was able to move on. Beatrice has been so good for him."

Jack looked at his partner. "Let's forget about the accident and get back to case of the missing laundry."

Greg answered, "We were only able to retrieve part of the clothing. Poor woman had to go shopping to replace sheets and blankets, but mostly personal items."

"I guess someone needed those items more than she did. Still, it was a major expense for a mother of eight children."

Greg nodded, watching the road as Jack kept an eye out for the trail that would lead the two of them down to the second homeless camp.

Eventually, Jack pointed out what looked to be a makeshift trail. "That's it."

Greg pulled the cruiser off the road. Both officers got out, and Jack took the lead on the trail. "Fingers crossed, partner. We sure could use a good clue right now."

"That's for sure," Greg said. "I hope Jenny is okay. If there's even a mark on her, Bill will put Tom away forever."

"And so he should."

They didn't have to walk far before they heard the crackling of a fire and voices nearby. Jack paused at the edge of the camp and announced, "Hello, gentlemen. I'm Jack Spencer and this is Greg Thomas from the Blue Ridge Police Department."

He glanced around the camp. A large blue tarp had been hung over the sleeping area, offering a draft-free and mostly dry shelter. Unfortunately, it had several holes that allowed water from last night's rain to drip onto some of the homemade huts beneath it. Somehow this group of men had managed to weave branches together to form walls and roofs to sleep under. Blankets were layered on the ground inside these enclosures, providing soft beds to sleep on. Jack counted about a dozen people all huddled around the fire, rubbing their hands to warm them up.

One of the men inquired, "What can we do for you, officers?"

Greg looked directly at the man. "Nice set-up you have here. We're sorry to hear about the cannery disaster."

"It was just a matter of time before we lost the building. If it snows this winter, we expect the last of it will be completely gone." He glanced between them. "Are you here for a reason?"

Greg responded, "We were just over at the cannery, and talked to a gentleman there. He told us one of you might be able to help us with an existing case."

"What's the case?"

"A man arrived here last night and has mysteriously disappeared this morning."

"Let me guess: He took a woman with him."

Greg nodded. "He did. Can you help us out at all?"

"Sure can, but what's in it for us?"

"Same offer we agreed to with the cannery camp."

"And what was that?"

"A free load of firewood to help you get through the winter. And it looks like you could use a new tarp to protect your site."

The man's hand shot out. "You have a deal."

They shook on it.

Now that Greg had a captive audience, he moved closer to the fire to warm his hands. Jack moved next to him.

"We know that someone entered town yesterday in the early evening," Greg said. "We're just wondering if any of you may have seen or heard anything regarding this person. It could be something simple like a flashlight shining where it shouldn't be, but also as important as seeing someone trying to enter a house." He paused, waiting for anyone to speak.

When no one spoke, a smaller gentleman shuffled forward. His clothes were tattered and at least two sizes too large. He looked to be a teenager. "I saw something."

Patiently, Greg asked, "What did you see?"

The boy looked nervous. "I never planned on being a bum and living on the streets, but this is where I ended up. These people around me are my family."

Greg gazed at him with utter respect. "You can find some amazing friends anywhere you look. I'd say you have found a family here."

"We don't steal. I guess you could say that we keep the neighbourhood clean. I was on the west side of town when a bus pulled into the station and several people got off. The last one was a scruffy looking man all dressed in black. He seemed lost, and I was about to approach him to see if he needed directions when he started walking towards the center of town. I followed him at a distance, and he stopped in front of a house. Before long, he walked onto the property and stared into a window, watching someone. Then he left and went to the local park and sat on a bench. He went crazy."

Jack encouraged him. "Crazy in what way?"

"He was yelling, 'I'll kill her, the unfaithful bitch. They'll never find her body.'"

"Why didn't you call the police?"

"He was very upset but he could very well be just venting his frustration. I don't own a phone and by the time I walked to the station he could have left the park. I chose to stay close and observe. In a crunch if it turned ugly, I could create a disturbance that would send him fleeing."

"What happened next?"

"I was concerned for the woman in the house, so I returned to her place to warn her about this crazy person. Just when I was about to knock on the door, I spotted a man in the kitchen next to her. I decided she wasn't in any immediate danger, so I returned to the park and found the bench empty, but his bag was still there. Hearing him rushing back to the bench, I hid in the trees. He was mumbling something, but I couldn't understand him. He sat on the bench for some time, but once it started to rain, he got up and went back to that same house. This time he approached the shed. I watched him unlock the door and go inside. I was quite concerned about the two people inside the house, so I stayed part of the night. Sometime during the early hours, the man came out of the shed and placed something behind the seat of a vehicle. When he went inside and the coast was clear, I snuck up, turned on my flashlight, and took a look inside the vehicle."

"Do you remember what was in it?"

"Sure do. Rope, lots of tie wraps, wire cutters, padlock and key, duct tape, gas can, and a pair of scissors."

"You remembered all that?"

"I might be homeless, but I was also gifted with a photographic memory. It can drive me crazy sometimes. I don't know how to shut it off. My brain always manages to keep it organized here." He touched his head. "Hope this helps you, and that the woman is going to be okay."

"Thanks for your help."

The two officers left. When they reached the cruiser, Jack called in their report.

"Daniel here, what you got?"

"We got an update on what's in Tom's toolbox from a homeless person." He read the list off, allowing Daniel time to write it all down. "We're on our way back to the office." He quickly added, "A second load of firewood needs to be delivered to the homeless camp at Suicide Hill. And throw in the largest tarp you can find."

After communicating with Jack, Daniel got up and approached Don's office.

Don looked up. "What do you have?"

"I just got an update from Jack."

"You have my full attention."

"One of the homeless people saw Tom last night and followed him over to Jenny's place. He was acting erratic, so the fellow stayed and observed. Sometime during the night, Tom left the shed and placed a toolbox behind the seat of Jenny's car. Once Tom was back in the shed, he crept up and looked inside the vehicle." Daniel looked down at a paper in his hand. "This is what was in Tom's toolbox: rope, lots of tie wraps, wire cutters, padlock and key, duct tape, gas can, and a pair of scissors."

"Thanks, Daniel. On your way back to your desk, would you put a line through 'Suicide Hill' tent camp? Also can you add the contents of the toolbox to the whiteboard?"

"Sure thing, boss." Daniel left Don's office and crossed off another location from the whiteboard.

Chapter Eight

1:30 p.m. – 2:20 p.m.

JIM AND MUHAMMAD LEFT THE station, Jim behind the wheel, and drove over to 22 Oak Crescent to check out the burned out, boarded up, and abandoned house. It was a craftsman-style home, with four red brick pillars holding up the roof over the front porch. Metal-framed chairs were strewn across the porch, their plastic coverings melted away. Debris lay over most of the front yard, but closer to the sidewalk, a child's plastic car was completely intact. The front door and windows were covered with plywood, probably put there by the people who owned the home. Nothing at the front of the house was salvageable; even the burned and twisted vinyl siding was partly melted. Trees that had once overhung the building, providing shade, were now a thing of the past. On the right side of the house, a red brick chimney stood tall and stately, appearing to be largely undamaged.

Jim was silent for a few seconds before speaking. "Do we have any information on what caused the fire or even when it happened?"

"Not that I'm aware of. Judging by the fact that it's boarded up, the fire could have happened weeks or even months ago. It's probably become an insurance issue."

"Then I guess my next question is why are we even checking out the place?"

Muhammad reminded his partner: "If Debbie is correct on her fifteen-minute theory, we need to check out the place. We just need to verify whether Tom and Jenny are here."

"Okay, then let's work our way around the house to see if anyone has entered since it was boarded up."

The two officers walked along the front of the house, turned the corner, and checked out the right side of the building. Two windows on that side of the home were tightly secured with plywood.

Muhammad glanced back the way they'd come. "The fire must have started somewhere along the front of the house."

"I wonder if we're able to get inside," Jim said.

"If any boards have been removed from the windows or doors, we have to check inside, but if everything is sealed up tight, then I don't see any reason to enter the building."

At the back corner of the building, a smaller piece of plywood that should have been attached to a window frame was propped up against the house. Jim knelt to move the board aside and spotted the broken window. It was low to the ground and most likely led into the basement. The plywood had originally been secured in place with screws that were now missing. Fragments of chipped wood lay on the ground below the window. It was obvious that someone had pried their way into the building.

Jim looked inside. "Someone might have climbed through this tiny window to get inside?"

"Maybe, but before we go and get filthy climbing through here, let's see if another entrance has been breached."

"I'll second that."

Jim put the plywood over the broken window and they investigated the rest of the home. The back of the house was boarded up like Fort Knox, as was the left side of the building. There was a shed set back in the yard and both officers went over to check it out. A window gave both men a clear view into the building.

Shining his flashlight inside, Muhammad said, "There's nothing here."

They returned to the basement window and moved the plywood off to the side.

Jim asked, "Did Don get a search warrant to enter the building yet?"

"Let me confirm that before we go in."

Muhammad called Don on his radio.

"Hey Muhammad, what you got?"

"Want to confirm that you got permission for us to enter the building."

"Yes, we got a judge to grant a search warrant."

"Thanks Don." Muhammad ended his call. "It looks like we're going in."

Jim said, "Okay, I'll go in first and you can follow." He lowered himself to the ground and went in head-first. It was a tight squeeze, but he managed to get in without tearing his uniform. There was a thud as he fell to the floor into a pile of soggy, soot-covered newspapers.

Muhammad inquired, "Are you okay?"

"I'm in, but I suggest you come in feet-first. There was nothing for me to hang onto once I was inside. I'm a mess."

"Thanks for the heads up." Muhammad took Jim's advice and landed on a chair that Jim had set by the window. He looked at his partner and laughed. "I'm really glad you went first. You look disgusting."

"I am, and I'm not returning to the office until I go home and get changed."

"Fair enough." Muhammad stepped off the chair and found his boots submerged in water up to the ankles. "Guess we both need to go home and get changed now."

Both officers turned on their flashlights and sloshed their way around the eerie basement. The floor that was covered with water, had soggy ash and fallen ceiling tiles floating around them. The gyproc walls were saturated with water from the fire hoses that had extinguished the fire. "I'm not sure if the house can be salvaged."

"Probably can't, but the owner can only collect the insurance if they rebuild. The location alone is worth replacing the home."

"You're right about that. Let's have a look around here before going upstairs."

Despite their best efforts, they were unable to determine whether anyone had entered the home through that tiny window. The basement had a musty, pungent charcoal smell that both officers were glad to leave behind them as they climbed the stairs to the main floor. The staircase came out in the kitchen, which was at the back of the house. Muhammad tried the light switch, but it was obvious there was no electricity in the building, so they kept their flashlights turned on.

The cupboards that faced the back of the residence were still intact, almost as if there hadn't been a fire in the house at all. The opposite side of the room showed charred beams, missing walls, and melted appliances.

Tables and chairs lay in a heap, while soggy couches were pushed up against the outer wall, most likely moved by the firemen before leaving the scene. There wasn't a clean surface to be found anywhere on the floor. All the ceilings had collapsed in the burning inferno.

Muhammad said, "I think it's safe to say that if someone had entered the building, they're no longer here."

Jim nodded. "It's possible that someone may have come inside, but left when they saw the state of the home. We'll need to go back downstairs and climb back out of that ridiculous window."

They went downstairs, and Jim was about to climb onto the chair and shimmy out the window when he thought he heard something. Muhammad heard the same sound, so they turned off their flashlights and stayed silent; hoping that whoever had made the sound would think they had left and come out of hiding.

Several minutes later, they heard the sound again, and now they could tell it was a quiet whisper. "The coast's clear."

There was movement in the far corner. They turned on their flashlights at the same time, illuminating two small children. The light startled them, and they stared at the officers like two deer on the road after dusk. Frightened, the children climbed back into their hiding place, a large cedar chest positioned just above the water line, and closed the lid.

Jim and Muhammad slowly approached the chest, and Jim lifted the lid. "We're not here to hurt you."

The child who looked to be the eldest covered the smaller child. "Leave us alone."

Muhammad looked around the smelly, damp shell of a house. "How long have you two been in here?"

Neither child answered.

Jim turned to his partner. "I'll call it in."

"That's a good idea."

The children jumped out of the chest and attacked Jim before he could make the call. The older boy shouted, "You leave us alone! We were here before you, so go find another place to hide out!"

Muhammad realized that the children didn't know they were police officers. He turned his flashlight to light up his badge. "We're not here to hurt you," he said. "Where do you live?"

"We live"—the younger boy paused—"here for now."

Muhammad glanced at the boys. "But this isn't your house?"

The older child whispered, "It's our safehouse."

Jim saw that the boys were trembling, obviously very cold, and probably hungry too. He inquired, "Why do you need a safehouse?"

The older boy looked scared. "Because some weirdo was chasing us and said he would kill us."

Jim looked at them with concern. "Why was he chasing you and why would he want to kill you?"

The younger boy answered, "We tried to steal his bag when he was in the park."

"You're safe with us," Jim assured them. "What are your names?"

The older boy answered, "I'm Adam and this is my baby brother, Michael."

"I'm not a baby. I'm just younger than you are."

"Where are your parents?" Muhammad asked.

Both boys broke eye contact with the officers and fidgeted nervously while saying that they lived with their uncle.

Jim took out his radio and moved to the other side of the basement, keeping an eye on the children as he called the station.

"Daniel here, how did you two make out?"

Jim answered, "Well, we're inside the house, but we've run into a slight problem."

"What's going on?"

"We found an unsecured window to the basement, so we entered the home. We investigated the entire building and were about to leave through the window again when we discovered two small children hiding in the basement."

"Who do they belong to?"

"I think they are orphans, no parents. They said they lived with an uncle." Jim paused. "Maybe send an officer to the house and tell him to bring a multi-headed screwdriver. We're not climbing back out of this tiny window when someone can uncover the back door."

"Copy that. We're short-staffed here, but I'll send someone."

"We'll be waiting, upstairs at the back door. See if you can rustle up some blankets. Their clothes are soaking wet, and they are really cold. It might be a good idea to scrounge up some food for them too."

"Copy that."

The call complete, the officers and the two boys climbed the stairs to wait near the back door.

Daniel walked to Don's office. "I just heard back from Jim and Muhammad. They searched the house on Oak Crescent and found two orphaned children. Someone needs to go over there and uncover one of the doors so they can get out."

Don looked around the office; six of his men were out in the field, and the rest were either glued to the phones or desks. "See if Sam can go over."

"Will do."

Don once again approached the whiteboard and added, "Found two children" next to "22 Oak Crescent" and put a line through the location. He stated, "Another dead end."

Daniel approached Sam. "Any chance you could go over to 22 Oak Crescent and help Jim and Muhammad get out of the house? They got in through a small window and found two young children in the basement. The windows and doors are boarded up and it would be easier if one of us went over with a multi-headed screwdriver to let them out."

"Sure. Where would I find a screwdriver in this place?"

"Check the toolbox in the basement. There should be one there."

Sam went downstairs and came back up a few minutes later, screwdriver in hand. "Found one. I'll be back as soon as I can."

Daniel returned to Don's office. The sergeant looked up from his paperwork. "Sam's on his way to the Oak Street residence," Daniel said. "Can I make a suggestion?"

"I'm all ears."

"We all know that Jenny's time is limited and we're short-staffed."

"Don't remind me."

"I was thinking of calling Sidville to see if they could spare a few officers to help out." He quickly added, "We should only need them for a couple of hours."

"That's an excellent idea. I'll call them right now."

Daniel left Don's office. Don picked up the phone and called Sidville to arrange for two officers to come over to Blue Ridge.

Sam drove over to the burned-out house on Oak Crescent. He climbed the stairs on the back porch and knocked on the plywood. "I'm here, guys. This looks like the safest way for all of you to get out of the house. May take me a few minutes, so be patient with me."

"Is that you, Sam?" Jim said from the other side of the door.

"It is, and I'm here to get all of you out."

He slowly worked his way around the plywood, removing one screw at a time and placing them in his pocket. When the last one was out, he put the screwdriver in his pocket and lifted the panel, exposing the door. Jim and Muhammad came out with the two children.

Sam looked at the two boys and gave them a reassuring smile. Sam suspected their ages to be about five and seven. The clothes they were wearing were far too big for their small frames. Their hair was tangled and matted with dirt and grime. Their fingernails had lines of dirt beneath them. All in all, they both could use a good bath, a haircut, and a new set of clothing.

With a surprised look, he turned to Jim and Muhammad. "What happened to the two of you? You're both a mess."

Muhammad answered, "Don't ask. I know you have to get back to the office, so do you mind taking the boys with you and we'll reseal the house?"

"I can do that," Sam said. He took the screws and screwdriver out of his pocket and handed it to Muhammad.

Muhammad added, "Do you think Jim and I could take an extra half hour before we get back to the office? We'd feel better if we showered and changed our clothes before returning to work."

"Sounds like a plan. See you both soon." Sam turned to the boys, and with excitement in his voice, asked, "Have either of you ever ridden in a police cruiser before?" Both boys shook their heads. "Then let's go, and you can even turn on the siren on the way back to the station."

Excited, the boys willingly followed Sam to the cruiser.

Jim and Muhammad chuckled when the siren started blaring as the cruiser disappeared around a corner. Then they got down to work sealing up the door.

Chapter Nine

1:30 p.m. – 2:25 p.m.

JENNY WAS UNCOMFORTABLE SITTING IN the hard chair. "Please, Tom, can I go back onto the bed? My back is getting sore."

Tom scowled at her. "I didn't bring you here to be comfortable." He did, however, cut her wrists free from the chair, his eyes on her as she crossed the room and lay down on the bed. She didn't look at him, but felt pressure on her wrists as he again fastened her to the headboard with the tie wraps.

"Thank you."

Tom returned to his chair and glared at Jenny. Neither spoke for some time, until Tom shouted, "Don't act like I'm not even in the room!"

Jenny looked at him sharply. "I'm more than aware that you're here."

"How long do you think you can hold off?"

"Hold off from what?"

"Resisting me. You know you want me."

She let out a loud laugh. "Hell would freeze over before that happens."

Tom jumped up from his chair and hurled himself on top of her, grabbing her throat. His eyes bored into hers. "You know I could take you right here and now."

Jenny twisted and turned, trying to escape his grasp. She was scared, but she shot him a deadly look and said in a raspy voice, "Go ahead. You won't get any satisfaction from me."

Caught off guard, he released her neck and backed off.

Jenny was still trembling and gasping for air. "Prison really changed you."

"Don't talk to me about prison. I had to fight for everything behind bars."

He returned to his chair, sat, and appeared to enter his dream world once more. "I almost died a thousand times when I was in the laundry department, but one day, my luck changed." He closed his eyes. "Every morning,

I listened as the guards released the prison bars, once again exposing me to the brutality of the other inmates. The squeal of metal upon metal was like a rusty nail being pulled out of a chunk of steel. This particular morning, right on schedule, I heard the cell doors slowly grinding open, one block at a time.

"As usual, I waited until most of the prisoners had left for the cafeteria before getting up. I rushed around getting dressed, used my rather public toilet, and washed my hands before leaving my cell. Only then did I make my way to the cafeteria, and after filling my metal plate with a light breakfast, I looked around for somewhere reasonably safe to eat. Empty seats were a rarity, so I had to select one that put me at the least risk. I chose a seat at the end of a long table, close to one of the guards, but also next to my only friend, Big John."

Jenny watched the expression on his face as he relived his hell yet another time. She whispered, "I'm glad you found a friend on the inside."

"He was my private bodyguard. I recall our conversation that day almost as if it happened yesterday. We exchanged our usual morning greetings, and I asked him how things were going. Big John looked so grim when he answered, 'Okay, I guess.' I was concerned for his safety, so I asked him what was up. Big John shoved a mouthful of powdered scrambled eggs into his mouth. They tasted like shit, but you either ate or starved. He looked defeated, but managed to whisper, 'After lights out last night, the guards left the block and didn't come back until morning. The other prisoners were yelling at me and telling me to watch my back, saying that sticking up for a wimp like you could cost me my life. I was really scared.' I didn't know what to do, or even what to say to John."

Tom appeared to be collecting his thoughts. "I said, 'Maybe you should lay low. If you don't interfere anymore, they'll leave you alone. I only have to survive another few weeks until my parole board meeting, and with a bit of luck, could be out shortly after that.' Do you know what he said to me?"

Jenny was speechless, but her eyes told him that she wanted to know what his friend had said.

Tom got up from his chair and went to the window. He spoke so softly that Jenny barely heard Big John's reply. "'Friends don't abandon each other. If I'm meant to die, so be it. I will at least go out defending my friend.'" Tom turned to Jenny, his voice a mere whisper. "I was overwhelmed and thanked him. I assured him several times: two more weeks. Only two more weeks. Big John softly inquired, 'How's your talk going for the parole board?' I wasn't sure how to respond, so I just said, 'Slow, but I'm working on it each day. Want to get out but can't avoid the fact that I killed a woman. I ruined her husband's life, and mine, too, but I deserve what happened to me. That woman's husband didn't.'"

Tom was in deep thought, no longer completely aware of his surroundings. Jenny looked at the man that was once the love of her life. "I wish you'd talked to me about how you were feeling sooner. I may have been able to help you."

Tom considered her comment but soon turned back to his story. "Big John looked at me and said, 'Anything you want to share?' I told him that once I was released, I couldn't allow these prison memories to control my life. If they did, I could very well end up back in this hellhole. I had to stay in control. Some days, I wish my brother Charles was here to defend me, but he isn't. I'm glad my brother is dead." He turned his attention back to Jenny. "He shot you in the back!" Tears streamed down his face, and he collected his thoughts again before speaking. "If Bill and his team hadn't killed him, I would have done the job myself. The police did me a favor in eliminating him, but I still want compensation from them. Half a million dollars could set us up for life."

Jenny knew he was really hurting, but rather than comfort him, she waited for him to continue.

Tom was quiet for several minutes before he spoke again. He looked directly at her. "I just had to survive another few weeks, get through the parole board hearing, and then I hoped to be back with you. Assuming I was even able to find you. I was afraid that maybe you had moved away, lost your job, that you were no longer welcome in town. I thought that if I was lucky enough to find you, it would take you some time to trust me again, but I hoped you'd fall back in love with me."

Jenny looked sad as she said, "I'm really sorry Tom, but you hurt me. I was so alone when you were gone. A few of the neighbors were nice to me, but mostly I felt like an outcast. You broke my heart and I'm not convinced it'll ever heal."

Tom continued, "I'm truly sorry and wish I could turn back the clock and change what happened that day when I shot Joan Wilks, but I can't. How can I win you back?"

Jenny never answered.

Tom looked sadly at her before continuing, "Without Big John, I probably would have committed suicide. He was my rock within those four walls. He reassured me that you would be waiting for me. My thoughts of you helped me get through each day." He sat in his chair. "We ate in silence most mornings, keeping our eyes down and avoiding the other prisoners. One morning, I saw a second guard approach the one standing behind us. He said, 'Morning, Alex.'

"'Morning, Fred. You're late for work again?'

"'Damn vehicle's still giving me headaches.'

"Alex responded, 'Why don't you get it fixed?'

"'Oh, hell, there's no time to even get it to a mechanic. They have me working straight ten hour shifts five days a week. No mechanic works on a weekend, so I'm screwed.'

"Big John and I looked at each other. He whispered, 'Here's your chance, buddy. You said you were a mechanic.'"

"I chuckled. 'Why would a guard trust me to fix his vehicle?' Big John reassured me. 'He needs a vehicle fixed and you need to get out of laundry. If you actually fix it, they may keep you in the garage until your release date. I won't have to protect you anymore if they move you to a different department. I'll miss you, buddy, but at least you will be safe. Go for it.'"

Tom glanced over at Jenny. "I wasn't sure if I could convince the guard to let me look at his vehicle, let alone repair it."

Jenny responded, "You were a very good mechanic, well respected in Blue Ridge."

Tom smiled. "Thank you for saying that."

"I'm not just saying it. It's the truth."

Tom seemed to collect his thoughts before continuing, "I took several deep breaths to build up my courage and turned to the guards, keeping my eyes down as I spoke. 'Didn't mean to eavesdrop, but I hear that one of you is having problems with your vehicle. Maybe I can help.' The guards looked at each other before eyeing me. 'Are you always poking your nose into other people's business?' I expected to get a slap on the side of my head, but found the courage to speak further. What did I really have to lose? 'I was a mechanic before I came here. Don't mind looking at the vehicle to see if I can fix it for you.' I took a chance and glanced up at them. Neither appeared ready to hit me, so I asked, 'What's the vehicle doing?'

"They glared at me, but then the one named Fred inquired, 'So you're a qualified mechanic?'

"'Have the papers to prove it, but of course, they aren't with me. Not allowed to bring anything personal inside.'

"Fred glanced at me before asking, 'What's your name?'

"'Tom Lockman. What's the vehicle doing?'

"Fred hesitated before answering, 'Damn thing is making a horrible grinding noise when I try to start it.'

"I told him, 'If you don't get it looked at, it could damage the fly wheel.'

"Fred looked confused. 'What the hell is a fly wheel?'

"'It helps start your engine and balances it to reduce drive train stress. Is your dashboard engine light on?'

"'All the time. Damn thing just clicks when I turn the key, but eventually it does start.'

"I told him that it sounded like the starter. 'It can get expensive if you hire a mechanic. I don't mind fixing it for you. It will be a nice change from the laundry department.'

"He looked at me. 'I'll get back to you.' Then they turned and left the room.

"I remember turning back to Big John and asking him, 'When they leave, does that mean I'm screwed?' Big John laughed. 'Who the hell knows? Just have to wait and see if it goes anywhere.' The rest of that day was uneventful. Just hours spent in the laundry room sweating up a storm.

"The next morning, that Fred fellow hunted me down at breakfast. He growled at me, 'Eat fast. You have a vehicle to fix today. Damn thing sounds like it's fried.'

"I glanced at Big John, grinning ear to ear. 'Looks like I won't be joining you for lunch today.'

"Big John responded, 'You have better things to do. See you tomorrow.'

"I wolfed down my breakfast and followed the guard to the mechanical department, where a single vehicle sat next to a work bench with all the tools I would need to complete the job. I popped open the hood and asked the guard, 'Did you test the battery?'

"'I charged it, but it made no difference.'

"'It has to be the starter, then. How did you get the new part so quick?'

"He answered, 'Phoned the wife yesterday and told her to go get the part before the shop closed. It was waiting for me when I got home.'"

Tom looked at Jenny with a wide grin on his face. "I knew that if I fixed this fellow's vehicle, it was my ticket out of laundry and into the mechanical department. I was finally where I belonged, fixing a broken vehicle with all the top-of-the-line tools at my disposal. I removed the negative battery cable, then the positive one. Picked up a ratchet and disconnected the bolts that held the starter to the block. I then carefully lifted the old starter out and replaced it with the new one. Once the negative and positive wires were reconnected, I turned to Fred. 'It should work now. Give it a try.'

"Fred slipped behind the wheel and turned the key. The car started. 'Nice job, Lockman. What cell you in?'

"'East wing, cell fourteen.'

"Fred grinned. 'Not anymore. We need someone like you in this department.' He then inquired, 'Do you have any personal stuff in your cell?'

"'Nothing.'

"'Then let me show you your new accommodations.'"

There was relief in Tom's voice as he continued, "Being moved to the mechanical department meant I was finally safe from the constant bullying, but there was still free time outdoors where I was constantly watching my back. Big John would still be there to keep an eye on me, but now I was worried that I was putting his life at risk, so I shied away. We still remained friends but only from a distance."

Tom looked sadly at Jenny.

Jenny became bewildered. Rather than continuing he got up, crossed the room, and went into the bathroom. How could he leave without a single word spoken?

When he came back, he made for the door. Before he could leave, Jenny asked, "Please Tom, can I use the washroom too?"

Tom sighed and went to clip the ties that held her to the bed. "Be quick. I need to get ready for my next call with Bill."

Jenny quickly used the washroom, and then allowed Tom to secure her to the bed again.

He glared down at her and then scrunched up his forehead. He appeared to be thinking. Tom refused to believe that Jenny was lost to him forever. There had to be a way he could win her back, but for the life of him he didn't know what to do. How could he convince her that he could once again be gentle and loving? He could change if he only knew that she still loved him.

He was turning to leave the room when she said, "I'm hungry. Do you have any food here?"

Over his shoulder, he responded, "If there's one thing I learned while behind bars, it's that food is a scarcity and meals kept you strong. The meals however were a culinary disaster. How could anyone ruin mashed potatoes? Hence my weight loss." He paused before continuing, "It turned out they were instant potatoes. But I soon discovered that if I didn't eat whatever they put in front of me, death would be in my future. Lack of food would only make me weaker and subject to harassment and more beatings. If you really want to know how I survived behind bars, you can go hungry, besides missing a meal will help you understand what I went through."

Tom's voice softened and he faced Jenny. "How I missed your fried chicken and steak meals." He shook his head. "At first, food fights in the cafeteria were funny, but they became scary after an inmate was stabbed with a homemade weapon and was sent to the infirmary. The strong men formed groups and constantly searched out the weaker ones, and I was definitely the latter. I woke up to a living hell everyday."

Having nothing else to say, Tom picked up the axe and left the room.

He stood in the shadows of the front porch. The sun peeked between the clouds, causing him to look up at the sky. The flash of light threw him back into his prison days. Rather than seeing the sun, he saw food being dumped over his head. His sensitivity started when the guards came around at all hours of the night flashing light into the prisoner's eyes, startling them awake. His eyes became sensitive to these flashes of light. This soon became apparent in the cafeteria when his food was dumped over his head causing Tom to look up towards the overhead lights above him.

As he became frailer, other prisoners considered him the runt of the pack. The same group of three bullies took it upon themselves to make his life miserable at every opportunity. Several times a day, he was pushed and punched, and numerous times a week, his food was stolen. The largest of the three bullies constantly approached him. "No need to waste food on you." The bully would either steal the food or dump it over Tom's head. The guards saw it as a joke, obviously at his expense. Unless there was an outright fight, the guards overlooked what he considered bad behaviour.

Tom snapped out of his nightmare and took a seat on the chair outside the door. He needed to think about his next call to Bill. Jenny wasn't willing to give him a second chance, and since he wouldn't allow her to move on without him, he had no choice but to plan his future without her. Hopefully, Bill would come up with the money, but if not, he needed a plan.

He stood and went to the next empty room, kicking open the door. Walking inside, he picked up an overturned chair and the dirty blanket on the bed. He left the room and walked around the back of the building, set down the chair and blanket, and proceeded to unlock the container. From inside, he brought out his toolbox and placed it on the ground. Getting into the vehicle, he backed it out and parked it as far into the forest as was possible, out of sight of prying eyes.

Next, he placed the chair just inside the container, put the blanket on the chair, and turned towards the woods. With his axe in hand, he started collecting twigs and firewood, which he then piled under the chair. If Bill decided to play dirty bugger, Tom was willing to sacrifice Jenny.

He returned to the room ready for his two o'clock call. Jenny waited for him so say something, but he just placed the axe on the table and sat in silence as he looked at his watch, counting down the minutes.

He then picked up the phone and entered Bill's number.

"Hi, Tom, you're right on time."

Tom got down to business. "Do you have my money yet?"

"Let me talk to Jenny."

Tom glared at Jenny before crossing the room and placing the phone next to her ear. "No tricks or you die."

Jenny spoke into the phone. "Hello, Bill."

"How are you, Jenny? Still hanging in there?"

Her voice broke as she answered, "I'm okay."

Bill quickly asked, "Are you close to town?"

"Yes."

"Hang in there and I'll see you soon."

"I'm counting on it."

Tom grabbed the phone away from her, walked back to his chair, and sat down. "The clock's a-ticking, so let's get back to business."

Bill cut him off. "What, no chit-chat?"

"I have nothing to say to you."

"Well, buddy, I have lots to say to you. If you as much as lay a hand on Jenny, my team will hunt you down."

"You can't even find me, so how do you plan on doing that?"

"The same way I caught your brother. Good old-fashioned investigation and legwork."

Tom was livid. "You're just trying to act smarter than me, but it won't work."

Bill laughed. "I am smarter than you. Once we find you, it's back behind bars where you belong. I'm sure your buddies there have missed you."

"There isn't a hope in hell that I'm going back. I would die before that happens."

"Duly noted. I'll make sure you end up in a body bag, if that's what you prefer."

Tom was taken aback. "I'm sure that isn't taught in the police academy."

"Once you're dead, who will care? My team has better things to do than play games with a wacko."

Curious, Tom asked, "Tell me, Bill, which officer killed my brother?"

"Doesn't matter, he's still dead."

"It matters to me."

"I wasn't there when it happened. Your bother shot me, and a fellow officer took him out."

"My brother shot you? That's wonderful."

"How do you figure? I'm alive and he's dead." Bill then added, "He's buried in the local cemetery, but being a criminal, he has an unmarked grave. If by some slim chance you should survive, you won't know where to deliver flowers. But I can promise you one thing."

"What's that?"

"I'll have you buried in the same grave, still unmarked."

"You're funny, Bill. You assume that you're going to win."

"Think about it, Tom. You are one person against the entire police force of Blue Ridge. If by some chance you escape, the whole country will be looking for you."

"My plan isn't to get caught. With the half a million dollars you give me, I'll disappear where no one will find me."

Jenny already knew that this very well could be the last time she talked to Bill, so she shouted, "I'm not sure you'll find me in time, Bill, but I know you tried your best! Just do me a favor."

Bill shouted, not even sure if Jenny could hear him. "Anything for you!"

Jenny was pissed and had nothing to lose. She could only see death in her future. "Put him back behind bars, or even better, kill the bastard."

Livid, Tom set the phone on the table and picked up the axe. Raising it above his head, he ran towards the bed.

Jenny screamed. "No, Tom! Don't do it!"

In a fit of rage, he smashed the dull blade into the headboard and screamed, loud enough for Bill to hear. "When Jenny is dead, I'm coming after you, or maybe someone close to you!"

Shaken, Bill shouted into the phone. "Jenny! What's going on?" The line went dead.

Jenny trembled when she saw how close the axe had come to her arms. Her mouth moved, but no words came out. Tom glared at her, and she turned away, afraid to say anything. He left the axe embedded in the headboard, and then clipped the tie wraps around her wrists and the ones binding her to the headboard.

He roughly pulled her to a standing position. "Take off your dress," he snarled.

Jenny's eyes grew large with fear. Was he about to rape her? She stood tall and watched him move the chair that stood by the table in front of the desk. When he turned back and saw her still clothed, he became furious, crossed the room, and ripped off her dress in one fell swoop. Jenny could hardly breathe. Tom was like a raving lunatic. He went to the table and opened his duffel bag, then pulled out his well-used, dirty prison clothes and tossed them in her face.

"Put them on," he snapped. "You keep saying you want to know what I went through. Well, here's your chance."

Jenny turned her back to him and dressed quickly. She didn't like the way Tom looked at her.

He noticed the scar on her back from across the room, and knew it had to be a result of Charles shooting her. He wanted to go over and touch it, but knew better. Instead, when she was dressed, he grabbed her and forced her onto the chair. She once again felt the tie wraps bite into her wrists. Jenny watched him go back to his duffel bag and was shocked to see a pair of scissors in his hand.

"What're you going to do?" she demanded.

He laughed. "If I can't have you, then no one can." Standing behind her, he grabbed a handful of her gray hair and roughly cut it off close to her scalp.

She tried to pull away, which earned her a slap across the head. Jenny was sure that she saw stars. She watched in horror as he cut off most of her hair and let it fall to the floor. Looking down, Jenny realized that her hair blended in with the dirt, the dust, and the mouse droppings. He placed the scissors in his pants pocket.

Sneering, Tom said, "Who the hell would want an ugly girlfriend?"

Tears streamed down Jenny's face as she looked at her reflection in the mirror in front of her.

Tom cut the tie wraps, roughly pulled Jenny to her feet, and marched her outside. Jenny was surprised to find she was standing in front of a dilapidated motel, unfamiliar to her. "Where are we?"

Tom dragged her to the back of the building and Jenny came face to face with a box car brown, rusty, banged-up, container. She then realized Tom really was capable of killing her.

Studying the container, she noticed a chair was placed just inside the door with firewood piled up under it. Jenny couldn't believe her eyes. Not only was she terrified, but she also started screaming, already knowing that there was no one around to hear her pleas for help. She fought him as he began to shove her toward the chair, but to no avail. He threw her down on the chair and secured her arms and legs to it with rope. He then covered her legs with the dirty blanket.

"Are you crazy, Tom? What are you planning to do?"

His eyes bored into hers. "I guess your fate is now in Bill's hands. If he doesn't come up with the money, you'll either suffocate, or die from hypothermia, or I'll burn you alive. I haven't decided how to end your life yet. It'll be a last minute surprise for you. Now that there's no hope of us getting back together, I have a confession to make. All my whining and sniveling about my time in prison was supposed to soften you up. But you're a tough bitch. I might have been smaller than the other guys in prison, but I was also faster. I could kill anyone I wanted and never get caught. I actually killed the guy who took out Big John. I became known as the stab-and-grab villain. That's how I got free packages of cigarettes. I learned that to survive, if you acted innocent, then no one would suspect you." Taking a final look at her, he turned and started to close the container doors. "Enjoy your last breaths."

She screamed as he closed the doors and locked her inside, only stopping just long enough to hear him singing.

"Ding dong, the witch is dead."

The thin lines of light around the doorframe slowly started to disappear. It was then that she realized that Tom was taping the door closed, so that once there was no oxygen left in the container, she would suffocate. Jenny wasn't ready to succumb to death yet, so she quit screaming, hoping to save oxygen. Now she was faced with her greatest fear: complete darkness. She closed her eyes and prayed that Bill would find her in time.

Tom took a seat at the front of the motel, satisfied with his decision to put Jenny well into his past. His thoughts went back to the only person in the world he had ever trusted: Big John. The two of them had had lots of laughs together, but they were also too smart to let their guards down. They had always kept their backs against the wall, mostly for protection, but still found time to walk around the complex during free time.

Tom remembered the day his friend was fatally stabbed as if it had happened only yesterday. Free time had ended, and as the two of them were about to enter the building, someone grabbed Big John and brutally pushed Tom against the wall, separating them. Beady eyes glared at Tom, challenging him not to interfere. From the corner of Tom's eye, he saw Big John trying to escape and come to his rescue.

A burly man approached Big John, carrying a homemade weapon, which he thrust deep into Big John's back. He laughed as Big John's huge body fell to the ground. Tom tried to scream, but nothing came out of his mouth. All he heard was, "Take that, you interfering son of a bitch."

Big John succumbed to his injuries a few days later. His death meant that Tom was now alone inside a cage of overgrown, overzealous tigers, out to destroy the weakest link: him.

Tom lit another cigarette and went inside as a chill descended in the air.

Chapter Ten

1:45 p.m. - 3:10 p.m.

AS DEBBIE AND ELI DROVE to the bunker, Debbie glanced at her partner. "According to the city, we turn off here, as if we're going to the Panorama Room." She made the turn onto the twisting road that followed the picturesque coastline. "The hidden road should only be a few miles ahead." She watched her odometer so she would know when they were drawing close. "Keep your eyes peeled. The city said the road would likely be overgrown and could appear as a hidden trail among the trees."

Eli carefully scanned the side of the road, looking for that mysterious break in the trees. He laughed. "How do we find a hidden road that may not want to be found?" He glanced over at Debbie. "It might not be easy, but we must be getting close now."

"If we miss the road, we'll circle back. Maybe we'll see it better coming from the other direction." Debbie cut her speed in half and soon spotted the break in the trees. She pointed it out to Eli. "That's it. Mountain View Road." The sign had fallen over as if it had been hit by a vehicle, and was partially covered in mud, but was still just visible to the observant lookers.

Eli responded, "Good eyesight, partner. Why is it that no one on the force knew about this turnoff, let alone that it led to an old bunker?"

"Beats me, but you know the old saying."

"What's that?"

"You learn something new every day." Debbie parked the cruiser on the opposite side of the road and they got out, locking the doors behind them.

They stood facing the start of what looked like a very rough trail.

Eli said, "That definitely looks more like an overgrown path than a road. How are we going to find our way to the bunker?"

"I'm not totally sure, but as long as we only hike about fifteen minutes uphill, we'll find it. One thing I know for sure, we'd better get to the bunker and back by mid-afternoon, or we may find ourselves using our flashlights to get back to our cruiser." Debbie climbed over a few fallen trees and started up what she thought might be the trail.

Eli was right behind her. "Wait for me!" he called out. "If we get lost, who's going to come and find us?"

"No one, so let's not get lost." As they got several steps into their venture, the trees overhead blocked out most of the sun, leaving the officers to think they had lost an hour of daylight. "Not too many people know about this place, so the city said the road might not be well marked. I understand it's quite a climb from here. The bunker is on the top of a hill overlooking the water. It's supposed to be an excellent vantage point."

"Did the city give you any history on the bunker?"

"A little. Apparently it was built at the beginning of the Second World War. The channel that leads into Blue Ridge would have been an ideal invasion point for our enemies. They could've overtaken Blue Ridge before anyone even knew they were here. According to the city, it was manned twenty-four hours a day, seven days a week, until the war was over. Some were built below ground, but this one is above ground and provides an excellent view of the coastline. They said that it should be deserted, but couldn't say if anyone would be there or not. It's a long way out for any homeless."

Eli kept his eyes on the trail, but glanced up occasionally. What he saw was breathtaking. The leaves on the trees were a rich red, and the branches hung heavy with clumps of moss, some of it hanging down a great distance. These were famously known as grandfathers' beards and they clung to the bark as if their lives depended on it. Some of the moss appeared to start at the top of a single tree and ran down to forest floor, then disappeared into the ferns. This provided a soft bed for the officers to walk on. Eli felt like the two of them had entered a true rainforest, as the droplets from the previous evening's downpour remained on all the leaves and pine needles. It fell as a soft mist onto both officers.

Debbie turned to Eli. "Do you hear that?"

"What?"

"Nothing but the sound of silence. Isn't it wonderful?"

"It's rather pleasant, but let's not forget why we're here."

"Don't spoil the moment for me. I'm a mother, so between home and work, I never get any silence."

"I stand corrected."

The two officers continued along what they hoped was the path to the bunker. They came alongside a small stream and planned their strategy to get to the other side. Debbie picked up an old plank that she thought might withstand their weight and laid it across several larger stones. "I'm going first in case it doesn't hold up under your weight."

Eli laughed. "Did you just tell me I'm overweight?"

"No. You took that out of context. I merely meant that you have more body mass than I do."

While Debbie was crossing the stream, she couldn't help but enjoy the sound of the water as it passed under her. It was like a well synchronized orchestra, each splash of water leaving what sounded like a different note as it rushed against the stones. It was a mesmerizing sound that was hard for her to get out of her head. Once she was on the other side, she turned to Eli. "Your turn. Good luck."

Eli had a huge grin on his face. "I bet you would think it was funny if the board broke and I fell into the water."

"I would, but I would try not to laugh too hard."

Eli was skeptical but successfully crossed the stream and then looked at his watch. "What do you think? Are we about halfway by now?"

"We should be." She took one step forward and froze. "Son of a bitch!"

Eli was right behind her. "Are you okay?"

She composed herself. "Just a damn mouse ran across my boot."

"You afraid of mice?"

"Not normally, but I like to see them coming."

"Good thing you didn't draw your weapon and shoot the poor thing."

"It would have been a waste of a bullet, plus lots of paperwork to fill out. Every bullet has to be accounted for and I have better things to do with my time, plus the little creature would've been obliterated for no fault of its' own."

Eli looked ahead and saw the trail slowly peter off. "We really need to be very careful from here on in. Neither one of us can afford to get injured." Off in the distance, he noticed that the path resumed and turned slightly upwards. "I guess this is where we start climbing."

Both officers grabbed hold of branches along the trail and pulled themselves along. The climb was slow and strenuous and they stopped several times to catch their breath.

Eli perked up when he thought he heard something. He scanned the area before looking up, and in a panic, he shouted, "Look out!" And he threw himself forward, shoving Debbie well into the bushes.

Surprised, Debbie shouted, "What the hell?" just as a heavy, jagged branch slammed to the ground where she had been standing. Far too close for comfort. She slowly lifted herself from the soggy ground, brushed off her uniform, and said in a shaky voice. "Thanks, Eli. I didn't mean to yell at you."

Eli also picked himself up and scraped the mud off his uniform. "That's okay. I'm just glad I prevented a serious accident." He glanced at Debbie and saw her distress. He gently moved her towards a fallen tree and the two sat down. "We'll take a short break so we can regroup." He changed the subject. "Do you hear that?"

With a joking voice she answered, "It's not another falling branch, is it?"

"No, it's not. Forget about the branch. What else do you hear?"

Debbie tilted her head, listening. "Wow. I was so wrapped up in the case I never heard the birds."

"Doesn't it sound like they're talking to each other?"

"It does. And I think I know what they're saying."

"Really? What's that?"

"'That lady's one lucky son of a bitch.'"

Eli laughed. "I don't think birds swear, but maybe they do. Have you heard of the term 'widow-maker'?"

Though she had joked about it a moment earlier, now her voice broke. "I have, but now I can say I've experienced it. How in heaven's name did you even hear it?" Her voice broke. "Thanks to you, I'm still alive. I have a husband and small child at home. It's important for me to walk through my front door every day and find the two of them waiting for me. I can't imagine leaving them alone."

"Stop thinking like that."

She laughed. "I'm a woman, so shouldn't the fallen branch be called a widower-maker?"

"Not sure if that's even a real term, but I guess you just made it one. If you're ready, then let's keep moving."

They got up and hit the trail again, dodging branches, climbing over fallen trees, pulling themselves up the steep hill, and slowly trudging forward through muddy patches. Most of the trail was covered with fallen leaves, making the journey slow going. Debbie spoke over her shoulder. "This trail is really slippery, so let's take our time. There's no way I'd be able to carry you back to the vehicle if you got injured."

Eli responded, "I agree." He was silent for a few moments before speaking again. "I'm glad that Don pulled the entire team together to brainstorm the clues on the whiteboard. That fifteen-minute window was driving everyone crazy, especially when Jenny used it twice." He then asked, "What made you think the fifteen-minute window could mean Tom hadn't taken her too far away?"

"I don't know this Tom character very well, as I was on maternity leave when he killed Joan Wilks. I got to thinking, that maybe the fifteen minutes meant he stayed close to town. If he'd spent the entire hour and fifteen minutes traveling after kidnapping Jenny, he wouldn't have been able to restrain Jenny and still make his ten a.m. phone call to the precinct. And I'm almost positive she would've given him resistance." Debbie paused. "I sure hope I'm right, or the entire team will be losing valuable time searching for her in the wrong places. I very well could be responsible for Jenny's death."

"Don't start thinking like that. The team was behind your idea. I'm pretty sure Bill and Don were also on track with your theory." Eli slowed just long enough to look up, and then he caught Debbie's attention. "I think I can see sky, so we must be getting close."

Debbie pointed. "Look up ahead."

Eli glanced past Debbie and saw a series of large stones that appeared to form a set of stairs in front of them. "These stairs have to lead somewhere, so we must be getting close. Plus, it looks like there could be a clearing just beyond them." He added, "They're covered in moss and rotting leaves, so watch your step. Let's hope the bunker is just over the crest of this hill."

The two officers took the stairs one step at a time, both wishing there was a rail to hang on to. Once at the top, the old bunker stood like a soldier in front of them. Debbie paused to take it in before speaking. "And just like that the bunker stands in front of us, majestic but hiding behind the trees, moss, and debris. She's a real beauty."

"Almost breathtaking."

They scanned their surroundings before approaching the dark abyss that beckoned them inside. The bunker was a massive concrete structure covered in a thick layer of moss. Branches partially blocked the entrance, and one of the rusty doors hung askew. Beyond that door, the two officers could see a second door that was propped open. They both drew their weapons and slowly moved towards the door, listening for any noises or movement. When they passed through the first door, the cold air hit them like a brick wall. Their damp, muddy uniforms provided no warmth. They immediately became aware of the smell of mould and rotting vegetation. They had also passed from daylight into almost total darkness, so both reached for their flashlights and turned them on.

Eli indicated that he would take the lead, so Debbie hung back to cover him. Eli slipped through the second door and into the bunker with Debbie right behind him. They scanned their surroundings with their flashlights, looking for anything, or anyone, that could be a threat to them.

Eli announced, "Coast's clear."

They placed their weapons back into their holsters and walked farther into the room, flashlight beams scanning over the mess in front of them.

Debbie commented, "People must have been living in here after the bunker was shut down."

"I agree, but how recently?"

"Your guess is as good as mine."

The walls were built of thick concrete and the ceilings were low. The floor was covered in blankets, plastic pop bottles, and newspapers. Along two sides of the room stood a series of shelves that must have been part of a makeshift kitchen. A rusted-out charcoal barbecue still sat in a corner, covered in grease and mouse droppings. Next to the barbecue were a few broken dishes that were covered in a thick layer of mud and cobwebs. On a separate shelf, they found old, rusty pots and cutlery. Two small windows on the far wall allowed a small amount of light to enter the bunker. There was a distinct smell of feces in the air.

Debbie held her nose. "I don't think anyone has been here for some time."

"You could be right, but let's check the entire building to be sure."

Debbie spotted a set of stairs off to the right. "This must be the way to the top of the bunker and the view of the coastline." She picked her way around the junk on the floor and started up the stairs, Eli in tow. At the top of the stairs, they found a series of slots in the outside wall. They each picked a spot and took in the view.

Eli was amazed. "Wow, the view is incredible."

Debbie was speechless for several moments. "Can you imagine building a house here and enjoying this view every day?"

"I can, but who the hell would want to walk up that godforsaken trail every day?"

Debbie laughed. "Not me, but anyone brave enough to build a home here could put a road in."

A clatter came from the floor below them. Instinctively, Eli and Debbie both drew their weapons, placed their backs against the outside wall, and listened. There was definitely movement below them. Carefully, they moved towards the stairs, flashlights and firearms in hand, and slowly descended. They turned their flashlights off as they approached the bottom of the stairs. Cautiously, they peered around the corner—and were stunned when they saw the silhouette of a bear sauntering across the room. Neither moved a muscle.

Eli whispered, "Great. If that bear sees us invading his winter hibernation den, we could be dead meat. You're tiny, so he'll start with me. After all, you did say that I have more body mass."

"Hush. He's not going to eat either of us," Debbie said, though she was unsure. She'd never been this close to a bear, and her mind wandered to what they would do if it attacked. They could always shoot the animal, but that didn't seem humane, although if it came to life or death, they probably wouldn't have an option.

If the bear was aware of their presence, it didn't seem too worried about them. She was trembling, but tried to slow down her heart rate. It seemed impossible that the bear couldn't sense their presence and hear her heart pounding deep within her chest. Somehow, she knew that if neither of them moved, the bear would settle down and they could quietly leave the bunker.

They watched the bear burrow into the far corner, wiggling under a pile of newspapers and blankets, appearing to be settling down for the winter. Once they thought it was safe to leave, they turned on their flashlights, covering the bulb with their hands in the hope of cutting down the glare. Slowly and carefully, they stepped around the debris on the floor, hoping the bear wouldn't hear them leaving. Eli constantly looked over his shoulder to check if the bear was approaching them. Once clear of the room, they quickly moved through the second door and left the bunker.

Outside, they rushed to the stairs and scurried down them, once again hanging onto branches as they descended the steep hill. It was more difficult going down than climbing up, as their feet were constantly slipping on the wet, mossy slope.

Eli was in front this time. He spoke over his shoulder. "I think it's safe to say that Tom and Jenny aren't here."

"I agree. Let's get the hell out of here."

By the time they reached the bottom of the hill, the two had fallen several times and were covered with mud and grime.

Debbie did a final check behind them in case the bear had followed and was relieved that it was nowhere in sight. They each grabbed a wad of moss and tried to at least clean their hands, then used a stick to pry most of the mud off the bottoms of their shoes.

Debbie glanced at her partner and broke into laughter. "You look positively horrendous."

"Do you think you look any better?"

"Probably not."

The two hadn't walked very far before Eli paused and turned to face his partner. "Debbie, this isn't the same way we came up."

"I noticed that, too, but as long as we're dropping, eventually we'll end up back at the road. We might not be close to our vehicle, but we can always hike back to it."

"I suppose you're right." He looked around. "I know it's still day light, but darkness is going to set in pretty quick. We need to find the road fast."

"I'm right behind you."

They set off again in search of the road. But Eli still felt that something wasn't quite right and stopped dead in his tracks. Debbie almost walked into him.

Puzzled, she asked, "What's up?"

"I'm not sure, but something's wrong."

"What do you mean?"

"You don't hear that?"

"No. What?"

"I think we've come upon some kind of nest . . ."

"Do you mean mice? Rats? Squirrels? Snakes?" Debbie asked, "I'm not comfortable with any of those, so let's move it."

"No. It's more of a chittering and hissing sound."

Just then, they heard the sound again and both turned to their right. Not far off the trail was a hollowed-out tree trunk, close to the ground, and hidden in the shadows. An animal was crouched at the entrance, partially hidden with branches and twigs. It moved slightly and Eli was able to see the distinctive black face mask and ringed tail. A fully grown raccoon was protecting its' kits. Eli looked at the long, thin front legs and the sharp nails extending beyond its' paws. Racoons were known for scratching and biting, and for being aggressive when protecting their young, so he hoped to avoid that confrontation. The racoon started making clicking sounds, letting them know she was aware of their presence.

"What the hell do we do now?" Debbie asked nervously. "We'll never get back to the vehicle at this rate."

Eli responded, "They only attack if they're cornered, trying to protect their kits, or if they're sick."

"Well, let's hope it doesn't have rabies. That still begs the question, what do we do?"

"We leave this path and circle wide, staying as far away from the mother as possible."

"If you say so."

They turned into the bush and, once out of sight of the racoon, circled back and confidently worked their way towards the road. But they had one more encounter before reaching the road. As they walked the last of the path, Eli heard buzzing high above their heads. It was a steady buzz that slowly got louder. He turned to Debbie and pointed high above them. They had come across a swarm of paper wasps hiding beneath the treetops.

Debbie became concerned. "I'm allergic to bee strings."

Eli responded, "I didn't know that. Most of the time, they seem reasonably docile, but they will defend their nests if they feel threatened."

Debbie was nervous, but also amazed at the nests above them. "They're so delicate. Don't you think they look like upside down paper umbrellas?"

"They do." He saw that she was uncomfortable. "Don't worry, we are so dirty the wasps won't come close to us or even know we're here."

Debbie responded, "Let's hope for both."

The two officers slowly continued along the overgrown trail. Eli pointed ahead of them. "I see daylight."

"Finally."

They climbed over a series of stumps and came out on the highway. Their cruiser was visible in the distance. Eli glanced down at his watch, which showed it was two fifty p.m. He grabbed his radio and called the station.

Daniel answered, "Daniel here."

"Hi, Daniel, this is Eli and Debbie. We've just been to the bunker and it's all clear. We need to go home and shower before returning to the office, though."

"What happened?"

"Let's just say we encountered mud and debris, and we're too dirty to come straight to the office."

Daniel responded, "Copy that. See the two of you soon."

Don saw the look on Daniel's face and knew the bunker was a bust. He slowly approached the whiteboard and put a line through the location.

Back at the vehicle, the officers looked at their dirty uniforms and clean seats. Debbie shrugged. "Hell. Not much we can do about the cruiser. Let's just get home. I'll drop you off, then come back and pick you up after I've showered."

"I'd appreciate that."

On the way back into town, Debbie laughed. "It's been a hell of day, don't you agree?"

Eli chuckled. "You could say so. Glad we got to spend it together. Too bad Jenny and Tom weren't there."

"We'll find her. Don't give up hope."

"An officer has to live on hope."

Once they were both showered, Debbie covered the front seats of the cruiser to keep their new uniforms clean. She then picked up Eli and the two checked in at the station. Don had already put a line through "Bunker Debbie and Eli".

Chapter Eleven

2:15 p.m. – 3:15 p.m.

AFTER BILL'S CALL ENDED HE stared straight ahead, unaware of Daniel sitting across from him. Questions were mounting as he felt the room closing in on him. What had he done? Had he pushed Tom too hard? What did Tom hope to gain if Jenny was no longer in the picture?

Bill had failed her, and now would have to live with the biggest mistake he'd ever made in his entire career.

Daniel looked across the table at Bill, feeling sorry for him. The frustration and signs of defeat were written all over his face. "We'll find her, Bill."

Bill's answer was a mere whisper. "At first, I thought so, but now I'm not so sure. Maybe I was too cocky, thinking I could take him down. It'll be my fault if she's dead. I was analyzing him the same way I did Charles, and that could turn out to be my downfall. Tom thinks the same as his brother, but seems to always be one step ahead of me. These damn criminals are getting too smart. That's why I retired."

Bill got up from his chair and left the building. It was starting to cool down as late afternoon approached, but Bill felt only emptiness. He sat down on the cold top step and tried to understand what had just happened. Jenny had put her trust in him, and he had failed her. Tears openly ran down his face and he made no effort to wipe them away. He couldn't think straight; he didn't have a plan B. He was a shell of a man who had let down the team of officers working so hard to save Jenny. He felt defeated, diminished, as if a strong wind passing by would reduce him to a pile of dust. Jenny had trusted him, and he had screwed up.

He and his team had taken down Charles, but it looked like Tom was going to win this episode. Bill had been too pushy, and it had cost Jenny her life. How could he live with that failure? Staring into the mirror each morning, seeing his reflection, would be a constant reminder of his ineptitude.

Daniel had watched Bill leave the building, and now he went to Don's office.

Don looked up from his paperwork. "How did the call go?" The look on Daniel's face told him it didn't go well. "What happened?"

Daniel spoke softly. "I think Tom just killed Jenny. Bill heard it all before the bastard disconnected."

"Shit. Where's Bill now?"

"He left, but I'm not sure if he's outside or has literally left the premises. He's pretty choked up."

Don got up and rushed outside to find Bill sitting on the top step. His slumped shoulders and bowed head told the story of how the latest call had impacted him. "You okay?"

Bill hesitated before replying. "No, not really. I just got Jenny killed. The asshole had the balls to do it while I was on the line." He put his face into his hands and wept openly. "I failed her, Don. How can I face Beatrice, Richard, and Claire knowing that I just got Jenny killed? I shouldn't even be here. I thought I'd left my career behind me when I retired. Life just isn't fair." Sounding defeated, Bill said, "I need a drink. A really strong one." He stood up and without turning around said, "I'm done. She died, I failed her, and I'm going home."

Don interjected. "You're right, life isn't always fair, but what if she isn't dead?"

Bill turned and faced him. "What do you mean?"

"I don't know about you, but until we find a body, we have to assume she's still alive. He could be playing mind games with you, pressuring you into securing his half million dollars."

"I heard her scream, then a loud noise, then nothing."

"You heard what he wanted you to hear. Do you remember when Charles fired his gun in the cabin, and we thought it was game over for Jenny? Who's to say she isn't still alive? Do what you want, but I'm still working the case. If Tom calls at three o'clock and you aren't here to talk to him, then she really will be dead. Please, Bill, at this point, let's assume that Jenny's still alive. He still wants his money, so we have to continue to work the case."

Bill looked defeated. "I don't know what to do next."

"We're a team here. Until we run out of leads, we follow the evidence."

"We *are* out of leads."

Don responded, "Then we look somewhere else. Please don't abandon her, Bill. If there's a chance she's still alive, we need to keep looking. Let's hope and pray that another clue hits us like a bolt of lightening, then we'll hit the road running. The case isn't over until it's over. The force really needs your expertise."

"I don't think you're hearing me, Don. I really screwed up!" He pointed to the door behind Don. "There isn't an officer in that room who will want to work with me. I'm a screw-up."

Don placed a hand on Bill's shoulder. "You've gotten soft since you retired. You need to expand your boundaries. I've never known you to be a quitter." He then added, "Let's make a deal."

"What kind of deal?"

"When this is all over and we have Jenny home safe, the team goes out and has a few beers. First round is on me."

Bill ran his hands over his face to wipe away the tears and looked up at the sky. "We really need to find her before nightfall. After that, we're screwed. I don't have the money for him and it's too late for me to try and get it."

"Then we fake it. We tell him we have the money and ask him where the drop-off point is."

"Do you think he'll fall for that?"

"Let's hope he does, but until then, we work the case."

Don and Bill returned into the office. Bill approached the whiteboard, picked up the marker, and added "Close to town, yes."

Don looked at the board. "Another clue that makes no sense right now. Debbie already looked at all the local vacant building sites, and so far, we're no further ahead."

Bill set down the marker. "If it made sense, then Tom would realize Jenny is sending us coded messages. This might be our final clue, so the whole team needs to start thinking outside the box. The odds of us finding her alive are slowly diminishing."

Don looked around the bustling common area. "Do you see any officers sitting and doing nothing? We all want to find her alive."

When Jim and Muhammad arrived back at the office, they found Sam and the two children sitting in the lunchroom. Jim grinned as he watched the kids, who were wrapped up in warm blankets, finishing off their lunch. "Hamburgers, fries, and Coke?"

Sam shrugged. "Nothing but the best for them."

"Have they talked yet?" Muhammad asked.

Sam responded, "Not so far. Thought we'd feed them first."

Jim smiled. "They certainly are enjoying the food."

Muhammad agreed. "Probably the best meal they've had in some time."

Bill saw the two children as he was passing by the lunchroom and poked his head in. "Where'd they come from?" he whispered to Jim.

Jim motioned for Bill to follow him into the common area. "We found them at the burned-out house on Oak Crescent."

"What were they doing there?"

"The oldest boy said it was their safehouse."

"Safehouse from what?"

"We're not sure right now, but hopefully we can question them once they've finished eating." Jim then added, "We've contacted child services and they'll be sending someone over before the end of the day to pick them up."

Bill glanced back at the children. "Hopefully they can shed some light on the case before they go."

"Amen to that," Jim said.

Bill turned and approached Don's office.

Don looked up. "You need something, Bill?"

"If it isn't a problem, could I use your office to call Kimberley and then Beatrice?"

"No problem. Take your time." Don got up and left, closing the door behind him.

Bill took a seat at Don's desk and composed himself before making his call. He still wasn't quite sure this was the right time to make the call, but he picked up the phone and called the Jackson residence anyway.

Eric picked up the phone. "Hello, Bill. How's it going at your end?"

"Not as good as I had hoped."

"I gather you haven't found her yet?"

"It's not from lack of trying. How is everything going at the house?"

"We're all good here. Claire is quite a handful, but Richard and Kimberley have her under control. Poor thing doesn't understand why she can't play outside."

Bringing Eric up to speed, Bill said, "The clues Jenny has given us so far haven't panned out, but we're not giving up." He paused. "I wanted to give up, but Don told me that wasn't an option." Bill's voice broke as he continued, "On my last call with Tom, it sounded like he killed Jenny. I might have screwed up badly and pushed him too far."

Eric left the room for a more private place to speak to Bill. He chose his words carefully. "Whether Jenny is dead or alive, you have to follow through. If he killed her, her body needs to be brought back to Blue Ridge for a proper burial. It wouldn't be right to leave her out there. Besides, Tom needs to be accountable for her death if she is indeed deceased. No officer likes to know that a case remains unsolved. On a more positive note, if she's alive and we can save her, we have a lot to celebrate."

Trusting in Eric, Bill continued, "Across my entire career, if I could save just one person, it would be Jenny. She has been through hell not just once, but twice."

Eric inquired, "What happened on the phone?"

"I thought our call was going as planned, then out of nowhere, Tom screamed and I think he attacked her. I heard her scream, and a loud thud. Then Tom ended the call."

Eric grimaced but tried to sound positive. "It doesn't exactly sound good, but don't overthink the evidence. Until her body is found, we'll consider her still alive."

"I sure as hell hope you're right."

Eric returned to the living room, "You know, I have three people who really want to talk to you."

"I bet you do. Who's first?"

"I'll let it be a surprise."

Claire came on the line. "Hello, Grandpa."

"Hello, Claire Bear."

"Guess what?"

"What?"

"I have no school today and Mommy and Daddy have a day off work. We're playing lots of games, but Eric can't play because he's already playing policeman at our house. It's very dark here because he keeps shutting the curtains and I'm not allowed to play outside."

"You listen to Eric. He's practicing how to keep a family safe, so if he closes the curtains, you leave them closed. It's kind of a test for him. You don't want him to fail, do you?"

"No, Grandpa. I want him to pass with flying colors." She paused before continuing, "Grandpa, colors can't fly, can they?"

Bill smiled. "Sure they can, honey."

"But how?"

"Sometimes when it rains, and the sun comes out, you can see a rainbow in the sky. They're flying colors."

"Oh! You're so smart, Grandpa. I'll be a really good girl."

"I know you will, sweetheart. I love you. Can I speak to your mommy?"

"Sure. Love you too, Grandpa. Here she is."

Kimberley took the phone and said, "Hello, Bill. How are you doing and how's the case going?"

"We've had a few hiccups, but we're working our way through them."

"Guess that means you haven't found her yet."

"No, but our team is working extremely hard to locate her."

"I know they are, but how are you doing?"

"As good as can be expected. I'm an old man trying to keep up with officers half my age."

Kimberley knew her time was limited, so she reassured Bill. "I love you Bill, and I know you'll find her."

"Thanks honey. I need to speak to Richard."

"Here he is."

She passed the phone to him. "Hi, Bill. What's the update?"

"Richard, we haven't found her yet and we're not even sure she's still alive. Please don't say anything until we're sure."

"Okay." He then inquired, "How are you holding up?"

"I'm too old for this, but you know Jenny wouldn't give up, so neither can I. We will need you close by for the takedown."

"I'll be there, but I'll need my medical bag from the hospital. I want to be prepared for whatever she needs."

"I'll make that happen. I really need to go and call Beatrice. She's probably worried sick."

"Knowing her, she is probably praying steady and waiting anxiously for you to call her. Good luck, Bill, and call when you need me."

"Will do." Bill hung up and paused for a few moments before he called Beatrice. Somehow, he had to speak with confidence to set her mind at ease. He called Glen's number, knowing that if he waited too long, he would lose his nerve.

"Hello, Bill. I was hoping to hear from you. How's the case going?"

"Not as well as I had hoped. We seem to be running from one brick wall into another. We have eliminated lots of locations, but we're still no closer to finding her." Bill took a deep breath. "I'm not convinced she's still alive. I may have screwed up."

Glen responded, "I doubt that. Just remember, to catch a criminal you have to think like one. Tom has no idea what you and your team are capable of doing." He then added, "What's your gut telling you?"

"I'm not one hundred percent sure she's dead, and Don told me that if we don't have a body, then we have to assume she's still alive."

"Good advice. You remember the old rule we learned in the academy."

"What's that?"

"Follow the evidence, leave no stone unturned."

"Everyone is working hard, and they're being so positive, it gives me hope that we'll find her in time. If by some chance we don't, Tom won't know what hit him. I'm sure no one would say a word if I shot him at the scene."

"I'm assuming that you don't have a gun, Bill. Besides, that's your heart talking, not your conscience. Even if no one would say a word, that's not quite how it works, and you know it. He needs to be tried for kidnapping with intent to murder. That would put him back behind bars and reunite him with all his buddies." Glen chuckled. "Listen Bill, Beatrice is right beside me and trying to grab the phone out of my hands. She really wants to talk to you."

"I'm sure she does. Put her on the line."

"Hang in there and call once this case comes to a head." He then passed the phone to Beatrice.

"Bill, are you there?"

He could tell from the tone of her voice that she was about to break down in tears. He somehow had to be strong for her. "I'm here, darling. How are you holding up?"

"Are you kidding me? I should be asking you that."

"I'm doing okay, just a little tired."

"How close are you and the team to finding her?"

"We're slowly eliminating locations and hope to have her safely in our hands before the day is out." Bill really hoped she believed him. He couldn't let her down.

"You be careful out there. We all want Jenny back, but we also want you back in one piece too." Her voice sounded choked up as she whispered, "I love you, Bill. I sure hope this is over soon." More lightly, she added, "Maybe you'll be home for supper."

"I can't make any promises. Listen, honey, I have a phone call soon and I need to prepare myself for it. I love you and will call when I have any new information."

"Okay. I love you too."

Bill hung up and took a few moments to regroup before leaving Don's office. Once he'd returned to the common area, he walked over to the table where Daniel was waiting for him. "Two minutes to your three o'clock call," Daniel said. "Are you ready for this?"

"I sure hope so." Just like clockwork, the phone rang. Bill picked it up, deciding to test the waters. "Hello, Tom. You and your brother Charles are like twins. Charles was an excellent adversary and you're proving to be the same, but in the end, you'll lose just like he did. It's scary to think two wackos can exist in the same family."

"Let's cut the bullshit and get down to business."

"Before we continue with this conversation, put Jenny on the line."

"Actually, Jenny isn't available."

"Then this conversation is over."

Bill hung up the phone, still unsure whether she was dead or alive and hoping he hadn't made things worse. He looked at Daniel, whose face was also showing signs of stress. He felt like the wind had been kicked out of his lungs, and breathing wasn't an available option for him.

It seemed forever before the phone rang again, but actually it was only a few minutes later, and Bill signed in relief. He picked it up. "Hello, Tom. I told you that if I called and Jenny wasn't available, this game was officially over."

"If you don't want her dead, then you'd better shut up and listen."

"What's to say she's still alive?"

"If I say she's still alive, then she is."

"Do you expect me to believe a kidnapper and murderer?"

"Don't piss me off, Bill."

"Why not? You're pissing me off."

"Trust me, she's alive, but for how long depends on you."

"What the hell does that mean?"

"Let's talk for a minute, and then we'll get down to business."

"Without talking to Jenny, I have no business to discuss with you."

"If you hang up on me again, I won't call back. I'll walk away from here and leave Jenny to suffocate to death. The decision is entirely up to you."

"What do you mean; suffocate?" Bill demanded. "What have you done to her?"

"In time, Bill. Don't be so impatient. We need time to chit-chat before we get down to business. Do you know what your problem is, Bill?"

"I'm sure you're going to tell me."

"You're far too impatient."

"Why wouldn't I be? Jenny's life is on the line. She might not mean anything to you anymore, but she's important to all of us here in the force, and to Blue Ridge." Bill paused. "The force doesn't give a flying shit about you. I'm sick and tired of you grumbling about being abused in prison, taking a ride in a commercial dryer, and whatever else happened to you. Jenny was probably sick and tired of your bellyaching too."

Bill switched the receiver to his opposite ear. "When you killed Joan Wilks, did you honestly think you wouldn't be charged? When you saw the prison walls towering above you, lined with barb wire, did you think you were entering a five-star, all-inclusive resort? You were put there to keep you away from society until you served your time. Once you were given early parole, you weren't even smart enough to keep your nose clean."

Tom was silent at the other end of the line, but Bill could almost feel him seething. He went on: "Did you really think that if she rejected you, you could start over by wooing her? She might have fallen for you again, but instead, you took the wrong path. You lost your last chance to be with her."

Tom shouted, "You think you're such a big shot, but in my eyes, you're just a loser." Tom started laughing as he asked, "Were you ever good at math in school?"

"What has that got to do with anything?"

"I'm merely asking. Before we hang up, I have a math question for you to solve."

Bill felt nervous as he waited for Tom to speak again.

"If you can't solve it, then maybe one of your colleagues can help you." Tom paused for dramatic effect. "Okay, here we go. You have a steel container that is eight feet high, eight feet wide, and twenty feet long. It's locked shut, and all the cracks around the door are sealed with duct tape."

Bill waited. He didn't like how Tom's question was panning out.

"Oh, yeah, I almost forgot. Jenny is sealed inside. She's been in there for at least forty minutes. My question for you is, how long before she suffocates? Since you think you're so high and mighty, let's see if you can figure that one out."

The line went dead.

Bill felt sick to his stomach as he approached the white board and picked up the marker. He added, "Jenny put in container" and slowly replaced the cap onto the marker. Bill looked anywhere in the precinct as long as it didn't involve looking at any officers. He didn't want to be the center of attention and have the officers in the station staring at him, knowing that he screwed up. He had to keep his feelings to himself.

Tom was really proud of himself. The hours had ticked by and the afternoon was coming to a close, and he was in complete control. He took a seat outside the room and lit up a cigarette. He was slowly breaking Bill down; by the time this ordeal was over, he would be a mere shell of a man, overtaken by grief. Tom only wished he could see the high and mighty retired sergeant face to face. At some point, that would happen, because Bill still had to deliver the money. With that much cash, Tom could live anywhere on the planet, eat expensive meals, and load up on umbrella drinks as often as he wanted.

Tom decided to visit the container and see if Jenny was still alive. He slammed his fist against the metal container, but got no reaction. If she wasn't dead yet, she could be very soon.

"You alive in there?"

When he got no response, he returned to his chair on the porch.

Chapter Twelve

2:20 p.m. - 3:15 p.m.

WHEN JENNY HAD FIRST BEEN locked inside the container, she was overcome with fear. She'd twisted, turned, and pulled on the ropes that bound
her to the arms of her chair. All she managed to accomplish was sore wrists
from the ropes biting into her flesh. She suspected that they were bleeding;
as a warm, sticky sensation ran down both arms. The ropes around her legs
were so tight she couldn't move them at all. She was, however, able to move
her toes to keep the blood circulating. She could shift her bum slightly, but
that accomplished nothing.

She'd screamed in frustration. "Tom, you bastard, if I get out of here, I'll
kill you myself!"

Now reality had begun to set in. Would she ever get out of this hellhole,
or would she die in this dark, cold container? She wasn't sure of its' size or
whether there were cracks in its' framing to allow even the slightest bit of
air to seep in. How long before her oxygen ran out? Preserving air had to
be her top priority. Exertion meant depleting her oxygen supply that much
quicker. She had to remain calm and in control of the situation.

Jenny started shivering; as her body slowly succumbed to the late afternoon temperature. It was slowly starting to get cold in this metal container.
Her wrists were starting to swell, causing a throbbing sensation up her
arms and a tingling in her fingers. With the ropes holding her legs to the
chair, she couldn't move her bum around enough to distribute her weight
differently. How she hated Tom right now. She shook her head, determined
not to let Tom enter her thoughts.

If only she could turn back the clock and once again have the man she
married by her side. But she was haunted by the vision of his beady eyes,
looking at her with disdain.

She forced her mind off Tom and back to her situation. The temperature in the container was slowly dropping and Jenny could feel her body fighting to retain the little heat she still had. Maybe she wouldn't make it out alive after all. Tears streamed down her face, but she wasn't able to brush them away. If she was indeed going to suffocate, Jenny hoped it would be painless. She practiced shallow breathing in hopes of saving oxygen.

Time moved slowly in her confined space and the words that came out of her mouth were a mere whisper: "I can do this. I don't want to die. Find me, Bill, please find me in time." She kept repeating these words over and over until she finally fell asleep from exhaustion.

She wasn't able to control her dreams. She was going through a whirlwind of nightmares and emotions. Jenny was thrown back into the past where once again she and Claire were in that dirty rundown cabin with Charles standing over her. He was threatening her to keep that baby quiet or else. Jenny was constantly trying to keep him calm while secretly sending Bill messages. She started trembling and cowered in fear as she recalled the incident where Charles raised his gun and pointed it in her direction. At the last moment he turned the weapon away from her and pulled the trigger. He stormed out of the cabin in a mad rage. When he returned, she realized that Charles wasn't sure if he had shot her or not, so she held Claire close and pretended to be dead. She drifted in and out of her dream before once again being thrown back into her nightmare. Bill was in front of her at the cabin when Charles shot her in the back. Jenny relived the pain of that bullet tearing through her body, and then she passed out. Her next horror was visualizing Bill on the ground, having been shot by Charles and not knowing how he was.

She jarred awake, remembering the day that Bill was shot and was thankful for the fact that his badge took the bullet and deflected it away from his heart and into his shoulder. Her thoughts were of Bill and how was he holding up under the stress? He was a good man, dedicated to the force, a wonderful husband, father to Kimberley and, best of all, a grandfather to Claire. When she'd found out Charles had shot him outside the cabin all those years ago, she felt responsible for the event. If she hadn't gone willingly with Charles, it wouldn't have put Bill at risk. Bill had simply waved it off as being in the wrong place at the wrong time. He had found her back then, and he would find her now.

Darkness had always made her anxious, and she started hyperventilating, which wasn't a good thing to do right now. She closed her eyes and pretended she was sleeping in bed, warm blankets surrounding her, trying hard to think of better times. But Tom's beady eyes and yelling voice seemed to dominate her thoughts. His face, which had once made her want to cuddle up next to him, now made her feel nauseous. She felt disgusted to be wearing his prison uniform. He'd had no right to chop off her hair, purposely making her look hideous. At least Jenny's hair would grow back. If there had ever been a chance that they might get back together, it was now lost forever. When he put her inside the hideous container, she never wanted to see him again. Tom had to finally know that it was over between the two of them.

Jenny wasn't sure of the time, but the chill of the late afternoon was setting in on her. The blanket Tom had placed over her legs only kept the lower part of her body warm. Every other part of her was slowly succumbing to the chill that was seeping into the container. The metal of the unit seemed to attract the cold, and her feet were starting to go numb. The only thing Jenny could do was try to keep her toes moving in hopes of warming them up.

"Please find me, Bill," she murmured. "I don't want to die here."

The tears started running down her cheeks like a stream in the spring, melting the winter snow. Afraid of dying, Jenny chose to recall the good times, the ones that didn't involve Tom or his crazy brother Charles. She tried to push both of them into her past and bury them forever in the back of her mind.

She thought of all the people from Blue Ridge who meant something to her. She had kept close to home for a long time after the murder, mostly because she had nowhere else to go. Despite the threatening phone calls, Jenny had been determined not to be a recluse; she still had to go to work, do the shopping, and run all her other errands. On weekends, when she wasn't working, Jenny loved to sit on the front porch in the morning, cup of tea in hand. That became a special time for her, as she was able to meet some of her neighbors. They waved to her whenever they saw her outside.

She especially liked it when, on some Saturdays, they would join her on the porch with their beverage of choice, which was usually coffee. It didn't take Jenny long to discover that the gentleman across the street was blind, but when he went for walks in the morning with his dog, he somehow sensed her presence and greeted her verbally or sometimes with a simple wave.

One of the best decisions she had made was to rent out one of her spare bedrooms. It provided her with not only extra income, but also someone to talk to at the end of the day. She was tired of living alone and barely making ends meet. Slowly, life had started to come back into focus. She learned quickly that a woman doesn't have to be married to feel fulfilled. She had her job, her house, her neighbors, and the police, who were actively looking out for her and of course, her close friends, the Jacksons and the Smithes.

She hoped this chapter would end happily, with her being rescued, but right now she only saw doom and gloom and a cloudy future. It was like she was looking through a window covered in frost. If only she could use her hands, she could wipe the frost away and see what her future held. Tears welled up in her eyes again, running down her cheeks and wetting her clothing. She had to get control of her emotions, or that dampness would compound the chills running through her upper body.

Jenny slowly opened her eyes to total darkness, and then quickly closed them tight again. Maybe this exercise would help her overcome her fear of the dark and help her regulate her oxygen levels. Her decision was made. She took it slow at first, gradually allowing her eyes to stay open for longer periods of time before once again closing them. She wasn't sure how long she practiced this exercise, but it did get easier with time, and eventually, she realized the darkness didn't bother her so much now. If she could over-come that fear, then she could do anything.

The constant silence was starting to play mind games with her. There were two things she was determined to do: survive this hell hole and walk out of this container under her own steam. She also didn't want to walk out a raving maniac, so keeping her mind on positive thoughts was at the top of her list.

She thought of Claire. Back in that scary cabin, after Charles had kid-napped them, Jenny had held Claire—just a baby then—in her arms and known she had to protect her at all costs. When Claire's tiny fingers had grabbed onto her thumb, she was smitten. Jenny would have died before she allowed Charles to lay a hand on her. From that moment on, she and Claire had a strong bond that couldn't be broken. Jenny had given her the nickname of Claire Bear, after her favourite teddy bear that slept in her crib when she was a toddler. Being around her had made Jenny want to have children of her own, but sadly, Tom wouldn't be their father. Maybe someday she would find someone she could trust enough to settle down and start a family.

Jenny's teeth chattered. It was becoming difficult to stay within her dream world. Thoughts of the people she loved were comforting, but it wasn't enough to stop the effects of the cold on her body. Tom's uniform wasn't heavy enough to keep her warm, and her short hair no longer covered her ears. Chills were starting to set in. Was the end nearer than she'd originally thought? Would she die suffocating or freezing to death? Whichever it was, she just hoped it was quick and painless. Her head slumped against her chest as she began to slip into oblivion.

She was roused by a noise overhead. At first, she thought she was still within a dream. A very bad dream. Tears started streaming down her face once again as she realized her nightmare was real, but at least she was still alive. How long had she been unconscious? Was she out for a matter of minutes, or had it been hours? More importantly, how much oxygen was left in the container? She had no way of knowing when time was mysteriously moving forward. The total darkness inside the container didn't tell her much. All she knew was that it wasn't the next morning.

She heard that mysterious noise a second time. Pinecones were dropping onto the top of the container. She was relieved it wasn't the bogeyman, although she no longer feared the dark. She also heard scurrying around the inside of the container and realized that there were also mice inhabiting the space. She hoped and prayed they wouldn't find their way onto her body, knowing she couldn't stop them from biting her.

She whispered, "Where are you, Bill? I really need a miracle. I don't know how much longer I can last in here. I'm starting to lose my mind and I'm so cold." She paused when her stomach growled. When had she last eaten? "I'm also starving."

Jenny tried to visualize a warm blanket being draped over her after Bill and his team found her. Maybe the team would bring two blankets. How she longed for warmth.

She allowed herself to fall into another dream, one where she was with the love of her life, Tom. He would saunter into her workplace daily to get a cup of coffee and flirt with her. He was so handsome, and a perfect gentleman. She was thrilled to see him every day and was excited when he finally asked her out on a date. Everything had been magical until she was introduced to his brother Charles. It was obvious that he didn't like her. But Jenny wasn't concerned about Charles, as she was marrying Tom, not his brother.

Next, she dreamt of the two of them on their wedding day. She was in a white dress; Tom was in a suit. They had pledged their love to each other that day.

That vision dissolved. Now she saw Tom's beady eyes glaring into hers, and heard him swearing to kill her. Her body jerked as if hit by a lightning bolt, and she was suddenly wide awake.

Relieved that she was still alive, Jenny shivered, colder than she was before. Trying to shift on her chair, she felt a hint of warmth enter her body, but knew it wouldn't last long. Maybe if she slept again, death would be quick and painless. She realized she wouldn't get to say goodbye to her family and friends. Overwhelmed with sorrow, Jenny whispered, "Goodbye, everyone. I love you all."

Jenny closed her eyes for what she thought could very well be the last time, but was startled awake again as she heard the container's rusty doors opening. Bill was standing in front of her. Jenny was relieved when she saw him.

His voice muffled, Bill asked, "Are you okay?"

Jenny smiled. "You found me."

"I said I would, and here I am." He cut the ropes that bound her arms and legs. "Are you able to get up and walk?"

Jenny nodded, but when she tried to stand, she couldn't move. It was then that she realized the door wasn't open and Bill wasn't there. She had only dreamt it.

There was no controlling her tears at that point. They flowed freely until she was exhausted. Bill and his team had tried their best, but it was too late.

She visualized Beatrice, Richard, Kimberley, and Claire all sitting in the same room, the adults all worried sick. Claire wouldn't have a clue what was going on. It was better that way, less traumatic for her. But the Jacksons, Bill and Beatrice, and the force had a real connection to Jenny. They had all survived Claire's kidnapping, so Jenny knew they would survive this one too. The only thing that bothered her was that she wouldn't be alive to see the police take Tom down.

Defeated, Jenny chose oblivion until she entered the next life. She only hoped that Bill could accept that he had tried his best and would make sure her body went back to Blue Ridge for a proper burial, assuming he managed to find her body.

She dropped her head forward and went peacefully to sleep.

Chapter Thirteen

3:15 p.m. - 3:50 p.m.

BILL WAS OUT OF HIS league. A look of defeat overtaking his face, he got up and approached Don's office. He tapped lightly on the door before asking, "Can I come in?"

Don looked up from his paperwork, already knowing something else had gone drastically wrong. "Sure. Take a seat."

Bill stepped into the room, closing the door behind him, and fell into the chair.

"What's going on?"

"Jenny's going to die and there's nothing I can do to prevent it."

Don sighed. "There's always something that can be done. Talk to me."

"Tom's sealed Jenny in a container, and if we don't find her in time, she'll suffocate."

"Oh, crap, Bill. I'm sorry, but remember, we don't give up. All Tom did was push up our timeline. He's forcing our hand, so more than ever we need to step up our game. Stay in constant contact with him and hope he slips up. When he does, we'll pounce."

Bill sighed and looked up at the ceiling. "I'm like a fish out of water, floundering to breathe. I'm fresh out of energy and my luck is not far behind. Jenny was counting on me, and I've failed miserably."

"Did Tom say how long she'd been in the container?"

"Supposedly around forty minutes. I have no idea how long before she runs out of air." Bill looked at Don. "I'm not as worried about her running out of oxygen as I am about the temperature inside the container. If we don't find her soon, she'll freeze to death."

Don crossed his arms and appeared to be thinking. He got up and walked to the window.

Bill studied him. "What you're thinking?"

Don turned back to Bill, crossed the room, and opened his door, finding Daniel about to knock on it. Behind him stood two uniformed police officers.

Don was surprised. "What's up, Daniel?"

"Here's our backup from Sidville," Daniel said. "These are Constable Cassandra Clarkson and Constable Butch Mitchell."

Don and Bill shook both constables' hands. "Thanks for coming," Don said. "We sure could use the extra help."

Cassandra responded, "Glad to be of service. What've you got so far?"

Don motioned the group over to the whiteboard. "We'll fill you in on what we know so far." Don started at the top of the board and worked his way briskly to the bottom, not forgetting any details.

Butch took in the information on the board. "That's a lot of clues. This Tom Lockman has a record for murder and now he's added kidnapping to his wrap sheet. What's his history?"

Don answered, "He and his brother Charles had a sister that died of crib death years ago and the parents blamed both boys for her death. The two boys were abandoned shortly after that and managed to survive living on the streets for years. Charles was the aggressive one and fought battles for the two of them during their youth and teenage years. Tom became a successful mechanic in town, while Charles remained homeless and was constantly in trouble. Years later when Tom heard that his parents committed suicide, he went off the deep end and killed a woman. Of course he went to jail. Five years later Charles found out that his brother Tom wasn't doing too well behind bars, so he tried to get him released. He tricked his brother's wife Jenny into helping with his charade. She was unaware of his plan until she was in the midst of it. In the dark of night he kidnapped a small child, who unfortunately had medical problems. She was born with infant diabetes and Charles wasn't aware of her condition." He paused before continuing, "Unfortunately that child was the granddaughter of Bill Smithe who was the Sergeant at the time. Bill had testified against him in court. The child also belonged to one of our local doctors, Doctor Richard Jackson, who also testified against Tom Lockman. The team had to find both Jenny and Claire before the child died."

Bill added, "We did find them in time, but Claire was in poor condition. Luckily her father was there to treat her immediately and monitor her until she arrived at the hospital. Unfortunately the team had to take Charles down." He added, "Charles was diagnosed with schizophrenia years earlier and it seems that Tom is now experiencing the same symptoms."

Cassandra listened before asking, "He sounds like a real piece of work. What's your next move; and how can we help?"

Daniel approached the group standing in front of the whiteboard. "Sorry to interrupt, boss. When I heard that Jenny was sealed inside a container, I took it upon myself to make a few phone calls. I phoned the municipal office and asked to speak to anyone who would know where empty containers in town are located. I spoke to a Colin Brooks, who just faxed me a list of locations. There are only two places in Blue Ridge that have containers. One is the local train station and the other is a construction site beside the local swimming pool. I called the pool first and found out that the container on site is used as a contractors' lunchroom and for tool storage, so that was a dead end. Next, I called the local train station and spoke to the supervisor there. He reassured me that the few containers they had on site weren't taped shut."

Daniel continued, "He did, however, also tell me that there are about half a dozen more a few miles outside of town. They're bound for the scrapyard, so they've been removed from the train station, to a few miles out of town and placed by a side track. Sounds to me like this location is a container grave site."

Don looked at Bill. "If Tom somehow heard about these containers, then that would be a good place to hide Jenny. It's isolated, no one around for miles, plus Debbie's theory around the fifteen minutes clue falls into play. We need to send a team to check out the site."

"I agree." Reinvigorated with hope, Bill turned to Daniel. "Thanks for making those calls."

"Anything for you, Bill."

Don turned to Cassandra and Butch. "I hate to throw the two of you into the deep end, but drastic times call for drastic measures." Don picked up the marker and added "Butch and Cassandra containers in town."

Butch responded, "Where do we find these containers?"

"The train station is on the north side of town. You and Cassandra go over there and get the location of those containers. Tom told us that Jenny is sealed inside, so look for signs that they're sealed shut. Call for backup if you need it."

Butch responded, "On our way." The two officers left the building.

Bill looked over at Don. "Hopefully this is the break we need to solve the case."

"I hope so too."

The train station was barely five minutes from the precinct, so Butch and Cassandra were there in no time. In the lobby, Cassandra saw the secretary and approached her. After introducing herself, she said, "I'm looking for your supervisor."

She responded, "I'm sorry. He had to step out."

"When will he be back?"

"He didn't say. Is there anything I can help you with?"

Cassandra looked around the room and spotted a map of the rail lines between Blue Ridge and Sidville. She approached the map and turned to the secretary. "We understand that there are about half a dozen empty containers just outside of town. By any chance, do you know where they are on this map?"

"I do. Just give me a minute to find the paperwork." A few minutes later, the secretary approached the map and placed a red tack on their location.

Butch inquired, "How far is that from here?"

"Approximately twenty minutes."

"Is it possible for us to drive the entire distance?"

"I'm not sure what condition the road is in, but you should be able to drive the entire distance. It's a rough road that runs beside the tracks."

"Thanks for your help."

"Not a problem. I hope you find what you're looking for."

Both officers returned to their vehicle and set off down the access road that ran parallel to the tracks.

Butch sighed. "Blue Ridge shouldn't be going through this nightmare a second time. Those Lockman brothers are both bad news. Once Charles was eliminated, one would've thought that Tom would get his shit together. Sounds like this Jenny is living her worst nightmare again."

Cassandra nodded. "This team has been working hard since ten o'clock this morning." She paused. "They are committed to finding her before it's too late. Fingers crossed that it has a happy ending."

Butch responded, "They certainly are pulling out all the stops to find her in time."

"They must be frustrated as each lead proves to be a dead end." She then added, "They won't quit until the case is solved. It could be a long day for everyone."

"Tired officers can sometimes get sloppy."

"That's why we work in teams. We cover for each other. Besides, there's no room for sloppiness. Not when it means someone could die. Jenny sounds like a strong woman, a real fighter. Let's just hope she doesn't give up."

"I get the impression she isn't a quitter."

"I sure hope you're right."

Butch picked up his radio. "I'm going to call it in."

Cassandra responded with a simple nod.

Daniel picked up the radio. "Hey, guys. How did you make out?"

Butch updated Daniel. "Secretary told us the location of the containers and we're on our way there now. We should be checking them out in about fifteen to twenty minutes."

"Perfect. Keep me updated."

"Copy that."

Butch hung up the radio and looked across at his partner. "You might want to consider slowing down. This road isn't ideal for high speed."

The cruiser hit a pot hole, jarring the two officers.

Cassandra braked slightly. "I should but time isn't actually on our side. Jenny is on borrowed time, and if luck is on our side, the vehicle won't let us down."

"I sure hope you're right."

Cassandra glanced at Butch. "Judging from what we heard back at the station, do you have any ideas about Tom's overall plan?"

Butch looked over at his partner. "My gut tells me that maybe the money isn't his initial plan. Killing Bill has to be at the top of his list. Revenge can be overpowering. What concerns me even more is, if he manages to kill

Bill, will he go after the Doctor who also testified against him. His revenge has to go deep."

"I agree. Do you think he's capable of killing Jenny?"

"If she rejected him; definitely. My best guess is that he thinks this is a game. It reminds me of my college days when my roommates and I used to play chess."

Cassandra laughed. "That goes back quite a few years." She swerved to avoid another deep pothole, but quickly regained control of the vehicle.

"It does, but the rules of the game still apply here."

"How so?"

"Tom is treating Bill and the team like chess pieces. He plans to slowly eliminate the team until only Bill is left."

"Are you saying that we're going to lose officers?"

"Not at all. I think Tom wants the team scrambling off in all directions in hopes of getting Bill all to himself."

"That's not going to happen. The team is committed to finding Jenny and protecting Bill at all costs. We need to outwit the bastard and take him down. We can win this, can't we?" She added, "Without losing any of our players?"

His answer was one word: "Checkmate."

They drove along the gravel road slowly getting closer to their search site. Butch was looking out the passenger side window when Cassandra slammed on the brakes. The vehicle skidding to a stop.

She looked across at him, and then screamed. "Shit. Hang on!"

The road beneath them was falling away leaving their cruiser's front and back bumpers perilously stuck between two sides of the embankment.

Both officers were thrown forward, and Butch put his hands forward to avoid impact and hit his head on the side window. Cassandra avoided the same injury by grasping the steering wheel tightly and hanging on to it. She looked over at her partner and noticed the gash on his forehead.

Butch grabbed his forehead. "What the heck?"

"You okay?"

Butch was disoriented. "I think so, although my head hurts like hell."

A torrent of swirling water had opened beneath them and was about to gobble up their cruiser with them in it.

"Hang in there, partner." Cassandra looked out her window, assessing their situation. She noticed that the tires on her side of the vehicle were still spinning. Below them ran a raging stream. Glancing to her left she saw the culvert that ran under the train tracks. It was still intact, but the portion under the access road had obviously failed.

She looked at Butch. "Okay, partner. We need to get out of here. I don't know how long before the bank gives way, and we're not hanging around to find out. Can you undo your seat belt?"

Butch nodded and hit the release button. "I'm assuming you have a plan?"

Cassandra undid her seat belt and carefully opened her window. "I'm going to climb out the window and get on the roof. Once I'm there, you need to follow me. I'll be standing on the opposite side of the cruiser to distribute the weight."

"What happens if the vehicle falls?"

"We don't have far to fall, so we'll probably live, but I'm not sure how deep the water is below us."

"Let's hope it isn't too deep." He looked at Cassandra. "What're you waiting for?"

Butch watched Cassandra slip through the window, knowing that she would grab the light bar on the roof, to pull herself up. The vehicle rocked as she climbed onto the roof and moved to the passenger side.

"Okay, Butch, your turn."

"Wish me luck."

"Just take it slow. I may have to move up here to counteract your weight."

Butch slowly moved towards the window. "Do you think our station will forgive us for destroying their cruiser?"

"Damn it, Butch. Stay focused."

"I am. I'm just nervous. I weigh a lot more than you, so I'm not totally sure how you can judge the weight distribution."

"Just leave that up to me."

Butch worked his way out of the window and was soon on the roof at the opposite end of the vehicle. He looked at her. "What do we do now?"

"I'm going to slowly work my way towards the end of the vehicle. I think I can climb back up to the road. Once I'm there, you'll do the same thing. Whatever we do, we don't do it suddenly."

"I'll be right behind you."

Cassandra slowly worked her way down to the trunk and found a root dangling in front of her. She gently pulled on it and hoped it would hold her weight. She glanced back at her partner. "Here goes nothing." Using the root as leverage, she pulled herself up onto solid ground. "That was easy. Now it's your turn."

Butch wiped the blood from his forehead. "Here goes nothing." He crept toward the back of the vehicle, and with each movement, the cruiser shifted. Once on the trunk, he took hold of the root and started to pull himself up. But then the vehicle started to drop out from under him, and he panicked. "Nooo."

Cassandra quickly flew into action. She yelled, "Grab my hand!"

Butch reached up with his free hand to grab hers. He looked into her eyes. "If you can't pull me up, you have to let me go."

Cassandra was straining to speak and hold him at the same time. "That's not going to happen. Use the root to try and lift yourself higher. I can get you out, but I'll need you to help me."

Butch was scared. He wasn't convinced that Cassandra was strong enough to pull him up. His right foot found a large stone deeply embedded in the soil. Taking a chance, he used it as leverage to move several feet closer to the surface while Cassandra strained to pull him to safety. Butch managed to get his right knee on solid ground and Cassandra grabbed the back of his uniform to haul him all the way onto the bank. Both officers collapsed into a heap, gasping for air.

Butch turned to his partner. "Thanks. You're stronger that you look."

"Must be all the weightlifting I do at the gym three days a week."

"I owe you my life."

"You would've done the same for me, although I would've been easier to lift out of that damn hole."

The two officers looked down into the hole that had just swallowed up their cruiser. Butch commented. "It's no wonder that the road collapsed. Look at that culvert."

Cassandra glanced at the void below them. The culvert was completely rusted out. "I'm surprised that it didn't collapse earlier. Lucky the tracks haven't gone out yet."

She glanced across at Butch. "How's the head doing?"

He touched it gingerly. "Well, it's stopped bleeding and it's not too sore." Butch pulled the radio from his pocket. "Good thing I didn't lose the damn radio. I guess we have to call Don and tell them about our vehicle."

"Glad it's you and not me."

Butch called the station.

"Daniel here. What's up, guys?"

"Well, we haven't made it to the containers yet."

"I thought you were only fifteen to twenty minutes away."

"We were but we ran into a glitch or should I say gulch."

"What happened?"

"There's no delicate way to say this, but we fell into a sinkhole. There was an underground stream raging beneath the road and as luck would have it; it fell away when we were on top of it."

Daniel was in disbelief. "Are you serious?"

Butch answered, "I'm not making this stuff up."

"I'll send someone out to pick you up."

"Not yet. We're still able to get to the containers so will call once we've checked them out."

"Keep me updated."

"On our way." Butch put away the radio and turned to Cassandra. "Let's check out those containers."

Daniel went to Don's office to give him an update. Bill was also there, waiting for news.

Don could already tell from the look on Daniel's face that it didn't go well. "What's up?"

"I just heard from Butch and Cassandra." He paused. "They ran into some trouble on the way to the container site."

Don looked worried. "What kind of trouble?"

"They lost their vehicle in a sinkhole; fortunately the two of them are fine. They're walking the rest of the way and will search the site. They'll get back to me once they've checked out the area." He then added, "We'll have to send someone out to pick them up once they're finished."

Bill shook his head. "Oh shit. Can anything else possibly go wrong today?"

Don answered, "One would hope not. Thanks Daniel. Keep me and Bill updated. See if anyone from the team can spare thirty minutes to go get them."

"Will do." Daniel returned to the common area and glanced around the room, looking for someone who didn't seem too busy. He walked over to Sam's desk. "Are you available to pick up Butch and Cassandra from the train station?"

Sam looked confused. "Sure, but what happened?"

"Apparently a sinkhole swallowed up their vehicle." He then added, "They're fine."

"Sure. Just let me know where and when to go."

"Will do. Thanks."

After walking along the tracks for five minutes or so, they came upon the containers. Both officers drew their weapons and walked in two different directions. The containers were set well away from the tracks in a neat row, with a slight gap between each unit. Butch took the back while Cassandra walked along the front, examining the containers as she moved from one to the next.

They regrouped at the other end.

Butch looked at her. "No sign of any vehicle here."

She responded, "And none of the units are taped shut. Guess we're finished here. Let's head back towards the train station."

Butch picked up the radio.

"Daniel here. Are you two okay?"

"We are, but the containers were a bust. No sign of any vehicle and none of the containers were taped shut."

"Okay. I'll send Sam out to pick you up."

"Tell him we'll be the two officers who look like they've been dragged through hell."

"Copy that."

Daniel nodded and Sam picked up his vehicle keys and left the building.

Daniel approached Don's office and shook his head. "Sorry, boss, another dead end." He could see the disappointment in Bill's face.

Bill just couldn't handle another dead end. "Is there anything else that could possibly go wrong today?" He sighed. "I'm going outside for some fresh air before my four o'clock call." He chuckled wearily. "You wouldn't by any chance have alcohol in your desk, would you?"

"Sorry, can't help you with that one."

"It was just wishful thinking. You can't blame me for asking." Bill topped up his coffee and walked outside.

Don watched Bill leave the building. He got up from his chair, walked to the whiteboard, put a line through "Butch and Cassandra containers in town" and then once again studied the evidence in front of him.

A short time later, Sam arrived back at the station with Cassandra and Butch.

Chapter Fourteen

3:55 p.m. - 4:45 p.m.

AT FIVE MINUTES TO FOUR, Bill sat next to the phone to wait for Tom's call. He was tired and losing hope that Jenny could be found in time. No one in the office knew how long she could remain in that confined space before she died. There were too many variables. Was she screaming? Hyperventilating? Just plain giving up? Bill refused to believe that Jenny was a quitter; he had to believe she was a survivor.

When the phone rang, he hesitated before answering. Looking at Daniel to confirm the recorder was turned on. He answered, "Hello, Tom."

"Hey, Bill, you don't sound too upbeat."

"Why would I? There's an asshole out there trying to kill his wife."

"I'm sure, by now, you must realize that Jenny won't be alive by morning, so we need to step up the exchange to an earlier time."

Bill started to feel a glimmer of hope. "What time were you thinking? And where's the drop-off point?"

"Not sure right now, but I'll let you know on our five o'clock call."

"You're playing with fire, Tom. You need to get her out of that container right now."

"There's no rush. She has plenty of air left inside that box. But I never thought about how cold it would be in there. I did give her a blanket, but the temperature is dropping fast. It might actually go below freezing tonight."

"If she dies, you're as good as dead too."

"Let's not talk about Jenny right now. I would rather talk about myself."

"You go ahead and talk, but don't expect me to actually listen to your bullshit."

Tom asked, "Did you ever smoke?"

Bill was confused. "What's that got to do with anything?"

"I was just making small talk."

"Jenny doesn't have enough time for me to listen to your small talk."

Tom continued, "I never smoked before going to prison, but it became a habit that all inmates took up. Did you know that a cigarette could be a form of torture?"

Bill was silent.

"Are you still there?"

"Yes, I'm still on the line. What's your point?"

"I've never counted the scars on my back and chest to see how many times I was burned, but it was a lot. Those burns took a long time to heal, and in some cases, before that happened, I was burned again in the same spot. That really hurt."

Bill was growing angry. "Let's meet face to face. I can add a few more burns on you from Jenny."

"That wasn't nice."

"I'm nice to people who are nice to other people. Do you know what your real problem is?"

"You're my problem. I still don't have my money."

"I'm sick and tired of listening to you bitching." He mimicked Tom's voice. "'Oh, I was constantly beat up, took a ride in a commercial dryer, and then lost my best friend.'" Bill paused before continuing in his normal voice. "Now I have to listen to you complain about being burned with cigarettes. You're just a whiner. There's no simple way to get through to you. You were in prison among criminals. Did you think they would all turn out to be your best buddies?" Bill changed the subject. "If you have a brain in that stupid head of yours, you'd release Jenny before it's too late."

"You're too dramatic, Bill. She probably has lots of air left."

"And you know this because you got all A's in math at school?"

"Not exactly. I'm just hoping that you come through with the money, and when you open the container, she'll still be alive."

"I won't be opening the container; you will be. My team will have guns pointed directly at your head. If she's dead, you'll be treated like a living target. Unfortunately, you'll be dead after the first bullet, so you won't actually experience the other several dozen shots."

Daniel caught Bill's attention and whispered, "Zip it Bill. Don't let him suck you in. He's not worth it."

Bill paused, acknowledged Daniel, but reached across the table and turned off the recorder.

Daniel wasn't happy however he sat quietly listening to Bill's side of the conversation.

Bill never skipped a beat. "Maybe the team will start shooting your legs and work their way up to your head. Then you can experience the real meaning of wanting to be dead."

Tom was becoming angry. "You can't talk to me like that."

"I just did asshole."

Bill hung up. He took a deep breath before balling up his hands, allowing his nails to dig deep into the palms of his hands. He felt no pain, just frustration and a sense of failure. Bill was once again on a crazy roller coaster ride that he had no control over. He couldn't stop the falling sensation. He just hoped that at the bottom of the hill, the car would be able to maneuver around the bend and stop at the platform to let him off. He really needed to get off this crazy ride and put his mind back on the case.

He murmured, "Hang in there, Jenny. Come hell or high water, we'll find you." Bill looked across the table at Daniel. "He's pushing me too hard and I'm about to snap."

Daniel looked concerned. "Take a few deep breaths, it'll help."

Bill took his advice. "Thanks. I'm having trouble imagining a happy ending to this case."

Don had walked up behind Bill, and he could tell by his gestures that the latest call didn't go well. He placed a hand on his shoulder.

Bill turned to Don. "He won't let her out of the container. Unfortunately, no one can even guess how long she has."

"We'll figure it out, Bill."

"Time isn't on our side. We might be too late to save her."

"Let's go into my office. We need to talk," Don said.

Bill followed Don into his office and the two sat down. Don looked at Bill and saw only a shell of a man sitting across from him. "I know you're upset and feel like you're backed into a corner, but Jenny's really counting on us to find her."

Bill looked sadly at Don. "I can't let her down. I've never broken a promise in my entire life, and today isn't going to be that day." Bill paused. "You know, when we went to the police academy, we graduated thinking we could conquer the world. One thing we weren't taught was that the world is nothing but one problem after another. When we solve one case, another one always stands in front of us. How can the world be so screwed up?"

Bill got up and walked to the window. "That's why I left the big city and moved here. I thought a smaller town would have less crime, and then Charles Lockman threw that theory out the window. And just when I thought I was free of him, Tom appears out of nowhere. I guess he would've shown up eventually, but why didn't he take his second chance at freedom seriously?"

Don answered, "I'm not totally sure, but he seriously screwed up."

"Charles was the main reason I retired, but I was also afraid of what waited for me down the road. I could deal with B&Es, druggies, and the minor problems of a small town, but murder and kidnapping were deal-breakers for me. I was drowning in a world that I had no control over. Beatrice was my only reprieve. She was there every night when I got home from the office. She loved me unconditionally, but my job always worried her, especially after Charles shot me. She was so relieved when I chose to retire. It was the right thing to do for both of us."

Don got up and joined Bill at the window. Placing his hand on Bill's shoulder, he said, "Every town has problems. That's why the force is more than one person. Come with me." He directed Bill to his office door, and they looked out at the common area. "Do you see anyone sitting out there and doing nothing? I'm not even convinced that we've gone through much coffee today because everyone in this office is too busy working to find Jenny to make a pot. The burden is on all our shoulders, not just yours."

"You're right, but I still feel a failure."

"That's not fair. It sounds like you're giving up before we find her. I don't think that was a lesson taught at the academy." Don slapped him on the shoulder. "Let's go back and look at that damn whiteboard one more time."

They approached the whiteboard together, but still, it all seemed to muddle together for both men. Don frowned. "What're we missing?"

"I'm sorry, Don. I just can't clear my head. This case makes no sense." He turned to walk away, but then focused on the two children standing just inside the lunchroom door, watching him. He asked, "Are those the two boys that were found at that burned out house on Oak Crescent?"

"They are."

"Have they spoken yet?"

"Not yet. They're very shy, but if you talk to them, they might open up. You've always been so good with children. Besides, it'll take your mind off Jenny, even if it's for a short time."

Bill wasn't hopeful, but needed a change of pace. "You're probably right. I'll give it a shot."

Don returned to his office, while Bill walked towards the lunchroom and stood in front of the boys. "Hey, boys. My name is Bill Smithe. What're your names?"

The oldest boy looked Bill up and down before replying. "My name is Adam, and this is my brother, Michael."

Bill smiled. "It's nice to meet you boys. Do you have a last name?"

Both boys were silent.

"Have you ever been in a police station before?"

"No. This is our first time."

Bill glanced at the empty food wrappers on the table. "How was your lunch?" He could tell by the look on their faces that they'd enjoyed it. "How about I give you a tour of the building?"

Michael beamed. "Wow that would be cool."

Bill led them to Don's office and introduced them to him. "Don, this is Adam and Michael. He then turned to the boys and said, "This is Sergeant Don Wilson. He runs this entire office."

Adam studied Don and grinned. "He's what we would call a big shot."

Don broke out in laughter. "You might say that. Where are you boys from?"

Adam said, "We're from nowhere. We live near the old cannery with a bunch of older people."

"Where are your parents?"

Michael grabbed hold of his brother's hand and the two boys remained silent.

Bill interceded. "I'm just showing them around the place."

Don winked at the two boys. "Don't let him handcuff you."

Michael answered, "No, sir."

Bill turned the two boys towards the common area. "Let's go and meet a few of the officers. They're really busy, so we'll just say hi and leave them to their jobs."

The officers on duty were very responsive. Although they couldn't actually talk to the boys, they either waved or winked at them.

Bill took them around the perimeter of the room first, and showed them his picture on the wall next to all the previous sergeants—of course, the current one of Don.

Michael looked the photo and then looked at Bill. "Why is your picture on the wall? Are you a bad man?"

Bill laughed. "No, I used to be a big shot here until I retired."

Adam asked, "If you're retired, then why are you here today?"

Bill looked between both boys before speaking. "I'm just here to help with a case for a few days."

Michael saw a group of photos on another wall. "Did these people used to work here too?"

Bill answered, "No, these are missing people. We keep their pictures up to remind us that we still need to be looking for them."

Michael spotted the whiteboard and asked, "Can I draw on your board?"

Bill chuckled. "Sorry, but that board is too important to just draw on it."

Adam studied the board. "What does it all mean?"

Bill looked at the board. "This is a case we are actively working on. Every line is a clue to solving a mystery. We have solved some of the clues, while others we're still working on."

Adam pointed to the whiteboard and saw the address 22 Oak Crescent. "That's where you found us."

"It sure is. Do you mind if I ask you why you were there?"

Michael leaned into his older brother. "It's where we go when we're scared. We call it our safehouse."

Bill was concerned for the two boys. "Why do you need a safehouse?"

Adam answered, "It's a rule among the homeless people. If a child feels threatened at all, they go to a safehouse and wait for an adult to come and bring them back to the camp."

Bill took the boys back into the breakroom and sat across from them. Choosing his words carefully, he asked, "How long were you in that safehouse?"

Adam, being the oldest, answered Bill's question. "We went there last night."

"Why didn't you both go back to the cannery?"

"It wasn't safe."

"The cannery wasn't safe?"

"No, just the walk back to it."

"What happened last night? Did someone scare you?"

Michael whispered to his brother. "Don't tell him or he'll lock us up."

Bill was concerned, but smiled. "No one here is going to lock you up."

Michael now had tears in his eyes. "If we go outside, he might be waiting for us."

Bill reassured the boys. "No one is going to be waiting for you outside." He then asked, "What makes you think I would lock you both up?"

Michael answered, "Because we did something really bad."

"I doubt that, but let me be the judge of that. What did the two of you do?"

Adam answered, "We were in the park looking for food, and there was a man sitting on a bench. He had a bag next to him. We thought that maybe there was food in the bag, so we went to steal it, but he caught us. We got away, but he was chasing us, screaming and yelling. He said that he would cut off our hands for stealing his bag and then kill us. He told us that no one would find our bodies. We were really scared."

Michael started trembling and had tears running down his cheeks as he grabbed his brother's hand.

Bill felt sorry for the two boys. "I bet you were both really scared. What did this man look like?"

Adam appeared to be thinking. "It was dark and he wore dark clothes. It was hard for us to hide from him. He was getting so close to us, I threw a rock to distract him. When he turned to go back to the bench we ran to our safe house."

Adam looked at the whiteboard and asked, "That name at the top of the board, is he the man who was chasing us?"

"We're almost certain it was him."

"And you haven't found him yet?"

"No, but we're not giving up."

Adam then looked at the board again. "What does hostage mean?"

"It means that a person is taken against their will."

"So that lady doesn't want to be with him."

"That's right."

"How do you get her back?"

"Our team follows the evidence and sometimes a lucky tip solves the case."

Adam looked directly at Bill. "I want to be a policeman when I grow up. I like solving mysteries."

"I'm sure you'd make a fine officer one day."

Michael asked, "What do all those other lines on the board mean?"

"They're clues that we gather and follow up on."

"How do you get those clues?"

"The lady that he kidnapped has been able to talk to us on the phone and she has been giving us some of the clues."

Michael looked confused. "Doesn't the guy know what she's saying?"

"Nope. She is very good at the game."

Michael added, "I love games. Can we play?"

Bill responded, "How about we leave the clues for our police officers to solve."

Bill spotted Don walking towards him and got up to leave the room. "I'll be right back."

Michael looked excited as he asked, "If I had a clue, could I add it to the board?"

Bill stopped abruptly and turned to look at Michael. "Do you have a clue?"

Adam responded, "I think we might."

Don watched Bill and the two boys approach the whiteboard. Don looked puzzled as he joined the three of them.

Bill held his breath and took the cap off the marker and handed it to Michael. "Go ahead, son, give us another clue."

The entire force stopped what they were doing and watched the child move the marker to the bottom of the board. He stood still for a short time and then looked up with tears in his eyes.

Bill felt like the floor was falling out from under him. Maybe Michael didn't really have a clue at all; maybe he just wanted to draw on the board.

Adam went to take the marker from his younger brother. "I'll write it down."

Michael rebelled. "I'm not a baby. I can do it." He turned towards Bill with tears running down his cheek. "I really do have a clue, but don't know how to spell the word."

Adam took Michael's hand and smiled at his little brother. "I'll tell you the letters and you can print them on the board."

Bill's glimmer of hope immediately returned. He stood behind the two boys and watched as Adam whispered into Michael's ear. Slowly and with childlike printing, Michael formed the letters on the board. When he was done, he stepped aside revealing the word "Motel".

Bill stood for several moments in shock and disbelief.

Bill glanced at Michael and then at Don. He returned his attention to Michael. "Are you sure?"

Michael nodded. "He yelled that if he caught us, he was going to take us there and kill us. We were both really scared."

Bill turned to Adam. "Is this true?"

Adam acknowledged his younger brother with a simple nod.

Bill comforted both boys. "He can't hurt you anymore."

The team now came alive by the possibility that Jenny very well could be found alive.

Bill had tears in his eyes as he hugged both boys. "I think the two of you might have just solved our case."

Michael started jumping up and down. "Yeah! We're heroes."

"That you are."

The boys returned to the lunchroom while the team flew into action.

Debbie approached Bill. "I guess that solves our fifteen-minute window puzzle. I just don't understand. I asked the city about that location, and I was told that the building had burned to the ground. They said there was nothing left to investigate. I should have followed through on it."

"Don't beat yourself up, Debbie. We really need you right now, more than you know."

"How's that?"

Bill answered, "You're the only one that Tom can't identify."

"Have you forgotten that I was the one who delivered the news of Tom's parents committing suicide?"

"Think about it, Debbie. No offense, but back then, you were a blonde and tiny. Today you're a brunette and—"

"Don't say it, Bill. My figure has changed after childbirth."

"Exactly."

Debbie thought about it. "Shit, you're right."

Debbie and Bill joined the rest of the team in the center of the common area, where Don was outlining his plan for the takedown. "I want everyone armed, wearing headsets, and in bulletproof vests. Daniel, you and Bob stay here at the station and hold down the fort."

He then turned to Cassandra and Butch. "How's the head Butch?"

"It's just a scratch. How can we help?"

"I need the two of you to take Bill in one of the cruisers to pick up Richard. Take him to the hospital so he can get whatever medical supplies he needs. Once they've been dropped off at the hospital, drive to the motel, but stay on the main road. Wait for us there, and no matter what, don't approach the motel."

Butch nodded. Cassandra grabbed a set of keys before leaving the station, Bill in tow.

Debbie stepped forward. "Don, do you mind if I make a suggestion?"

"I'm listening."

"Let's not be too hasty. We definitely need to go to the site, and yes, maybe Tom is there, but what if Jenny is being held somewhere else?"

Don thought for a moment. "That's a chance we have to take. Jenny is on borrowed time."

Debbie stood her ground. "Let me go undercover."

Don looked skeptical before inquiring. "What're you suggesting?"

"You arrested this Tom fellow over ten years ago, am I correct?"

"Yes, you're right."

"And you brought him here and put him behind bars. Is that also correct?"

"It is. But what're you getting at?" Don asked.

"Bill brought it to my attention that Tom Lockman was marched through the front door of this station, and then passed through this room full of officers. What's to say that he doesn't recognize everyone who was in the room that day? I was on maternity leave when he was arrested. I'm the right officer to go undercover."

Don studied her. "But you went to his house to deliver the news of his parents' death."

"Yes, I did, but Tom never even glanced at me. It was like he was in his own world. Besides, Bill has pointed out to me how different I look since then."

Don nodded. "You do have a point. What did you have in mind?"

Debbie grinned. "I think I'm going fishing. Can I borrow anyone's fishing tackle and gear?"

Daniel overheard the conversation and answered, "Mine's available. I'll call the wife and get her to deliver it here right away."

Don looked at Debbie. "I sure hope you have a foolproof plan. You need to be really careful out there. Tom is unpredictable."

"All I need to do is get close enough to draw Tom out, and hopefully spot the container. If it's not there, then he's holding Jenny somewhere else." Debbie squared her shoulders. "It's simple. If she's not there, then I come back and we start all over again. Until I know for sure, the team stays on the highway until they get the go-ahead from me."

"Okay, team," Don said, "We now have a plan."

Cassandra, Butch, and Bill arrived at the Jackson house unannounced. Bill knocked on the door and saw Eric look through the window before opening it. Then, over Eric's shoulder, he spotted Beatrice coming out of the kitchen. When their eyes met, tears ran down her cheeks and she flew into his arms. He held her so close she could hardly breathe.

"Bill, what're you doing here?" she asked. "Is Jenny okay?"

Bill buried his face in her hair to hide his tears from the others in the room. Then he turned to Glen with an accusing look on his face. "What's she doing here? I told you to take her somewhere safe, where no one could find her, and she's here?"

"You wouldn't have found her if you weren't here for a reason. Besides, what better place to hide her than here? She has two officers watching over her, plus I think Eric needed some extra help with Claire. She's a real fireball."

Bill backed down. "I guess you're right." He released Beatrice so he could quickly hug Kimberley. "How're you holding up?"

"It's been a long time since our family spent the day together. How about you?"

He answered, "Busy day, but hopefully it will be over soon."

"Does that mean you've found her?"

"The latest tip we have sounds really positive."

"Jenny was always clever sending out clues."

"I agree, but our latest tip came from two small children."

Kimberley looked somewhat puzzled. "Really. You be careful out there."

"I will thanks." He then turned his attention to Claire. "How're you doing, sweetie?"

"I'm behaving just like you told me to, Grandpa. I really want Eric to get a good mark on his test."

Eric looked confused. "What test is that, Claire?"

"Grandpa told me to not open the curtains when you closed them. You were practicing protecting people."

Eric glanced at Bill approvingly and smiled. "Oh, yeah, thanks, Claire. I really want to do well on my test."

Bill shook hands with Richard. "I just need a few minutes with Beatrice, and then we'll talk."

Richard nodded. "I like the sound of that."

Bill took Beatrice into the kitchen where they could talk privately. Once away from everyone, he kissed her passionately. As she drew away from him, the lack of expression on his face worried her. She could always read his facial expressions, but today she was unable to. "What's happening, Bill? Is Jenny okay?"

Bill wasn't sure how to answer her. "I'm not totally sure, honey. Tom locked her inside a container several hours ago and sealed it shut. No one knows how long she has before she'll suffocate."

"Oh, crap, you have to find her."

"I know." He then added, "We're almost positive that we have the location where Tom's holding her. We just need to go and check it out."

"So why are you standing here?"

"I came to pick up Richard. We want him with us when we find her. I didn't know you were here too. I've missed you so much."

"I've missed you, too, but if you know where she's being held, then go and get her. You don't need to waste any more time here with us. Just be careful and I'll see you later." She saw the concern on his face. Delivering a final kiss, she told him, "You'll be back before you know it."

"How can you be so sure?"

She smiled. "Because I told you I'll see you later. You wouldn't want to disappoint me, would you?"

"Not a chance."

They returned to the living room.

Beatrice took Claire into her bedroom to play dolls allowing Bill to speak openly to the family.

Bill turned to Richard. "We're taking you to the hospital to pick up your medical bag. We're also going to need an ambulance and two medics if they're available."

"I'll make it happen," Richard said. "Where's he holding her?"

Bill answered, "Do you remember that old motel about fifteen minutes out of town?"

"He can't be holding her there. Didn't it burn to the ground several years ago?"

"Apparently not. It's still standing."

Richard asked, "Does anyone know what condition Jenny is in?"

"We're not one hundred percent sure of Jenny's status. All we know at this time is Tom locked her inside a container and sealed it shut."

Richard looked concerned. "How long has she been there?"

Bill thought back to what time Tom had said he put her inside the container and did the mental calculations. "At least two to three hours."

"It's approaching freezing outside," Richard said anxiously. "She'll be showing signs of hypothermia. I'll make sure we have lots of blankets and oxygen onboard." He added, "We need to get to her fast."

Bill glanced at Kimberley and saw that she was as pale as a ghost, looking like she was about to faint. Crossing the room, Richard moved her towards the couch and sat down next to her.

"Are you all right, honey?"

The color slowly returned to Kimberley's face. Dazed, she said, "How could he do such a thing? She's his wife."

Bill shook his head. "I think prison did a number on him. He's not all there. I've talked to him several times and at this point, he's unpredictable. Believe it or not, she is safer inside that container right now, well away from him. But our biggest concern is the temperature and oxygen levels inside." Bill continued, "We just need to confirm that we're right about her location, and if so, take Tom down."

Richard gave Kimberley a kiss on the cheek and turned to Bill. "I'm ready if you are."

Concerned, Kimberley said, "You two be careful."

Bill responded, "You'll be able to see her soon. Say goodbye to Beatrice for me."

"I will."

The two officers, Bill, and Richard left for the hospital. Eric locked the front door behind them.

Beatrice returned to the living room just in time to see Bill, Richard, and the two officers drive away. Seeing Kimberley sitting on the couch, obviously in distress, she sat next to her. "Everything will be okay, Kimberley. Let's go into the kitchen and put on some tea."

Claire responded, "Can I have some too?"

Beatrice smiled. "Of course, honey. You can help me make it."

Chapter Fifteen

4:45 p.m. – 6:00 p.m.

BACK AT THE STATION, DEBBIE went into the washroom to put on Daniel's fishing gear. Everything was far too large for her, but she could tell Tom the gear belonged to her husband. She came back to the common area and saw some of the officers grinning.

"Well, guys, do I look like a fisherman?"

Greg laughed. "If I were a fish, I'd be trying to swim upstream before you arrived."

Debbie laughed too. "I've never fished before, so hopefully I can pull this off. All I need to do is find out whether he's there and if there's a container on the site." Debbie paused as a thought occurred to her. "I can't exactly arrive in a police cruiser."

Daniel tossed his keys to her. "My old beater's out back. She's a bit touchy, so go easy on the clutch."

Debbie removed the fishing gear, picked up the rod, and tackle box and left the station. She loaded the tackle box, hip waders, and fishing rod into the back of Daniel's truck. She climbed behind the wheel and started the engine. Remembering Daniel's warning about the clutch, she slowly eased it into gear and rolled out to the front of the station. Three cruisers full of officers were waiting there to follow her to the motel.

As she approached the turn-off to the motel, Debbie spotted an ambulance parked on the side of the road. She drove past and turned into the motel driveway, where she stopped. The cruisers parked behind the ambulance and the officers got out. Debbie rolled down the window of the truck as Don approached.

"Are you ready for this?" he asked.

"Sure am."

Don watched her insert her earpiece. "Be careful."

Nodding, Debbie restarted the engine, shifted the truck into gear, and turned the radio up to maximum before driving the short distance to the motel.

Greg looked confused. "Why did she put the radio so loud?"

Don answered, "She wants him to know she's coming. The music will draw him out into the open."

Cassandra, Butch, Richard, and Bill stood by the ambulance, while the two medics waited inside. From a distance the four of them listened to a recap of the takedown plan. Don gathered his officers close to him. "Once Debbie confirms that there's a container on the site we split up into two groups. Half of you walk the length of the motel and approach the back of the building from the right side. The remaining officers walk along the left side with me. Nothing happens until we hear from Debbie."

When everyone was on the same page, Richard approached Don and inquired, "Where do you want me?"

Don responded, "Stay in the back of the ambulance, well away from danger." He handed Richard a radio. "We'll let you know when you and the ambulance should come in. Until then, you stay put."

"Got it." Richard walked back to the ambulance and climbed into the back.

Bill turned to Don, about to speak, but Don cut him off. "The same goes for you, Bill. I'm not taking any chances with you. He'll be gunning for you."

Bill was angry. "What the hell? We don't even know if he has a gun! Besides, Jenny has a better chance of surviving if I'm there. I'm already going to miss his five o'clock call, so he's going to be pissed. I want him dead for what he's done to Jenny, but I also want him back behind bars. Let me try and talk him down."

Don looked at Bill. "You're not wearing a bulletproof vest."

"I don't plan on getting shot. Besides, I'm not going back into town to get one. I'm going in whether you want me to or not."

Don shook his head. He knew that Jenny's time was limited, so didn't want to waste any more of it arguing. "Fine, but stay close to Cassandra and Butch." He then turned to Butch. "You're both in charge of keeping Bill safe."

Butch responded, "We'll be next to him if he confronts Tom."

Debbie dodged all the potholes and slowed down on the washboard sections of the road as she approached the dilapidated motel. There were definite signs that a fire had occurred in the building, but it only seemed to affect one unit in the center of the motel. The building was in sad disarray, with paint peeling from the siding. A good number of the windows were shattered and shredded curtains hung in their empty frames. She looked around, took a deep breath, and slowly climbed out of the vehicle, purposely slamming the door shut behind her.

Casually, she walked towards the box and lowered the tailgate. She moved the fishing gear closer, and then pulled on the hip waders. From the corner of her eye, she spotted movement at the far end of the motel. She whispered, "There's definitely someone here, but I didn't get a good look at who it is yet."

Don responded, "Do you want us to move in?"

"Negative. I still haven't located the container. Until I find it, keep the team at bay."

"Copy that."

Just then, Debbie saw a man come around the building and approach her.

"What're you doing here?" Tom demanded.

Debbie feigned a startled look. "Shit, you half scared me to death."

Tom glared at her. "I asked you, what're you doing here?"

"I could ask you the same question."

Tom was ready to blow a gasket.

Debbie could sense his anger. He clearly didn't want her anywhere near the motel. With a nonchalant smile, she pulled the fishing tackle and rod out of the back of the truck. "My hubby told me that if I caught a fish for supper tonight, he'd cook it and also do bath time with both our girls before bed. That means I'll get to sit in my pyjamas under a warm blanket with a glass of white wine in my hand." She chuckled. "He forgets that I'm an excellent fisherman; or, should I say, fisherwoman."

She started to walk towards the back of the building, but Tom cut her off. "You can't be here. You're trespassing."

"What do you mean, trespassing? This place has been abandoned for years, which begs the question, what are *you* doing here?"

"I'm in the process of buying this building, so you're trespassing." Tom snapped.

Debbie tried to look behind him. "You're actually going to purchase this motel? That's great news! It will definitely give the area a boost." She moved around him and caught a glimpse of what she thought could be a container.

Tom cut her off again. "You can't be here!"

Debbie did her best to sound disappointed. "Please, this is the best fishing hole in the area. It's not every day that my husband offers to cook me dinner."

Tom yelled, "You're trespassing! Get off my property!"

Debbie backed away from him. His beady eyes glared at her, and she was worried that her pushiness would help him figure out that she was an officer. "Okay, okay, don't throw a hissy fit. I know a second fishing hole that I can go to, but this one's the best." Turning to walk away, she spoke over her shoulder. "Good luck with the motel. In future, you might want to be nicer to your potential guests."

She felt his eyes on her as she returned to the vehicle, removed the hip waders, and put all her gear back into the box of the truck. Shutting the tailgate, she then climbed into the cab, started the engine, and turned around to drive away.

On her way back to the team, Debbie spoke into her ear piece. "He's really pissed, but on a positive note, it looks like there could be a container on site."

Don was relieved. "Copy that. Good work, Debbie."

Tom glanced down at his watch, livid. He was five minutes late making his five o'clock call. That bitch had thrown off his schedule. He stormed back to the motel room and called the station.

Someone who wasn't Bill answered, "Hello, Blue Ridge Police Department. How may I help you?"

Tom was dumbstruck. "I need to speak to Bill Smithe."

"I'm sorry. He's stepped out of the office."

"Where is he?"

"Family emergency. Can I help you?"

Tom shut off his phone. He was starting to panic. If that lady reported him to the authorities, he was screwed. It was now or never. If Jenny was already dead, he would pack up and leave; if she was alive, then he'd eliminate her and hit the road. Tom knew better than to take her vehicle. By now, there would be an APB out for it. Walking was his only means of escape.

His first thoughts were burn Jenny's vehicle, leave her body sealed inside the container and escape. That was all he could think about. But what if she was still alive. He should at least say good-bye to her.

Before Tom stormed out of the motel room, he made sure the scissors were still in his pocket. Finding them there, he trudged around the back of the motel and towards the container. For a moment, he stood in front of the door, staring at it.

Then he went to get his toolbox and gas can from behind the container.

Debbie arrived back at the main road and joined up with the rest of her team. Everyone was ready for the takedown.

Don took charge. "We've a mess ahead of us to clean up. Let's stay safe and watch each other's back. Debbie, you're with Greg and me on the back left corner of the motel. Jim, you're with us too, but you'll need to work your way to the front left side of the container."

Jim responded, "Got it, boss."

"Butch and Cassandra, you're in charge of Bill. We already know Tom will try and take Bill out. That can't happen."

Don tossed an earpiece to Bill. "Stay close to us, but well hidden in the bushes." When Bill nodded, he said, "Okay. Move out, everyone."

As the teams split up and went in different directions, Bill leaned in and whispered to Don, "Do you have a plan?"

"I'm hoping the element of surprise works to our advantage."

Bill turned to Don. "I hope we're able to bring him in alive. He needs to be accountable for kidnapping Jenny."

Tom put his ear against the container door and whispered, "Are you still alive in there?" There was no answer, so he kicked the door and still got no response. Even if she was still alive, Jenny was no threat to him, as she would still be tied to the chair. Tom drew the scissors out of his pocket and started cutting the duct tape and pulling it off. Once it was removed, he unlocked the door and swung the doors open before stepping just inside. He looked at Jenny. He couldn't tell if she was dead or alive, so he bent down close and studied her. He could see her chest slowly rising and falling.

"You bitch. Why won't you die?" He felt her cheek. "Oh, my dear wife, you're freezing. I know a way to warm you up."

He grabbed the gas can and poured it over the branches under her chair. Jenny slowly looked up at him, realizing suddenly that because she hadn't suffocated or frozen to death, he was going to burn her alive. Horrified, Jenny looked at her husband, who was now a raving maniac, and begged for her life. "Please, Tom! Don't do this."

"Tell me you love me, and that you'll run away with me, and this can all end here and now."

Jenny opened her mouth and in a defeated voice said, "I love you."

Tom was livid. "You don't really mean it. You're just lying through your teeth."

Jenny wanted her freedom more than anything, but if she went with him, her nightmare would continue until the day she died. Tears ran down her cheek as she felt the end was near.

Don walked along with Greg and Debbie, while Bill, Cassandra, and Butch were several paces behind working their way into the bushes. The three officers would be positioned on the left back side of the motel. Jim split off and disappeared into the forest, slowly working his way to the left front side of the container. He climbed over fallen trees, trying to be quiet as he found his position.

Meanwhile, Jack, Sam, Eli, and Muhammad drew their weapons as they approached the back side of the building and moved towards the main office. The door was open. Jack went in and came back out a moment later.

"It's all clear, but there are no room keys hanging on the board. He must have taken all of them so we wouldn't know which unit he's in."

As the four men approached the first window, Jack glanced in and saw no one. The door was also locked so he moved to the next unit. Passing each room, they first checked the window, then the door. The team bypassed the unit that had the fire damage. All was clear, except for the second unit from the end. The door had been kicked in, but Jack found the room empty.

The team then moved to the last door, which was unlocked, but they found it empty as well. All four officers turned on their flashlights and went inside. Glancing around the room, they saw Jenny's purse sitting on the bed, untouched. Upon further inspection they noticed hair and tie wraps scattered all over the floor. An axe was embedded deep into the headboard.

Jack murmured, "Looks like Jenny's purse. And now we know why he took the tie wraps from his shed. The bastard used them to control her movements around the room."

Sam responded, "It sure looks like it." He radioed the rest of the team. "We found the room where Tom held Jenny, but he's not here. We're heading towards our position."

Don responded, "Copy that. Once your teams are in place, let me know. Tom must be near the container, so tread carefully."

The teams were slowly getting into position. Eli, Sam, and Muhammad remained close to the back right side of the motel, but well out of sight.

Jack took his position just off the right side of the container and murmured to the team, "It looks like the door's been opened, but so far, I can't see Tom. He may be inside."

Don responded, "Hold your position."

"Copy that."

Jim reported, "I can confirm the door is partially opened, but there's no activity that I can see." He paused as Tom came into view. "I have a visual. Tom is just inside the door and—shit!"

"What's going on?" Don asked.

"The bastard just tossed the gas can into the bush. He must have just doused Jenny in fuel."

"Does anyone have a clean shot?" Bill barked.

He received four negatives.

Debbie flew into action. She spoke into her headset. "Under no circumstances does Tom light that fuel. I don't care which officer takes him out, just make sure it's a clean shot." She quickly ran towards the container, trying to get as close as possible before Tom saw her.

As she approached, he turned to face her. "I knew you weren't a fisherman. I could smell that you were a copper a mile away." He clicked his cigarette lighter on.

"You don't want to do this, Tom," Debbie said. "Jenny doesn't deserve to die this way."

"Don't tell me how she should die. Bill screwed up by not paying me, and now she has to die. I always follow through on my promises. Bill's the one to blame."

Bill whispered to Cassandra and Butch, "Cover my back. I'm going in."

Neither officer could stop him; as he was already moving towards the container.

Tom glanced up as Bill walked out of the bush and stood next to Debbie. "Hello, Tom. We finally meet face to face."

"Ah, the famous Sergeant Bill Smithe had the balls to show up. I don't see you carrying a bag full of money. That's not good for Jenny. I can see you didn't come alone. Call your men off." He glared at Bill.

"If I drop this lighter, the game's over. I may die, but Jenny will go down with me." He sneered. "Can you live with yourself knowing that you failed Jenny? Tell your team to do the right thing and lower their weapons."

Bill raised his hands. "Stand down, everyone."

"You never even tried to get the money, did you?" Tom snarled.

"No, I didn't"

"Not smart on your part."

"Think about it, Tom. I go into the bank and ask for half a million dollars, what's the first thing the bank is going to want to know?"

"I don't know, and who cares? It was up to you to get the money."

"You didn't plan this out very well."

"How's that?"

"Look at me. I'm retired with no job. What bank is willing to give me a loan of that size when I'm not only old, but also unemployed?"

Tom responded, "I guess you never hit up that Doctor. He probably has loads of money. Half a million dollars is probably petty cash for him."

"You really don't want to do this Tom."

Tom screamed, "Don't tell me what I want or don't want to do." Tom turned towards Jenny. "Look at her. She's pathetic."

Bill had to try and get control of the situation. "Look at me, Tom. I need to apologize to you."

Tom slowly turned to face Bill looking somewhat confused. "What the hell do you need to apologize to me for?"

"I failed you," Bill said sadly.

"No shit."

"I didn't mean about the cash. I actually meant about your brother Charles."

"Don't talk to me about my brother."

"I really tried to talk him down, but I failed. For that, I'm sorry." Bill got no response. "I wanted to bring him in with no incident, but he forced the team's hand when he shot Jenny." Bill added, "Don't do anything rash. Let's talk about it. All our officers have stood down, so this conversation is just between the two of us."

"This isn't one of our phone calls where you treat me like shit."

"No, it isn't. It's a conversation, face to face, between the two of us."

"I have nothing to say to you except that I'm disappointed. I didn't want to have to kill Jenny, but you forced my hand."

"Did I really? As I see it, you poured the gas around her before my team was even in place. You had no intention of waiting to see if I could come up with the money. You planned to kill her all along."

Bill switched into negotiator mode. "You have two choices. You either let Jenny go and you return to prison for kidnapping and attempted murder, or my team eliminates you. Is that really what you want?"

"I never get what I want!" Tom shouted. "I wanted a baby sister and then she died. Our parents blamed her death on Charles and me." Tears started to run down his cheeks, and in a trembling voice, he said, "They abandoned both of us. We lived under bridges and begged for food. It wasn't fair what happened to us. When parents die, they're supposed to leave something for their kids. Charles and I got nothing."

"No, it wasn't fair, but somehow you both pulled through it. You met Jenny and fell in love. I know she loved you too. You had a good job, once upon a time."

Tom looked at Jenny. She was visibly trembling, not only from the cold, but also from fear.

"You can stop this, Tom. Put down the lighter and let's call it a day."

Tom looked down at the lighter. After a moment, he extinguished the flame and threw it to the ground rather than on the pyre under her chair. He looked up at Bill as Jim and Jack appeared out of nowhere, grabbed his arms, and started to lead him away.

Tom trembled. "I just wanted her to love me again. Why couldn't she say I love you to me and really mean it?"

Bill shrugged his shoulders. "Maybe she just needed time."

Bill and Debbie rushed into the container to evaluate Jenny's condition. Bill spoke into his headset. "Jenny's here. We need the ambulance right now."

Richard confirmed. "We're on our way."

Bill pulled off his jacket and draped it over Jenny's shoulders. He took out his pocketknife and carefully freed her wrists from the chair, while Debbie cut the ropes binding her legs.

Debbie stayed in a squatting position as she held Jenny's hand. "We've got you, Jenny. You're going to be okay."

When Jim and Jack had Tom a safe distance away, they turned him around and were about to place him in handcuffs when Tom pushed both officers away from him and grabbed Jim's weapon. He turned around and faced the container.

Debbie was studying Jenny's face when her eyes suddenly went as big as saucers. Her voice was just a whisper, but Debbie heard it loud and clear. "No, Tom. Don't do this."

Debbie spun around and saw Tom pointing the weapon at Bill. In a split second, Debbie knew what was about to happen. She drew her gun, threw herself in front of Bill, and fired several shots. Tom froze as the bullets entered his heart and then forehead. He fell to the ground, dead.

Bill knew Tom was dead as soon as he heard the shots. Devastated, he looked at Tom's body. "Shit! I thought I had convinced him to turn himself in."

Debbie responded, "Did you ever think that maybe Jenny wasn't the target, but you were?"

Bill shook his head in disbelief. "I really wanted to save him."

"I know you did. But sometimes people come along who just don't want to be saved. We do our best and, hopefully, we can save most of them. Unfortunately, Tom wasn't one of them."

Bill looked at Debbie. "Why did you do that?"

"What? Save your life?"

"Yes. He could have shot you."

Debbie shrugged. "I guess I might have overreacted, but when I saw Tom had a gun pointed directly at you, I had to do something." She paused. "I wasn't going to be the one to explain to Beatrice why you took another bullet. I figured my bulletproof vest would protect me if he got off a round before I did. Turns out I didn't even need it."

"Thanks, Debbie. I owe you big time."

"Sorry about Tom. Even though things didn't quite pan out the way we wanted them to, it's all over and Jenny's safe."

"Yes, she is."

Within a matter of minutes, Richard and the medics were on site. Richard ran up to the container. "We heard the shots. Where's Jenny? Is she ok?"

Bill pointed to the ground several feet away. "Tom's the one that got shot." He stepped aside and Richard saw Jenny.

Richard and both medics approached Jenny. Richard placed his fingers on the side of her neck. "Her pulse is weak and breathing's shallow."

Bill couldn't believe the woman in front of him was Jenny. Debbie looked at him. "Why do you suppose he made her wear his uniform and chopped off her hair?"

Bill looked disgusted. "He wanted her to experience what it was like living in a hellhole."

"Poor Jenny."

One medic placed an oxygen mask over Jenny's face. Her eyes fluttered open, and she looked up and saw Richard. She smiled. "Where's Bill?" she asked. Her voice was muffled by the mask.

Bill stepped forward. "I'm here, Jenny."

"You found me."

"I said I would, and I never break a promise."

"No, you don't, but you cut it pretty close." With tears in her eyes, she whimpered, "Look what he did to my hair. And he made me wear his prison uniform."

Bill smiled. "You're safe now, Jenny. Your hair will grow back, and we can easily burn his uniform."

"I remember hearing shots fired before blacking out. Is everyone okay?"

"The officers are all fine."

Trembling, she asked, "And Tom?"

"I'm sorry, Jenny. He didn't make it. An officer had to shoot him."

"Is he dead?"

"I'm afraid so. I really tried to talk him down, but it didn't work."

She spotted Tom's body a short distance away and broke down in tears. "I really did love him once."

"I know you did."

The medics rolled the gurney from the ambulance up to the front of the container. Jenny was lifted out of the chair and placed on it. Warm blankets were placed over her to warm her up, and the oxygen offered her a new chance at life. Jenny watched one of the medics insert a needle into her vein, taping it to her arm, and then start the flow of intravenous fluids into her system. She still wasn't sure what had just happened. One minute, Debbie and Bill were talking to her, and then she'd spotted Tom with a gun in his hand before several shots were fired. Everything from that point on was a blur.

Jenny looked up at Richard. "Do you like my new haircut?"

"Do you want to know the truth or a lie?"

"The truth, of course."

"You're still a beautiful person, so the haircut means nothing."

Jenny smiled. "So, my clothing doesn't bother you either?"

"Clothes can be changed and hair will grow back." Richard placed a kiss on her cheek, and then watched the medics load her into the ambulance.

Closing her eyes, she concentrated on her breathing: in and out, in and out. Jenny allowed her body to relax.

When she woke up again, she wouldn't be inside that horrible container anymore.

Don approached Bill and Richard. He also signaled Jim to join them. Once Jim was there, Don spoke to him. "Can you drive Bill and Richard to the hospital? I'm sure Jenny will want to see both of them once she's treated."

"You got it, boss."

Bill protested. "Don't you need me here for the cleanup?"

"You don't work for the Blue Ridge Police Department anymore, so consider yourself relieved of your duties."

Bill grinned ruefully. "The force just doesn't appreciate me anymore."

The three left the scene in a cruiser, heading towards the hospital. On the way there, Bill called the Jackson house.

Eric picked up the phone, already knowing it was Bill. "Hello, Bill. Tell me you have good news."

Kimberley and Beatrice were listening intently, hoping the news was good, but they were also prepared for the worst. Claire was sitting on the floor playing with her dolls.

Bill let out a sigh of relief. "Jenny's okay. It's all over."

Eric winked to the ladies and went into the kitchen for privacy, in case it also came with bad news. He inquired, "And the team?"

"We're all safe and sound. Tom however didn't fare too well. I tried to talk him down and thought I'd succeeded until he tried to shoot me. Debbie took him out."

"I'm sorry Bill. I know you wanted to bring him in alive." He paused before asking, "How's Jenny doing?"

"She's suffering from hypothermia and dehydration. She's on her way to the hospital right now."

"That's good news, but you know everyone here is going to be asking about you."

Bill paused. "I'm fine. No bullet wounds."

"Good to hear. I'll give the ladies and Glen an update. When do you think they'll be able to see you and Jenny?"

"Not sure right now, but how about they come by the hospital in about an hour? Hopefully Jenny will be well enough for company."

"We'll all be there." Eric hung up. He went back into the living room with a big grin on his face. "Jenny's fine and Bill is too. We can go to the hospital to see them soon."

Kimberley and Beatrice broke down into tears. Claire looked confused and asked, "What's wrong?"

Kimberley laughed. "These are tears of joy."

Claire thought about it, and then seemed oblivious to the drama that had just unfolded. She returned to playing with her dolls.

Back at the motel, dusk was fast approaching, so with what little time they had left, the team walked around the site, looking for evidence.

Don approached Eli and Muhammad. "You two stay here until the body is removed."

Eli responded, "Will do."

"Let's lock the container for now. Tomorrow, I'll send a team to go over the area. Even though Tom is deceased, we need to collect evidence for our paperwork."

Eli answered, "We're on it."

Sam approached Don. "I have something I think you're going to want to see."

"Okay. Lead the way."

"We're really lucky we found her in time," Sam said.

Don responded, "You mean Jenny's lucky we found her in time."

"It's the same thing, just a different perspective."

Don looked at it in disgust. "He actually made her watch him as he cut her hair off."

Sam added, "Looks like he also tore off her dress before making her put on his prison jumper."

"Pathetic bastard. I already told Eli and Muhammad to seal off the container. I'll also get them to tape off this room."

Don returned to Eli and Muhammad and told them about the room.

Eli nodded. "We'll make sure it's sealed up tight."

Next, Don approached Butch and Cassandra. "Thanks for the extra help. Blue Ridge owes you big time. Hopefully we can return the favour one day."

Butch nodded. "Glad to help out."

Cassandra added, "It's always nice to close a case, especially when it has a happy ending. It didn't end well for Tom, but Bill really made the effort to talk him down. Hopefully Jenny realizes that."

Don responded, "I think she knows that." He then added, "You can take one of our cruisers to get back to Sidville. But before you go, we have a tradition in our office. Once a case is closed, all officers involved meet for what we call the 'cleaning off the whiteboard' ceremony. We'd love it if you both were able to attend."

Cassandra responded, "We'd both like that. Just let us know when it is, and we'll be here. Is it okay if we return your vehicle at that time?"

"Definitely."

Cassandra and Butch left the motel.

The rest of the team congregated around Don. He wasn't sure what to say.

So he said, "Let's get the hell out of here."

Chapter Sixteen

6:00 p.m. - 10:00 a.m.

JENNY WAS ONLY CONSCIOUS FOR the bumpy ride in the ambulance back to the highway. She was sound asleep by the time the ambulance arrived at the hospital. The gurney was wheeled inside to a private room, well away from other patients, where she was carefully lifted from the gurney and placed in a bed. She was covered with two sets of warm blankets surrounding her frail body. A doctor and nurse entered the room to assess her condition and determined that she had symptoms of dehydration and hypothermia. The two proceeded to carefully treat the wounds on Jenny's wrists and then her ankles.

Bill and Richard arrived a half hour later and Richard stopped at the information desk.

The receptionist looked up. "Oh hi Dr. Jackson. I didn't know that you were on call today?"

Richard answered, "I'm not. An ambulance arrived here about half an hour ago. Can you give me an update on the patient?"

The receptionist looked at her computer and asked, "Is the patient Jenny Lockman?"

"Yes. How's she doing?"

"We have a team working on her right now. She's in room four. You can go right in."

"Do you mind if I bring Bill in with me? He's very close to her."

She could see that Bill was worried sick. "Of course. Maybe check first with the doctor who is looking after her to see if it's okay for him to go into the room."

"Of course."

Bill followed Richard down the hall and waited outside the room until he was allowed to go in to see Jenny.

When Richard returned, he studied Bill. "You look awful. Do I need to get a bed for you too?"

"I'm fine, thank you very much, just a bit tired."

The two entered the room. The doctor and nurse were just finishing dressing her injuries with gauze.

The doctor turned to Richard. "Her wrists were tied so tight it cut off her circulation. She'll be okay, but the scars will be a constant reminder of what she went through to survive."

Richard inquired, "What's the update on her legs?"

The doctor answered, "The ropes were also very tight, but I think Jenny kept moving her toes to stay warm, and that allowed her blood to continue circulating."

"Will we be able to speak to her?"

"She's all yours, Richard, but I wouldn't rush her. She's been through hell. There's a good chance she may need counselling to get past her ordeal. Talking should help her along the way."

The doctor and nurse left the room, and Richard and Bill approached the bed.

Jenny was slowly regaining consciousness, but refused to open her eyes. If she did, where would she be? Would she still be inside that nasty container, or worse, was she deceased?

Somehow, something felt different. She was no longer restricted in a sitting position; she was now lying on a soft surface. Jenny felt warmth, and less pain. Maybe this was heaven. She visualized angels tending to her wounds and preparing her to meet her maker.

Half sobbing, Jenny realized she hadn't been able to say goodbye to her family and friends. Tears ran from the corners of her eyes, down her cheeks, and onto a pillow under her head. A warm blanket comforted her in her despair.

A hand took Jenny's, and Bill's voice whispered, "Hi Jenny."

Jenny stopped breathing for a moment. Had Bill also been killed in the takedown? Was Beatrice now left alone? She wept openly.

Bill kissed her cheek. "You're okay, Jenny. We found you."

Jenny took a deep breath, and then opened her eyes. "Am I alive?"

"Yep."

"Are you really here?"

"You bet I am."

Jenny pulled one arm out from under the blanket and reached out to touch Bill's cheek. "You really are here." Jenny scanned his body, at least what she could see from her bed. "Are you okay? Did he hurt you?"

"I'm fine. The only way he hurt me was when he hurt you."

Jenny noticed Richard standing off to the side. She forced a smile and said, "I hope you're real too."

"It's me in the flesh. The doctor on duty has treated your wrists and ankles."

Jenny tucked her hand back under the warm blankets. Crying openly, she spoke between breaths. "I really fought to stay alive in that container, but I knew my time was limited. I was struggling to breathe, so eventually I just went to sleep, not afraid of dying anymore." She looked at Bill. "How did you find me?"

"Two little boys helped us."

"Two little boys? Do I know them?"

"I don't think so."

"Who are they?"

"We think they are two homeless children who claim to be living with their uncle at the old cannery. They were in the park at the same time as Tom. The two tried to steal Tom's bag thinking it might have food in it. When they got caught and managed to escape, they heard him ranting about how he was going to kill them at the old motel. We put two and two together."

"The two boys came into the station and told you that?"

"No. We happened to be searching a site where we thought Tom might be holding you and came upon them. We took them to the station and arranged for child services to pick them up at the end of the day."

"They have no parents?"

"I'm not one hundred percent sure. Bob mentioned they were living with an uncle at the old cannery homeless camp, but we both suspect that wasn't true." Bill paused to collect his thoughts. "I was falling apart, Jenny. I promised to find you and I wasn't sure I could keep that promise. In trying to relieve my stress level, Don put me in charge of the two boys. He asked me to speak with them. Apparently, he thinks I'm good with children."

"He's right about that."

Jenny wanted to know more about the boys. "How did they connect Tom as the person who threatened them?"

Bill continued, "At first, I don't think they did. I decided to give them a tour of the precinct. When they saw the whiteboard, they became curious." He added, "Little boys are always curious about something. Adam asked me, 'What's that?' I told them it was an active case we were working on. He then asked if that was the name of the man who had chased them in the park. I was in shock."

"Those poor boys must have been really scared."

"I really think they were. Once they were sure he was gone, they went to their safe house. I allowed the boys to study the whiteboard further. They saw your name and asked if Jenny was his wife. They heard him say he wanted to kill you. I almost fell off my chair. They then spotted 22 Oak Crescent, the house where they were hiding, and asked why there was a line through it. I told them that we didn't find you there. They responded, 'But you found us there.' I had to laugh. Indeed we did."

"I finished the tour and took them back to the lunchroom. We chatted a while longer before Michael asked, 'How do you get the clues?' I told him some were from you and some were from our officers doing research. The little boy turned and looked at the board. I was about to leave the room when Michael asked, 'If I had a clue, could I put it on the board?' I almost had a heart attack. I smiled and said, 'Sure, let's do it.' The three of us left the lunchroom and stood in front of the board. I gave the marker to the youngest boy. At first, I was discouraged, as he hesitated to write anything down. He just looked sadly at me and eventually said he didn't know how to spell the word. His older brother whispered the letters into his ear, and I was shocked to see the word 'motel' on the bottom of the board. I could feel the stress leaving my body as I gave the boys a hug and the team planned the takedown."

Jenny sighed. "I have to meet them. They saved my life."

"I'll make that happen."

"Do these boys have names?"

"Adam and Michael."

Richard interjected. "We really need to let Jenny rest. Beatrice, Kimberley and Claire will want to have some time with her when they arrive."

"Thank you both for not giving up on me," Jenny said.

Bill answered, "Failure isn't part of our motto."

Bill and Richard left the room. Out in the hall, Richard turned to Bill. "We may as well stay here. Eric will be dropping off Beatrice, Kimberley, and Claire shortly."

The two took a seat to wait for them.

Richard glanced at Bill. "How're you doing?"

"Much better now that I know Jenny's safe. How about you?"

"Don't worry about me. I was safe under house arrest with two stressed-out ladies, two bodyguards, and a child full of energy. I didn't have much time to worry." He paused. "Can I ask you a question?"

"Sure, go ahead."

"Now that it's over, how do you really feel?"

Bill thought about it before answering, "Dealing with Charles was part of my job. When I retired, I thought my last days on earth would be full of rest. No more stress, and all my time spent with Beatrice. Then Tom came along. He almost beat me. Did you know that to catch a criminal, you actually have to get into their heads? It's mind-blowing and exhausting." He paused. "I almost lost Jenny."

"But you didn't."

"I couldn't bring Charles in alive, but I had hoped that I could bring Tom in alive. Sure, he'd be facing life behind bars, but at least he'd still be alive."

"He gave you and the team no choice."

The emergency doors slid open and both men looked up. In walked Eric, Glen, Kimberley, Claire, and Beatrice.

Beatrice started crying when she saw Bill. They hugged, then Bill took her into a private room, and they held each other, afraid to separate. They finally kissed and she moved away and studied him. "Are you hurt?"

"No, darling, I'm just too old for this job. I'm exhausted."

"How is Jenny?"

Tears formed in his eyes. "She's going to be okay, but I almost failed her. She damn near suffocated in that container, and if she didn't, hypothermia would have taken her."

"The important part is you were able to save her. When can we all see her?"

"She's resting right now, but she would love a short visit with all of you."

Kimberley, Richard, and Claire were off in a corner waiting to see Jenny, Claire sitting on her dad's lap.

Eric and Glen approached Bill and Beatrice. Bill shook Eric's hand. "Thanks, man, for watching over all of them. I hear that Claire gave you a run for your money."

"She was fine. Glad you and the team are safe. If you don't need me anymore today, I'd like to head home. I'll deal with the paperwork tomorrow, if that's okay."

Bill responded, "I'm sure that will work." He watched Eric leave the building, and then turned to Glen. "Thanks for always being there for me."

"You only seem to call me in emergencies. Maybe one day you'll make it a social call." Glen glanced across the room. "That Claire sure has grown up."

"That she has. Did you have any issues with her?"

"Not at all, it was your wife who was the real problem." He winked at her. "She didn't bake any cookies this time around."

Bill laughed. "She can be difficult sometimes."

Glen hugged Beatrice first, then Bill. "Go home, Bill, you look like shit."

"Thanks buddy."

Glen then left the building.

The Jacksons approached Beatrice and Bill. Richard said, "We can go in and see her, but it's suggested we don't stay too long. She's been through quite a lot."

The five walked into her room and saw Jenny sitting up in bed. A wide grin came over her face when she saw all of them. She reached out for Claire, and Richard sat her on the bed. "I've missed you, Claire Bear."

"I missed you too." She then studied Jenny. "You cut your hair."

Tears formed in Jenny's eyes. "It doesn't look very good, does it?"

Claire studied her again. "I like it. It just needs a few stray hairs cut and it'll be perfect."

Jenny hugged Claire with her one free arm. "Thank you, sweetheart. I love you."

"I love you too.

Jenny then hugged Beatrice. "I almost can't believe that Bill and his team actually found me."

"I know. The team never gave up on you. They worked their butts off."

Jenny looked over at Bill. "Take him home, he looks whipped."

Bill protested. "Hey, I'm not a spring chicken. Yes, I agree I look haggard, but I also got the job done." He shrugged. "I'm just not appreciated, so I'm leaving with my wife and going home."

Jenny whispered, "Thank you, Bill."

"You're very welcome."

The last person Jenny hugged was Kimberley. She apologized. "I'm sorry I couldn't pick Claire up from school."

"Oh my God, don't be ridiculous. It's not your fault that any of this happened. We're just happy that you are now safe. Get some rest, Jenny, and we'll be back tomorrow to check up on you."

Once everyone had left and the nurse checked her vitals, Jenny asked that the lights be left on in her room. She was still in disbelief, and terrified that if the lights were turned off, she would once again find herself inside that container, freezing cold and suffocating. The lights were her new comfort zone—at least for now.

Jenny lay awake for hours, and by the next time the nurse checked in on her, she was exhausted.

"Are you okay, dear?" the nurse asked.

With tears in her eyes, Jenny answered, "I can't sleep. I'm afraid to close my eyes."

"Let me check your vitals." She smiled at Jenny. "Everything is fine. Would you like me to get you a sleeping pill?"

Cautiously, Jenny said, "Sure. I'd like to try it."

The nurse left the room and returned a few minutes later with not only the sleeping pill, but also two more warm blankets. Jenny took the pill and allowed the nurse to wrap her up in the blankets.

As the nurse was leaving the room, she asked, "Do you still want the lights left on?"

"Yes, please."

Jenny's body started to relax, and she fell into a deep sleep. Her dreams were a mish-mash of emotions that she couldn't seem to wake up from. Tom was everywhere: sitting at the restaurant watching her work, and laughing with her at nothing in particular; then he was in that horrible motel room, scaring her half to death.

Although she was in a deep sleep, she kept repeating, over and over. "Wake up, Jenny, before he kills you."

Her dream suddenly went foggy like a fall morning, where the dew hadn't dissipated yet. Once it cleared, she saw the man she'd married. His voice was like an echo. "I'm so sorry, Jenny. I didn't mean to scare you. I didn't mean to hurt you. I pledged my love to you so many years ago, and if I could change anything, it would be how I treated you over the past day. No matter what, know that I loved you so much that it hurt, and I always will."

Even though Jenny was asleep, she shed tears for the man who had been her soulmate, even though he was no longer a part of her life.

Then, she dreamed no more, but slept peacefully.

She woke up feeling fully refreshed and was welcomed by the sun peeking through the window of her room.

A new nurse came into her room. "How did you sleep dear?"

"Very well, thank you."

"Let's just check your vitals before breakfast arrives." She took Jenny's temperature, blood pressure, and pulse. With a smile on her face, she winked and said, "All good."

Breakfast arrived, and Jenny was almost finished eating when Richard and Kimberley came into her room. "Good morning, Jenny. We have great news."

Jenny looked surprised. "What's going on?"

Richard smiled. "We're getting you out of here." He saw the concern on her face and added, "No, you're not going home to your place. Kimberley and I are taking you back to ours, just for a day or two." When she hesitated, Richard went on: "We can't go home without you. Claire would be devastated. She's already preparing your bedroom with lots of her favorite teddy bears."

Jenny smiled. "How can I say no to an offer like that?"

"I've taken a few days off of work to make sure you're okay," Richard said.

"Thank you, both of you."

Once breakfast was finished, Jenny looked around the room. "I have no clothes to change into."

Kimberley said, "Just wear what you've got on for now and I'll drop by your house and pick up a few things later."

The three left the hospital. When they got home, Claire was standing in the front window waiting for Jenny to arrive. Their neighbor had kindly watched Claire until her parents returned. As soon as the three walked through the door, Claire threw her arms around Jenny, almost knocking her over.

Richard came to the rescue. "Be careful, honey. Remember, Jenny needs lots of rest."

"Sorry Dad." Claire turned to Jenny. "Mom and Dad said you're going to sleep over here. Isn't that cool?"

"It sure is, honey."

Chapter Seventeen

10:00 a.m. the next day

JENNY ARRIVED AT THE POLICE station to a room full of officers, family, and two very special guests. Richard had insisted that she arrive in a wheelchair, as she was still experiencing discomfort on her wrists and legs. Once inside the building, the entire office greeted her with applause. This wasn't the reception she'd been expecting, and she shed a few tears. She knew all of the local officers, because at one point, each of them had kept watch over her house after Tom went to prison.

Bill approached her and bent over to kiss her cheek. "I have a surprise for you."

Jenny looked at him. "What?"

Bill stepped aside and two small children came into view. Jenny was overcome with emotion. Bill had told her he thought they were homeless, but this morning, they were all cleaned up and neatly dressed. Both needed a haircut, but that was minor in the grand scheme of things. What caught Jenny's attention at first was that they both had the most intense brown eyes she had ever seen. Those eyes pulled at a string in her heart. As she put her hand out, both boys slowly moved closer to her.

Jenny took a small hand in each of hers. "I understand that you boys are the ones who helped find me?"

Adam answered, "Yes, ma'am."

Michael was very excited. He pointed to Bill and said, "He said we're heroes."

Jenny chuckled. "You sure are. Thank you so much."

Adam answered, "You're welcome, ma'am."

Jenny released their hands and smiled. "We'll talk some more before you leave, if that's okay?"

They both nodded in agreement. Jenny then circulated around the room and thanked every officer personally. When she came to Bob, Jenny noticed the bandage on his arm. "Whatever happened to you?" she asked.

Bob raised his arm and chuckled. "Hell, this old thing? Chalk it up to being at the wrong place at the wrong time. It's just a scratch. Or should I say a bite."

Jenny wasn't satisfied with his answer. "Seriously, what happened?"

"Unfortunately for me, Jack and I were checking out a site and came upon a pack of wolves. I don't think they were happy to see us."

"They attacked you?"

"You could say so. Hey, don't worry, it's just a scratch." He glanced around the room, and then turned his attention back to her. "Everyone here is so glad that you're safe." He whispered, "You didn't hear this from me, but Bill worked his butt off. When those two boys pinpointed your location, you could almost see a weight lift off his shoulders."

"Bill said he would find me, and he did."

Jenny continued around the room, listening to each officer as they shared their contributions in finding her. She heard over and over. "Welcome home, Jenny. Glad you're okay." More than once, Debbie's name came up in the conversation.

Jenny finally approached her, and Debbie smiled when their eyes met. Jenny whispered, "Word's out that, apart from the two boys, you were instrumental in finding me. They're saying you went undercover as a fisherman or should I say, fisherwoman?"

Debbie chuckled. "They're just jealous." She sobered and added, "Actually, I was the only one who could do it. I was on maternity leave when"—she paused before continuing—"when Joan Wilks was shot. The team couldn't take the chance that your husband would remember them, so I was the correct officer for the job."

Jenny reached for Debbie's hand. "Don't feel bad. My husband made a serious mistake when he shot her, and he kept spiralling downhill after that. Just talking to him about his time in prison made me scared for my life, but also sorry for what he had to go through." She was quiet for a moment. "He used to be such a gentle man, but I guess prison can play mind games on a person."

"I'm really sorry that we weren't able to save him."

"I'm not convinced that he wanted to be saved. At least now he's at peace."

Debbie looked sadly at Jenny. "I can't imagine what you had to go through, and we're all so sorry that it took us so long to find you."

"I needed that time with him. Prison took away the man that I once loved. I so wanted to reconnect with him, but once he put me into the container, it hardened my heart. I knew he was lost to me forever."

Debbie smiled. "You need anything the force is here to help you."

"Thank you." She then released Debbie's hand.

Jenny turned and saw two officers she wasn't familiar with. She approached them. "I'm sorry but I haven't met the two of you before."

Cassandra smiled. "Butch and I were loaners from Sidville, brought in to help find you. I'm not so sure that we accomplished much."

Butch added, "All we managed to do was lose our cruiser in a sinkhole."

Jenny looked surprised. "Really?"

Butch grinned and nodded in Cassandra's direction. "Yes, really, and guess who was driving?"

Cassandra glared at him. "Yes, we got hung up over a sinkhole, but don't forget who saved you."

"I could never forget that. You wouldn't let me." Butch took Jenny's hand. "It's nice to finally meet you."

Cassandra also shook her hand. "Glad it all worked out for you."

Jenny smiled at the two officers. "Thank you so much for your help."

She then turned around and came face to face with the whiteboard. Approaching it, she saw Tom's name and hers, then focused on "10:00" written on it. That had to be when the police became aware she had gone missing. Seeing Tom's name on the board brought tears to her eyes. She scanned the rest of the board and saw the word "MOTEL" at the bottom, printed by a child. Her eyes locked onto that word. Those two small children had been instrumental in saving her. She owed them a lot.

Don came up behind her. "What do you think, Jenny?"

She looked up at him. "About what?"

"The board that's sitting in front of you, of course."

Jenny sighed. "I'm so glad that your team was able to decipher all my clues. I was so scared Tom would figure out what I was doing."

"You did give us a run for our money when the fifteen-minute clue came up several times."

"Who finally figured it out?"

"Debbie did."

"Of course she did. I'm forever grateful to everyone here in this room. Without them, I might not be here today."

She glanced back at the board and spotted "1692—Salem witch trials?" Jenny started trembling and Don immediately signaled for Richard to come over. Seeing her in distress, Richard knelt beside her and took her hand. "You're okay, Jenny. He can't hurt you anymore."

Sobbing, she turned to him. "He was going to burn me alive. How could he do that to me?"

"He shouldn't have. You're a wonderful woman."

Jenny wiped her eyes. "Thank you, Richard. Tom was a good man when we were first married, but somehow, he got lost along the way. I still love him for the good times, but it will take time before I recover from my imprisonment. He was delusional and I had hoped to bring him back to the man that I once loved, but that wasn't meant to be."

"It'll take time, Jenny, but you'll be okay. Now wipe those tears away. We're all here to celebrate our success in finding you."

She realized that the room was silent and quickly wiped away her tears. Then she turned around to face all the officers in front of her. "I want to thank all of you so much."

Don said, "Jenny, we have a tradition here in the Blue Ridge Police Department. The whiteboard only comes out of storage when we have a complicated case to solve. Yours was one of those cases. Usually, we have a senior officer wipe the slate clean, but this time, we have decided to ask someone else to clean the board. Rather, I should say two very important people who helped us solve this case." Don turned to Bill. "Do you mind if we bend the rules just this once?"

"I don't work here anymore, so you won't hear any complaints from me."

Don pulled a chair up to the whiteboard. "Adam and Michael, would you please come forward and do the honors?"

Both boys were beaming as they walked to the front of the group.

Don turned to Adam. "Would you please erase the top half of the board? Then Michael can clean the bottom half off."

Adam jumped onto the chair and proudly wiped the eraser across the top half of the board, leaving it clear. He then climbed down and handed the eraser to his brother. Before cleaning the board, Michael spotted, 22 Oak Crescent. "That's where you found us."

Don grinned. "Yes it is, and thanks to you, Jenny is safe and sound."

Michael made big strokes across the board, leaving the word "MOTEL" for last. He grinned. "I wrote that word all by myself."

Don smiled. "You sure did."

Tom Lockman

Phone call 10:00   Jenny Hostage
Called Bill Smithe

Check out Jenny's house and work place Bob and Jim
Tom called 11:00
Claire's new name Nancy
Medicine behind bathroom mirror 8:45
School out 15 minutes earlier 2:45?
Tom using burner phone
Bill and Greg check Jenny's house
Put Jackson's under protection Eric on duty
~~*Searched cabin Charles died at Eli and Bob*~~
Searched Jenny's house Sam and Muhammad
Collect evidence

2 roads to school under construction 15 minute delay
1692 ? Salem witch trials

~~*Old cannery Greg and Jack*~~
~~*Suicide hill tent camp Greg and Jack*~~
Items Tom took from the shed: Rope, tie wraps, wire cutters,
*   padlock & key, duct tape, gas can, scissors*
~~*22 Oak Crescent Jim and Muhammad;*~~ *found two children*

~~*Bunker Debbie and Eli*~~
Close to town yes
Jenny put in container

~~*Butch and Cassandra containers in town*~~

mO ⊥ƎI

Once the board was clean, the entire room applauded satisfied that another case was closed. Don waited for the clapping to stop, before announcing, "Cookies and cakes are in the staff room. Help yourself."

As the officers shuffled off to the staff room, Kimberley came and stood next to Jenny. "Are you okay? If it gets to be too much for you, then we'll take you back to our place for a rest."

"I'm fine." She glanced around the room. "I haven't seen Claire since we arrived. Where is she?"

"When Don mentioned the food, she was gone in a shot. You know more than anyone how important her sweets are to her."

"That I do."

"Did you want to stay a little longer?"

"Actually, I do." She turned to the clean whiteboard. "Seeing it empty is a relief. It means I survived."

"You sure did. You're an amazingly strong woman. Can I get you something to eat?"

"No, I'm fine, thanks. Just want a few minutes to myself, if you don't mind."

"Of course. You need me, you call." Kimberley then left, heading towards the refreshments.

Bill saw Jenny sitting alone, looking at the blank whiteboard. He approached her and pulled up a chair. "You have no idea how good a feeling it is to see that damn board empty."

"Yes, I do." She turned to him. "But I have no idea what you went through to find me. I'm forever grateful."

Bill took her hand. "This might not be the right time Jenny, but Tom's burial is in a few days. Do you want to attend?"

Jenny tensed up, incapable of speaking, but nodded her assent.

"We'll be there to support you."

"I know you will." She sighed. "It's time for me to start a new chapter."

Richard, Kimberley, and Claire returned then. Richard said, "I hate to break up this little party, but I think Jenny needs to get some rest. We're going to take her back to our place for the time being."

Bill acknowledged. "She's all yours."

And the four left the office.

Before the officers broke off their celebration, Don clapped his hands to get their attention. "Okay folks, we need four strong officers to deliver firewood and a tarp to the two homeless camps. First one is at the old cannery, but the actual camp is behind the building, down a short trail. The second one is at the bottom of Suicide Hill. Look for the trail on the left and follow it to their camp. Both groups know that you'll be coming."

Greg put up his hand. "Jack can drive one of the trucks and I'll drive the second one. We know where both locations are." Jim and Debbie also volunteered.

Don responded, "Thanks. The two trucks will arrive at about ten o'clock tomorrow morning. Which camp gets the tarp?"

Greg responded, "The one at the bottom of Suicide Hill."

"Both camps were very helpful, so let's follow through on our promise."

Chapter Eighteen

Two days later

JENNY SAT IN A CHAIR at the cemetery, a single red rose on her lap. The service was short, and when it was over, she stood, walked to her husband's open grave, and laid the rose on his casket. She kissed her fingertips and touched the wooden box that held her husband's remains. Bill watched, confused but nonjudgmental.

When the service was over, she turned to him with tears in her eyes. "Today I buried the man I loved, not the man that terrorized me."

And Bill finally understood.

He drove her home. Before getting out of the car, Jenny turned towards him. "Do you have time to come in? I have something I'd like to discuss with you."

"Sure."

He followed her inside her house.

"Can I offer you some tea?" she asked.

"I would love some, thanks." Bill watched her move around the kitchen, putting on the kettle, getting two mugs from the cupboard, and placing a few cookies onto a plate. She filled both mugs with hot tea and then sat across from him. "What's on your mind, Jenny?"

"I have a proposal, but you might think I'm crazy."

"Let's hear it and I'll be the judge."

She looked directly at him, and without wavering, she said, "I'd like to adopt Adam and Michael. Is that even possible?" She didn't wait for his reply. "I owe both those boys my life and I need a reason to carry on. I think they will give me a purpose. They need a parent and I need children around me. I know that I have Claire, but I want to be a mother. I just don't know how or even if it will work. I live on a waitress's salary, but I would do anything for those boys."

Bill smiled. "I can't make any promises, but let me look into it."

"Thank you, Bill. I appreciate it." Jenny sat silently looking at him.

He knew she had something else on her mind. "Is there something else we need to discuss?"

Jenny cleared her throat. "If I manage to get the boys, I don't want them to have Tom's last name. He threatened to kill them. I buried Tom and his last name will go to the grave with him." She waited to see Bill's reaction.

Bill was surprised, but also understood.

Jenny continued, "I'm going back to my maiden name."

"I completely understand." He gave her a reassuring smile. "What was your maiden name?"

"Jensen."

"That's a strong name. I'm sure the boys would love to be adopted and take your last name."

"I hope so."

They finished their tea and Bill left.

Several days later, Bill returned to Jenny's house. She opened the door and saw him standing there with Adam and Michael. Jenny beamed when she saw the boys. "Come in." The three stepped inside and Jenny looked at Bill. "Why are all of you here?"

Bill responded, "I thought, since you wanted to adopt the boys, that you might want to ask them yourself."

Jenny was tongue-tied, but she turned towards them. Taking a deep breath, she spoke nervously. "I would like to adopt the two of you, if that's okay?"

Michael was excited. "Does that mean you'll be our mom?"

Jenny cried. "Yes, it does."

Adam asked, "What would our last name be?"

Jenny proudly answered, "Jensen." She spelled it out for the boys: "J E N S E N."

Both boys hugged her.

"Bill, I don't know how I can possibly thank you."

"There'll be a short waiting period before the boys can move in. The system has to know that you're stable and have the means to provide for them."

"I understand. I want them so bad. I just hope they'll feel at home here."

"Don't be silly. You're going to be an amazing mother." Bill looked at Jenny. "I've contacted the prison in Edmonton and told them of Tom's death. They have agreed to pay you his entire wages from when he was inside. It's not much but it comes to just over twenty thousand dollars. It will help you set up their room, buy their clothing, and get anything else they might need right away. We just have to wait for an evaluation on how you're doing. Until then, the boys will be staying with me and Beatrice."

She hugged Bill. "I can't thank you enough."

Bill looked down at her fondly. "The entire police force is here for you if you ever need them. And so am I."

Epilogue

The boys moved in with Jenny; and she was prepared to raise them to adulthood.

Some readers may be wondering how she could raise two children on a waitress's salary. With the money she collected from Tom's prison wages, she was able to provide for their immediate needs.

She also went to a psychiatrist, who told her that the more she talked about her kidnapping, the faster it would help her heal. Those two boys were her inspiration.

Jenny spent several months interviewing the officers who had actively worked on her case. She then compiled their notes and her experiences into a novel, which took her two years to complete. It became a great success.

She titled it *The Container.*

Author's Note:

Thank you for purchasing and reading my book. I am extremely grateful and hope you found value in reading it. Please consider sharing it with friends or family and leaving me a review online. Your feedback and support are always appreciated, and allow me to continue doing what I love. If you would like to leave a review, please go to my web site and follow the links to where you purchased the book.

http://www.lucillelabossiereauthor.com

Lucille LaBossiere